Splatoon SQUID KIDS COMEDY SHOW

1

STORY AND ART BY

HIDEKI GOTO

TM & © 2020 Nintendo

Volume 1
VIZ Media Edition

Story and Art by
Hideki Goto

Translation **Tetsuichiro Miyaki**
English Adaptation **Bryant Turnage**
Lettering **John Hunt**
Design **Kam Li**
Editor **Joel Enos**

TM & © 2020 Nintendo. All rights reserved.

SPLATOON IKASU KIDS 4KOMA FES Vol. 1 by Hideki GOTO
© 2018 Hideki GOTO
All rights reserved.
Original Japanese edition published by SHOGAKUKAN.
English translation rights in the United States of America, Canada, the United
Kingdom, Ireland, Australia and New Zealand arranged with SHOGAKUKAN.

Original Design vol.ONE

Printed in the U.S.A.

Published by VIZ Media, LLC
P.O. Box 77010
San Francisco, CA 94107

10 9 8 7 6 5 4 3 2 1
First Printing, July 2020

PARENTAL ADVISORY
SPLATOON: SQUID KIDS
COMEDY SHOW is rated A and
is suitable for readers of all ages.

TM & © 2020 Nintendo

Splatoon
SQUID KIDS COMEDY SHOW

1

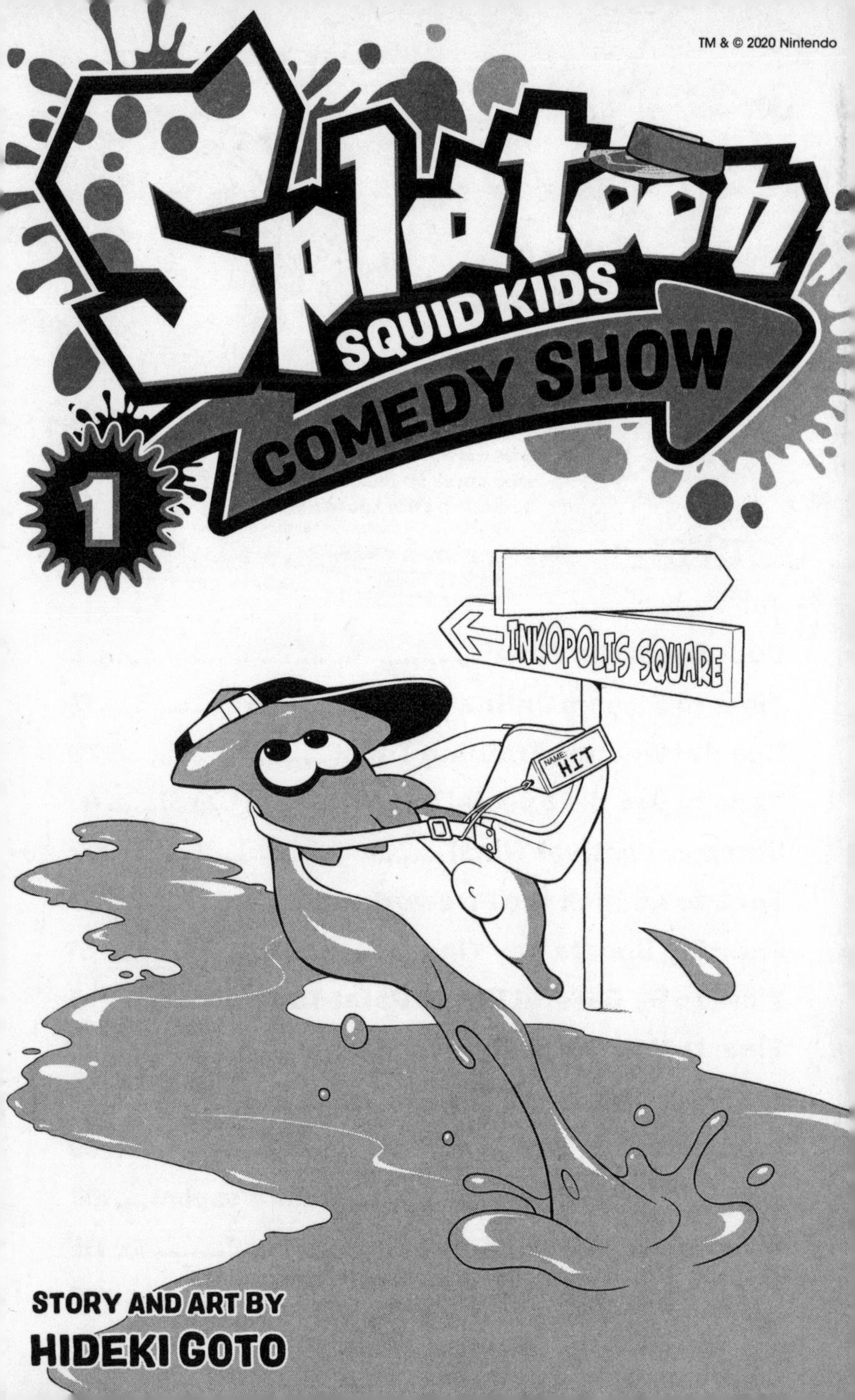
INKOPOLIS SQUARE
NAME: HIT

STORY AND ART BY

HIDEKI GOTO

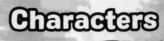

Characters

Maika
A city girl who
uses Dualies.

Hit
A boy from the countryside
who came to the city to
become a cool squid kid!

Contents

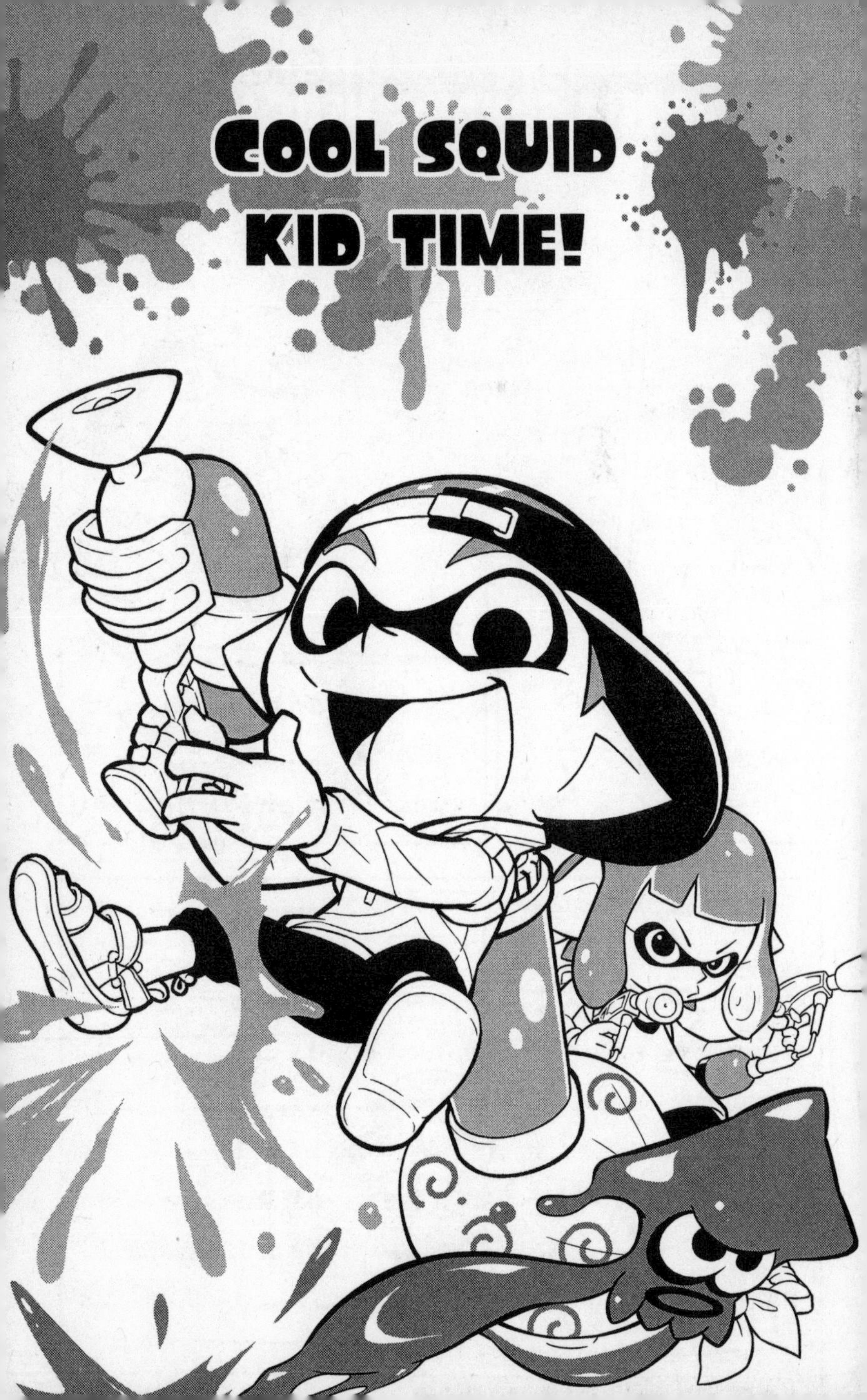
COOL SQUID
KID TIME!

INKOPOLIS SQUARE, HERE I COME!

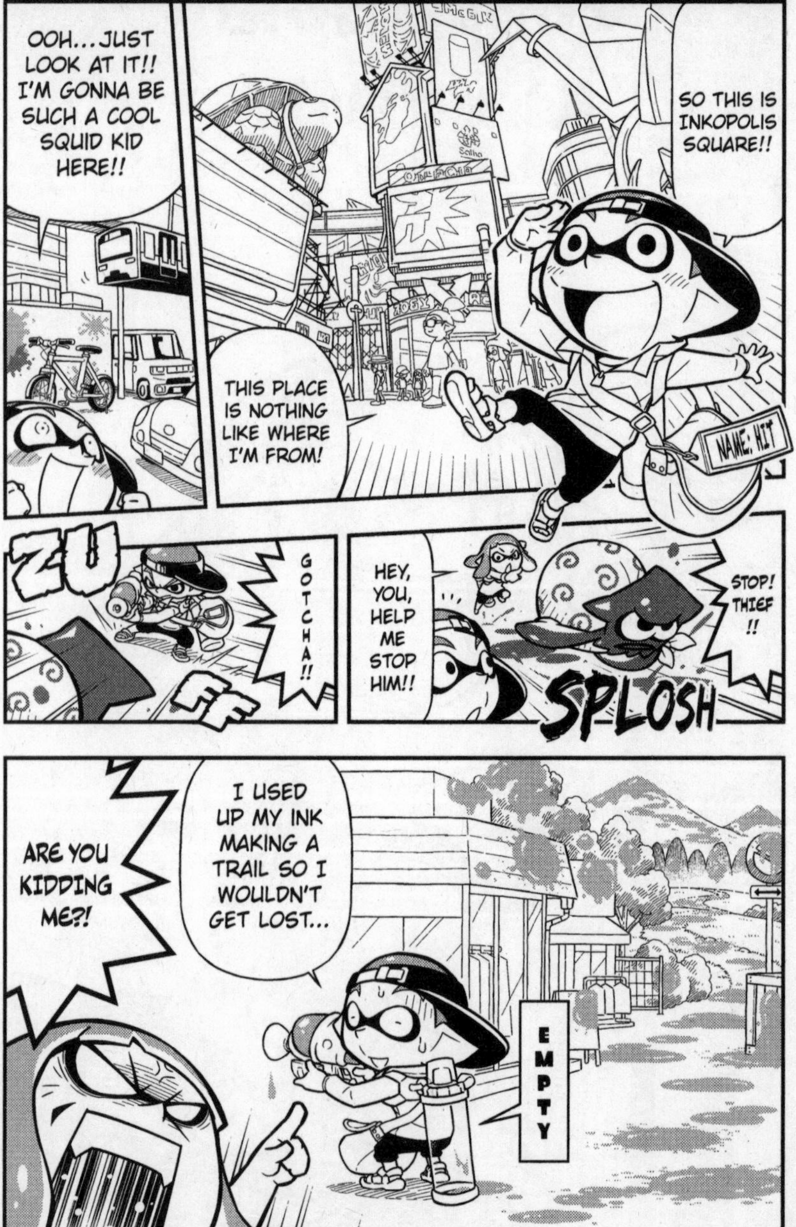
SO THIS IS INKOPOLIS SQUARE!!
NAME: HIT
THIS PLACE IS NOTHING LIKE WHERE I'M FROM!
OOH...JUST LOOK AT IT!! I'M GONNA BE SUCH A COOL SQUID KID HERE!!
STOP! THIEF!!
HEY, YOU, HELP ME STOP HIM!!
SPLOSH
GOTCHA!!
ZU
FF
I USED UP MY INK MAKING A TRAIL SO I WOULDN'T GET LOST...
ARE YOU KIDDING ME?!
EMPTY

INK TRAIL

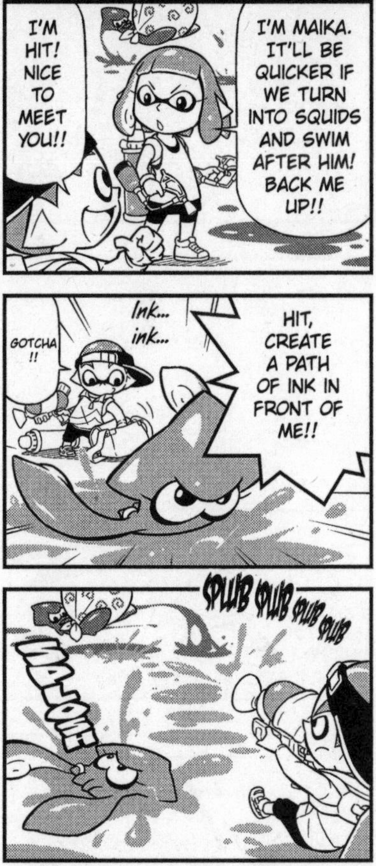
I'M MAIKA. IT'LL BE QUICKER IF WE TURN INTO SQUIDS AND SWIM AFTER HIM! BACK ME UP!!
I'M HIT! NICE TO MEET YOU!!
HIT, CREATE A PATH OF INK IN FRONT OF ME!!
Ink... ink...
GOTCHA!!
SPLUB SPLUB SPLUB SPLUB
SPLOOSH
EXTRA-HOT TABASCO
Oops! Wrong one!!
TABASCO
AIYEEEE!!

MAIKA'S NEW LOOK

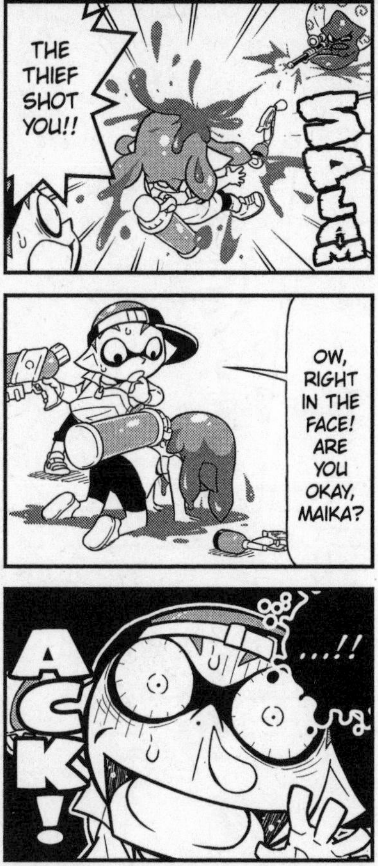
SPLAM
THE THIEF SHOT YOU!!
OW, RIGHT IN THE FACE! ARE YOU OKAY, MAIKA?
...!!
ACK!
HERE YA GO.
RAZOR
IT'S INK, NOT A BEARD!!

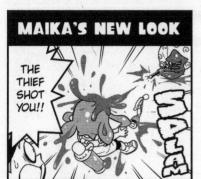

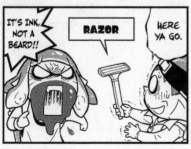

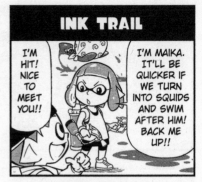

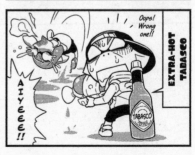

LIFESAVER

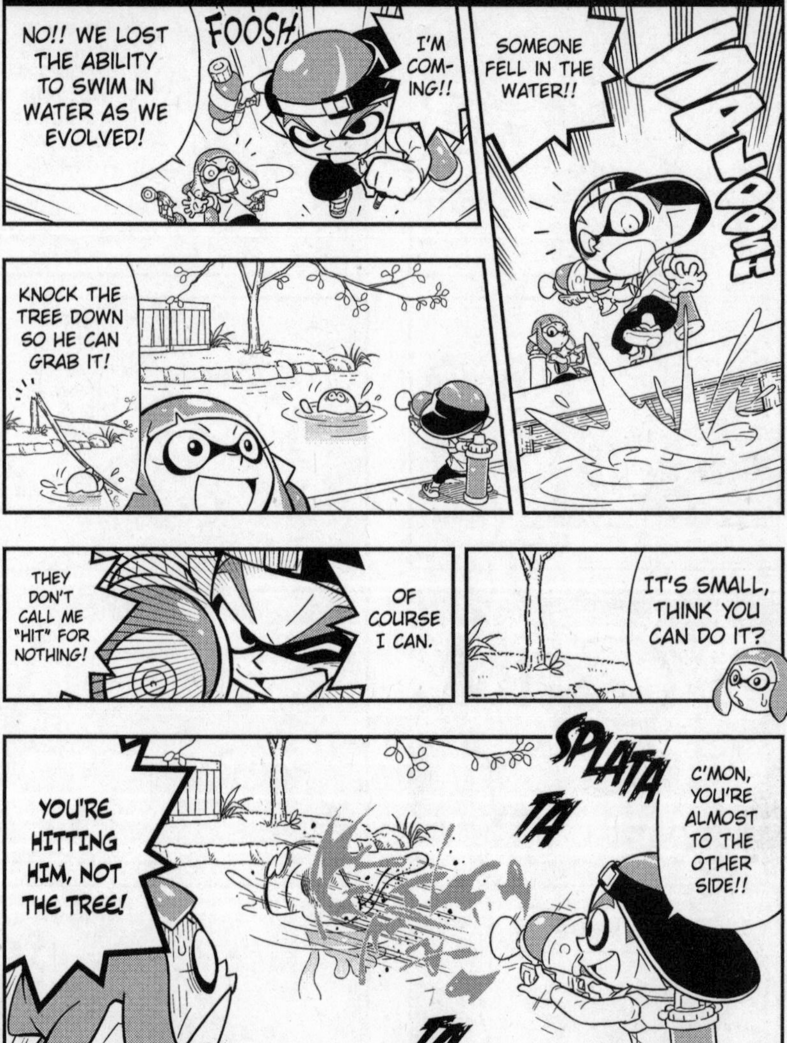
SOMEONE FELL IN THE WATER!!
WALOOSH
I'M COM-ING!!
FOOSH
NO!! WE LOST THE ABILITY TO SWIM IN WATER AS WE EVOLVED!
KNOCK THE TREE DOWN SO HE CAN GRAB IT!
IT'S SMALL, THINK YOU CAN DO IT?
OF COURSE I CAN.
THEY DON'T CALL ME "HIT" FOR NOTHING!
C'MON, YOU'RE ALMOST TO THE OTHER SIDE!!
SPLATA
TA
TA
TA
YOU'RE HITTING HIM, NOT THE TREE!

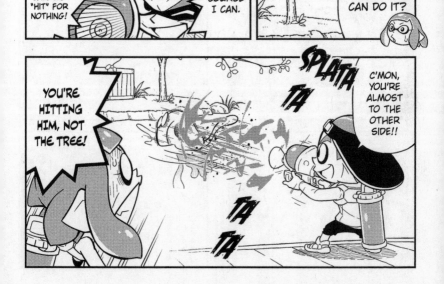

DARING RESCUE

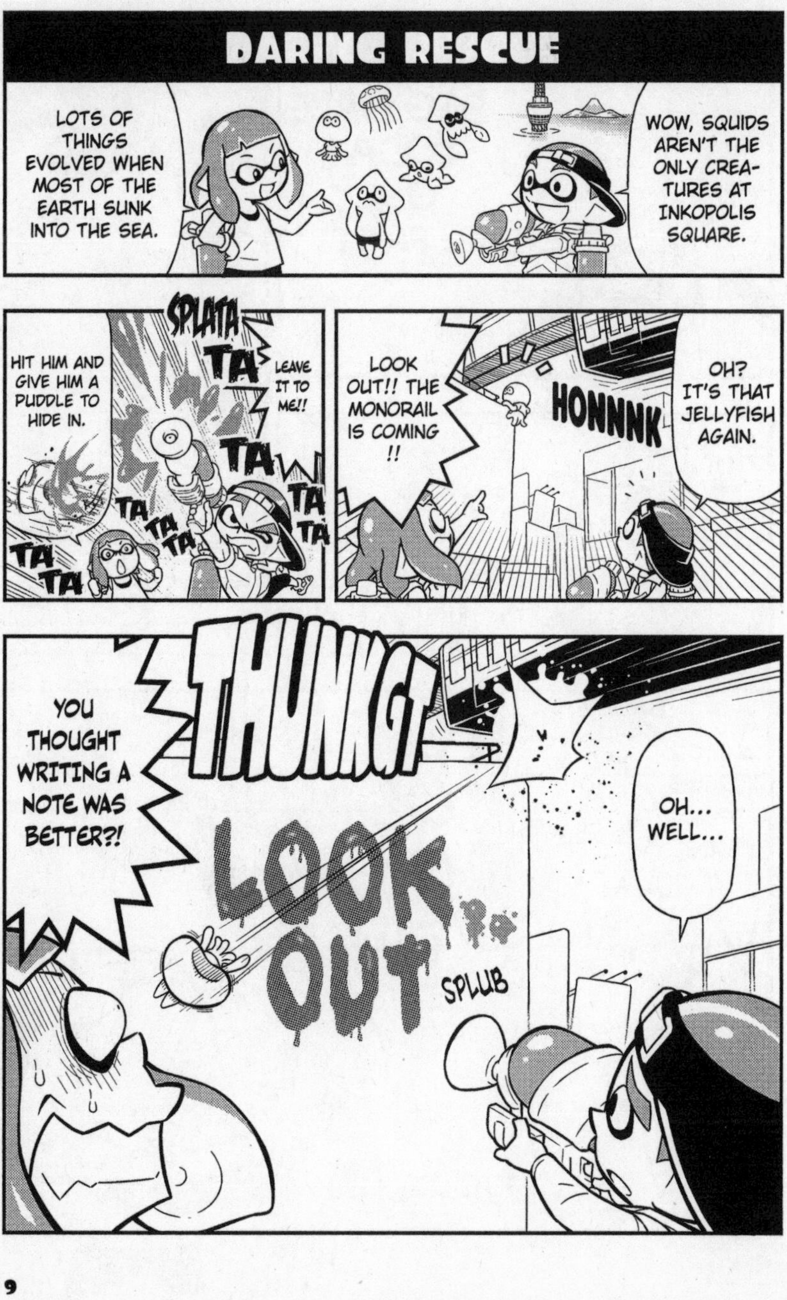
WOW, SQUIDS AREN'T THE ONLY CREATURES AT INKOPOLIS SQUARE.
LOTS OF THINGS EVOLVED WHEN MOST OF THE EARTH SUNK INTO THE SEA.
OH? IT'S THAT JELLYFISH AGAIN.
HONNNK
LOOK OUT!! THE MONORAIL IS COMING!!
LEAVE IT TO ME!!
SPLATATA
TA
TA
TA TA
HIT HIM AND GIVE HIM A PUDDLE TO HIDE IN.
TA TA TA
TA TA
THUNKGT
OH... WELL...
YOU THOUGHT WRITING A NOTE WAS BETTER?!
LOOK OUT
SPLUB

SALE'S OVER

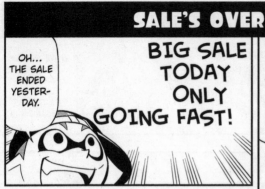

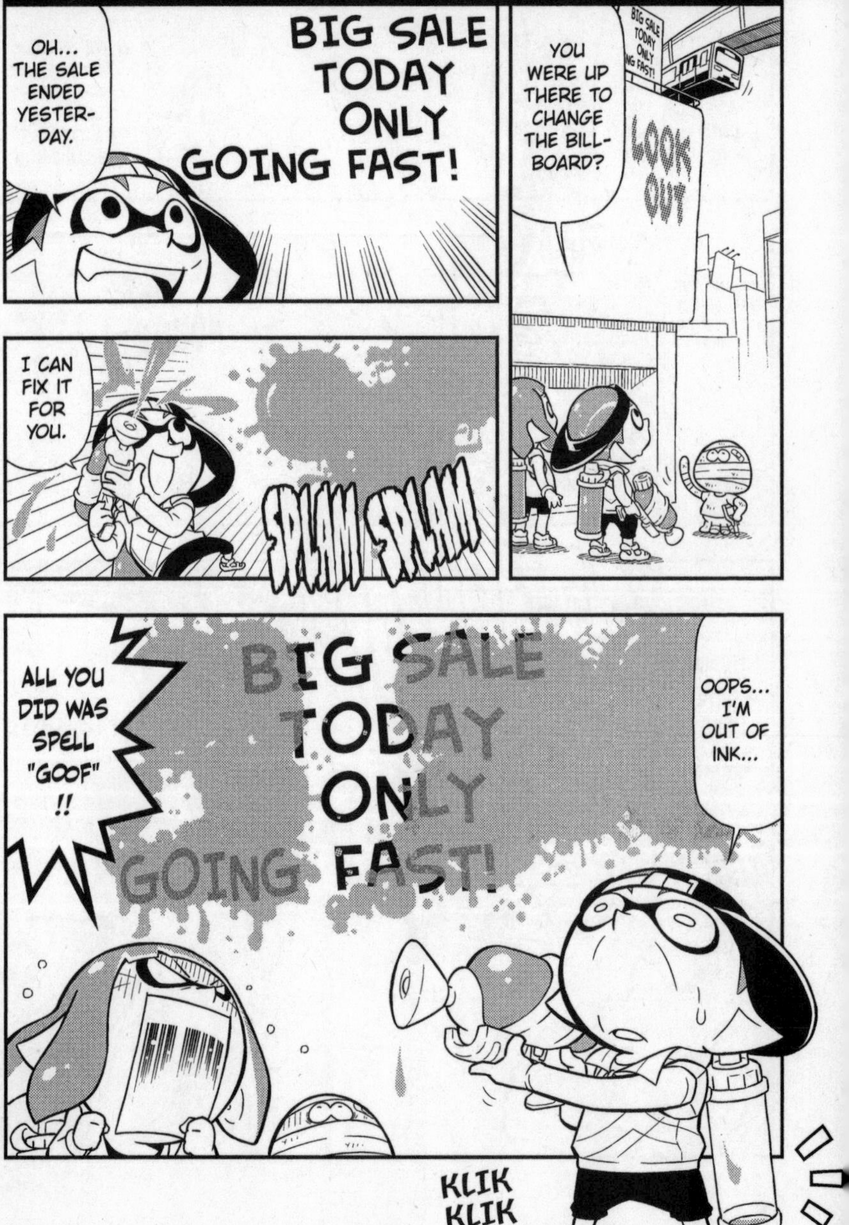
BIG SALE TODAY ONLY GOING FAST!
YOU WERE UP THERE TO CHANGE THE BILL-BOARD?
LOOK OUT
OH... THE SALE ENDED YESTER-DAY.
BIG SALE TODAY ONLY GOING FAST!
I CAN FIX IT FOR YOU.
SPLAM SPLAM
OOPS... I'M OUT OF INK...
BIG SALE TODAY ONLY GOING FAST!
ALL YOU DID WAS SPELL "GOOF" !!
KLIK KLIK

BICYCLE

OOH !!
YOU'LL LEND ME YOUR BIKE?
I CAN MOVE SO FAST.
NOW I'M A COOL SQUID KID!!
SHFFFFF
IN INK
SPISH SPISH
I think I'm stuck...
YOU CAN'T SWIM ON A BIKE !!
SWEEEE

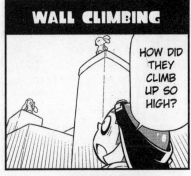

WALL CLIMBING

HOW DID THEY CLIMB UP SO HIGH?
YOU PAINT THE WALL WITH THE INK AND CLIMB UP.
SPLISH
SWEEEE
OH, NEAT !!
SPLAM
SPLAM
SPLAM
NOW IT'S MY TURN!
HNNRRGH!!
KRRRK
KRRRK
FORGET THE BICYCLE ALREADY !!

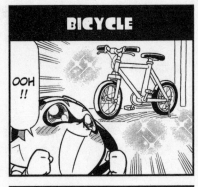

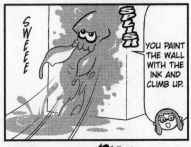

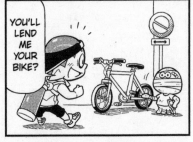

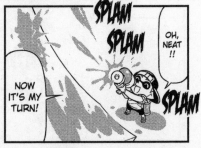

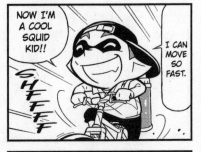

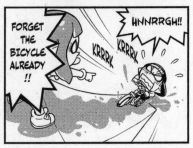

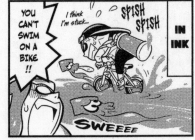

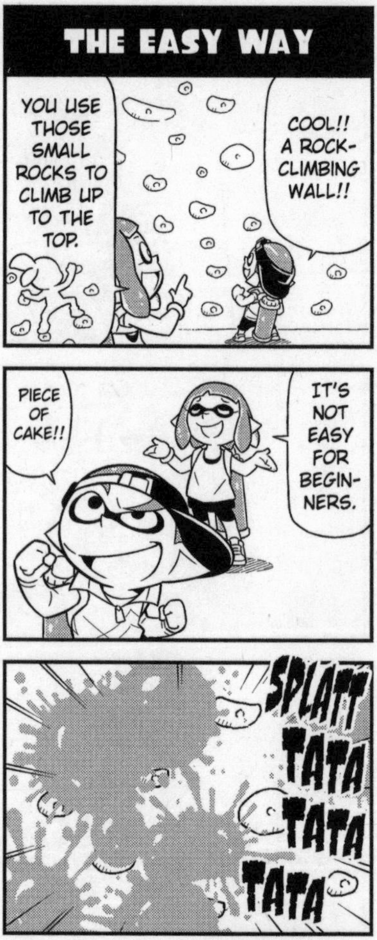
THE EASY WAY
COOL!! A ROCK-CLIMBING WALL!!
YOU USE THOSE SMALL ROCKS TO CLIMB UP TO THE TOP.
IT'S NOT EASY FOR BEGIN-NERS.
PIECE OF CAKE!!
SPLATT TATA TATA TATA
SWEEEE
THAT'S NOT HOW YOU DO IT!!

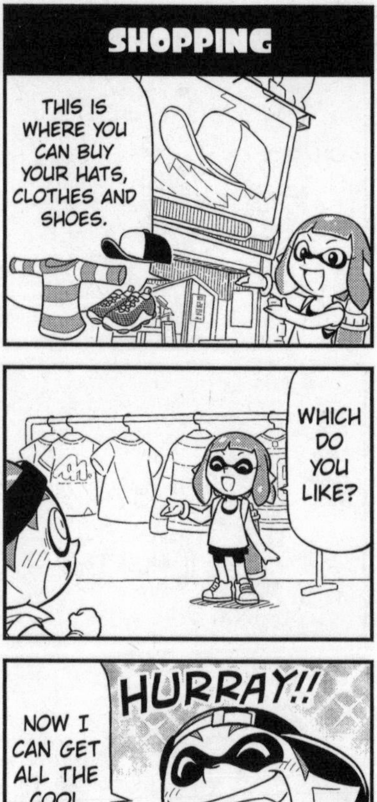
SHOPPING
THIS IS WHERE YOU CAN BUY YOUR HATS, CLOTHES AND SHOES.
WHICH DO YOU LIKE?
HURRAY!!
NOW I CAN GET ALL THE COOL GEAR!!
WE'RE GOING TO THE WEAPON SHOP NEXT.
I'M JUST HERE TO CARRY YOUR STUFF?!

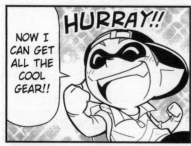

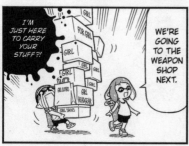

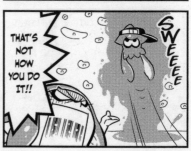

ROLLER

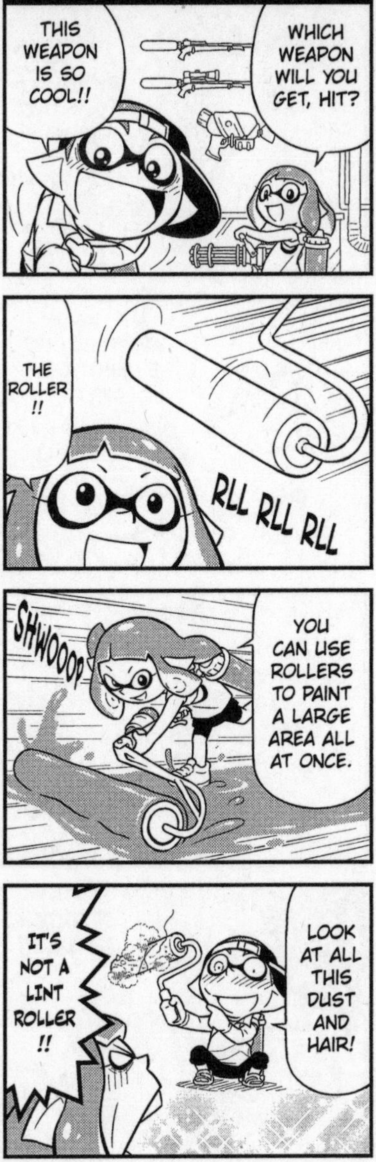
WHICH WEAPON WILL YOU GET, HIT?
THIS WEAPON IS SO COOL!!
THE ROLLER!!
RLL RLL RLL
YOU CAN USE ROLLERS TO PAINT A LARGE AREA ALL AT ONCE.
SHWOOOP
LOOK AT ALL THIS DUST AND HAIR!
IT'S NOT A LINT ROLLER!!

INK TANK

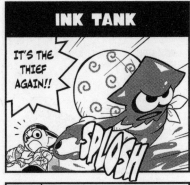

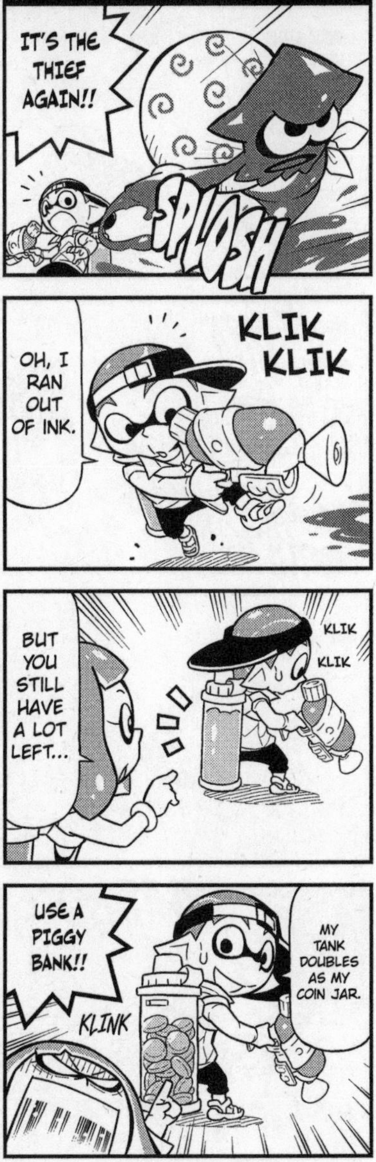
IT'S THE THIEF AGAIN!!
SPLOSH
KLIK KLIK
OH, I RAN OUT OF INK.
KLIK
KLIK
BUT YOU STILL HAVE A LOT LEFT...
MY TANK DOUBLES AS MY COIN JAR.
USE A PIGGY BANK!!
KLINK

MAIKA'S SKILLS
Ink... ink...
LOOKS LIKE I'LL HAVE TO DO IT.
SPLATT TATA TATA
TATA
YOU'RE GONNA LOVE MY FRESH SKILLS!!
TATA
IS IT RAINING?
AIYEEEE!!
SPLATATA
NOT RAIN, JUST LOUSY SHOOTING.
A LITTLE HELP
MAIKA, YOU WIELD TWO WEAPONS?! COOL!!
THIS IS A DUALIE, THE LATEST WEAPON.
MY HANDS ARE FULL, SO I NEED YOUR HELP.
GOTCHA!!
HIT, UPPER-RIGHT CORNER!!
WHAT?! WHERE?!
SCRATCH HARDER!!
SKRCH SKRCH
THIS ISN'T THE HELP I THOUGHT YOU WANTED.

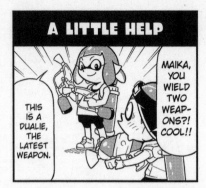

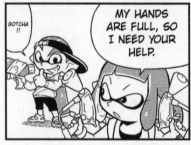

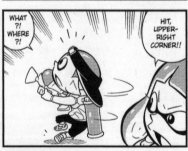

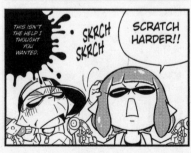

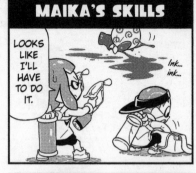

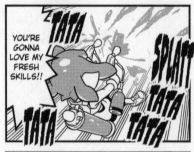

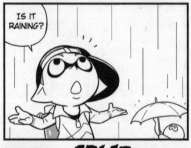

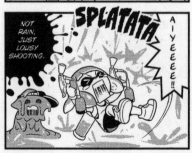

DODGE ROLL

SPLAM
LOOK!
THE THIEF IS SHOOTING AT YOU!!
BWOOSH
SHUP
WHAT MOVE IS THAT?!
SPLUB
DODGE ROLL. YOU CAN DO IT IF YOU USE DUALIES.
COOL!!
LET ME TRY!!
SWIP
SHUP
HIT, YOU DON'T HAVE DUALIES, SO HOW CAN YOU DODGE ROLL?
ONE MORE TIME!!
POOT
SWIP
OH, IT'S MORE OF A PASS-GAS PASS!!

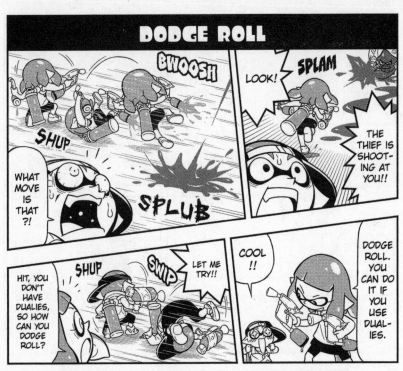

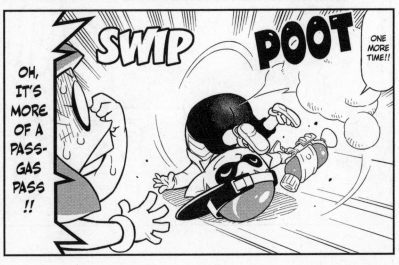

RED LIGHT

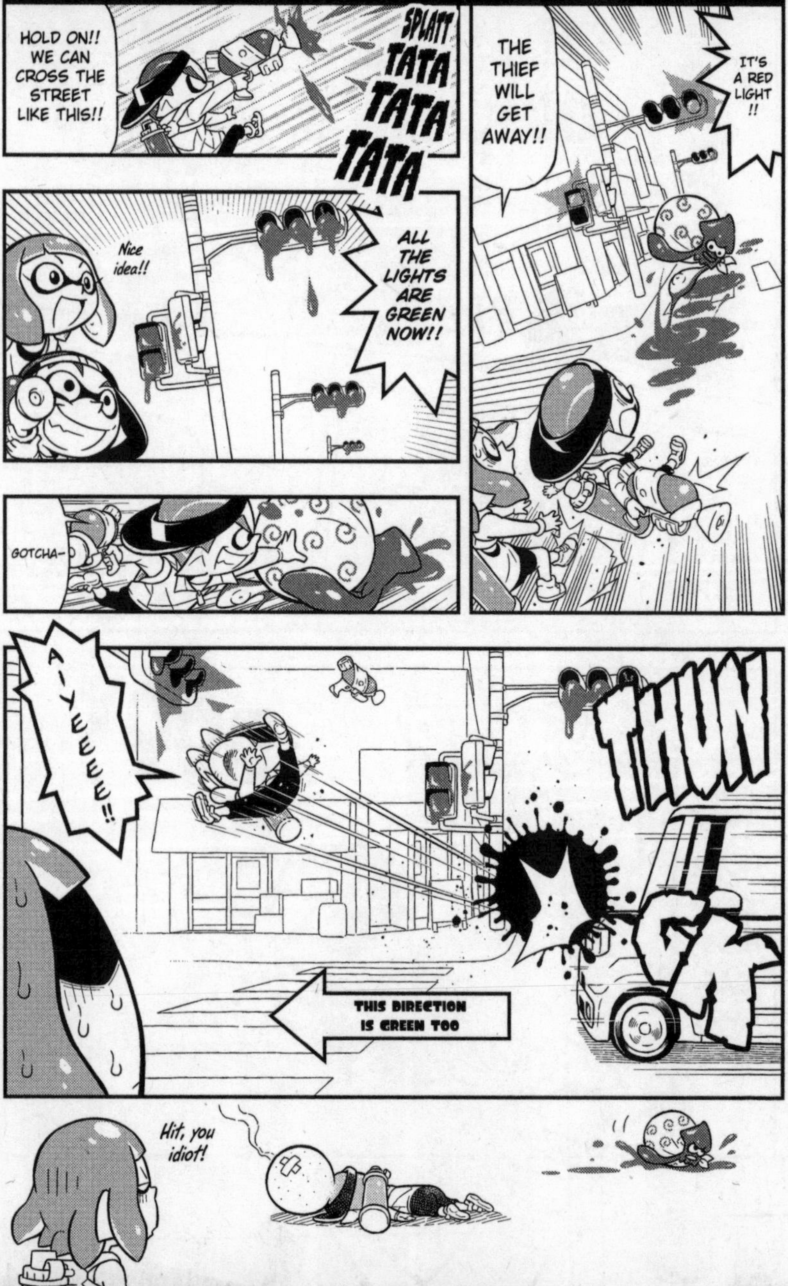
IT'S A RED LIGHT !!
THE THIEF WILL GET AWAY!!
SPLATT TATA TATA TATA
HOLD ON!! WE CAN CROSS THE STREET LIKE THIS!!
ALL THE LIGHTS ARE GREEN NOW!!
Nice idea!!
GOTCHA-
THUN
GK
THIS DIRECTION IS GREEN TOO
AIYEEEE!!
Hit, you idiot!

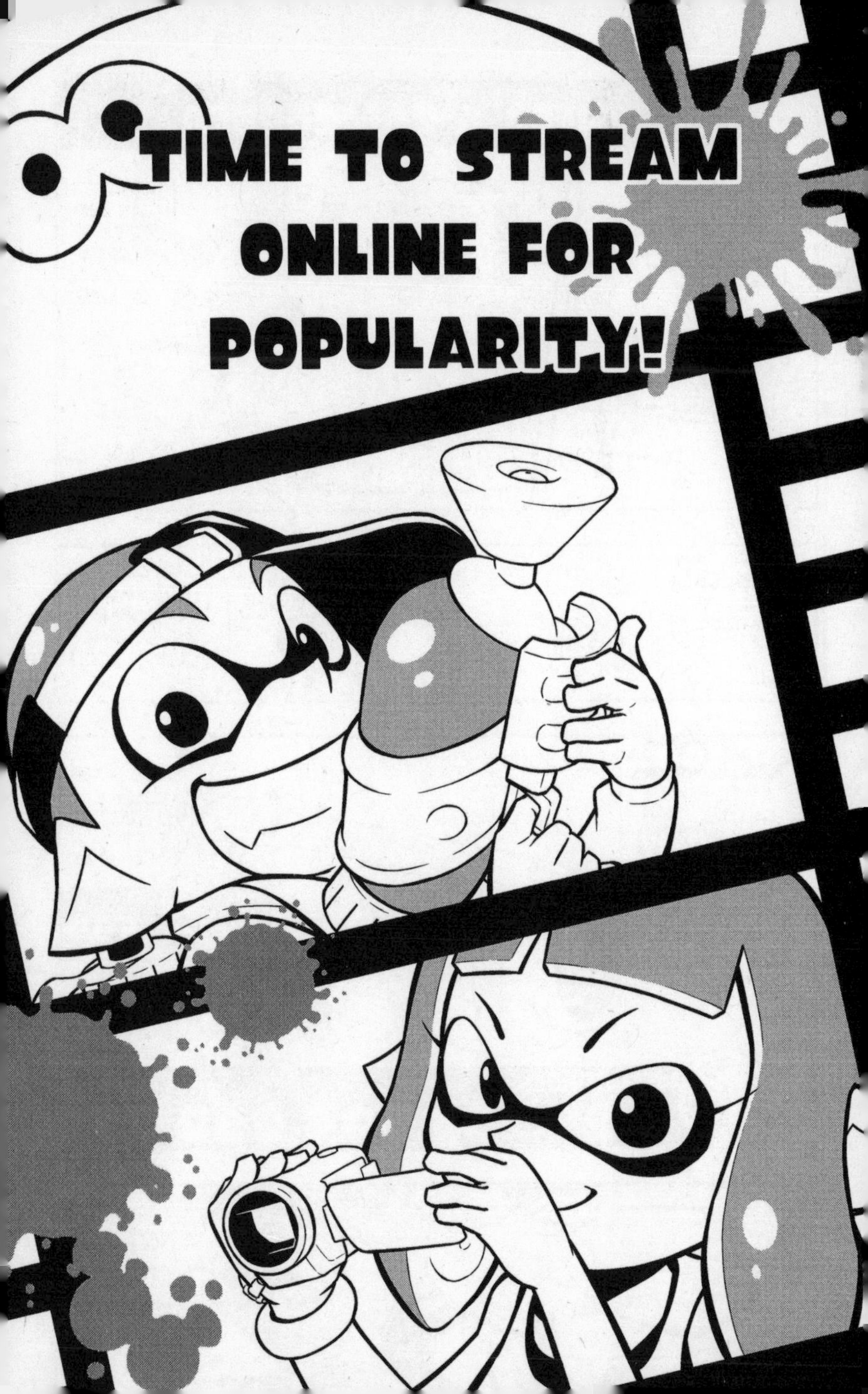
TIME TO STREAM ONLINE FOR POPULARITY!

NEED A CAMCORDER

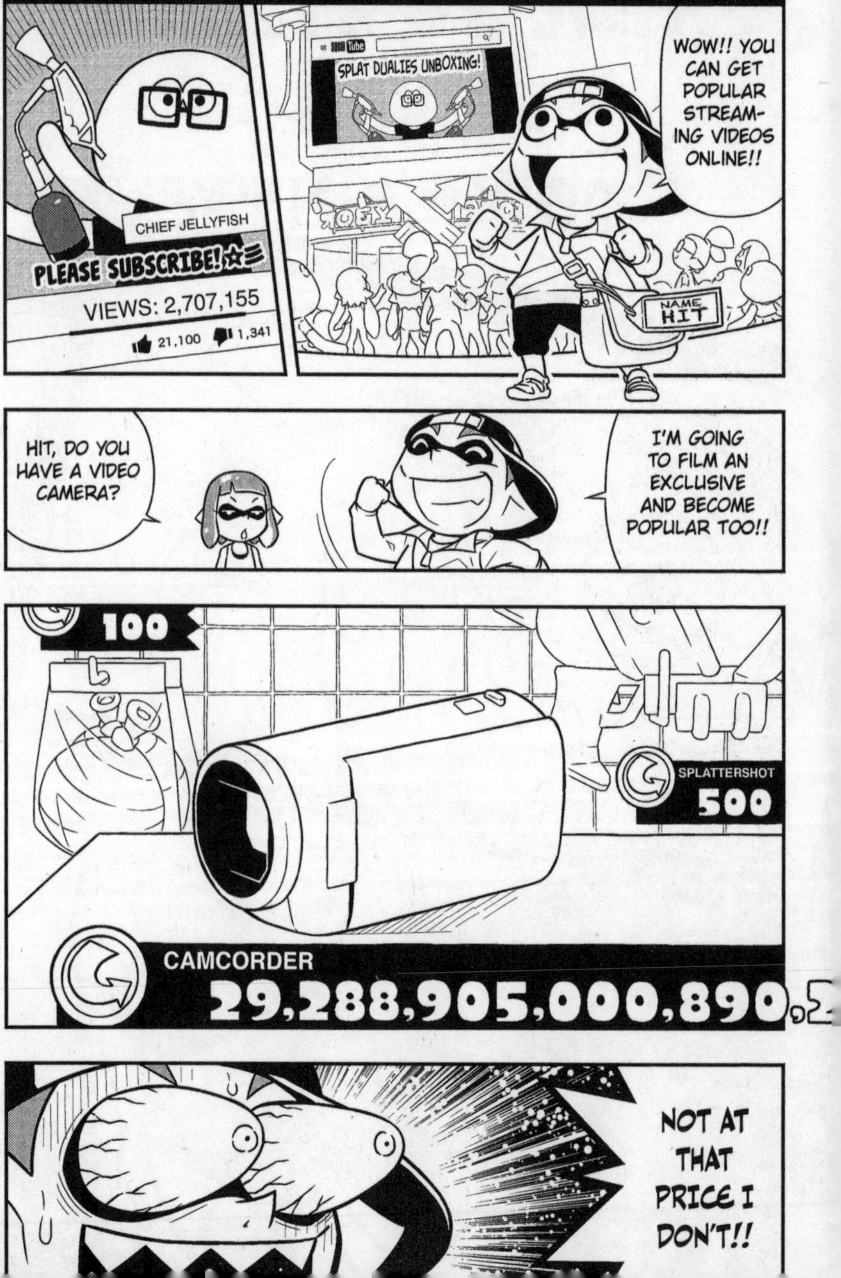
SQUID Tube
SPLAT DUALIES UNBOXING!
WOW!! YOU CAN GET POPULAR STREAMING VIDEOS ONLINE!!
NAME
HIT
CHIEF JELLYFISH
PLEASE SUBSCRIBE!☆彡
VIEWS: 2,707,155
21,100
1,341
I'M GOING TO FILM AN EXCLUSIVE AND BECOME POPULAR TOO!!
HIT, DO YOU HAVE A VIDEO CAMERA?
SPLATTERSHOT
500
100
CAMCORDER
29,288,905,000,890,
NOT AT THAT PRICE I DON'T!!

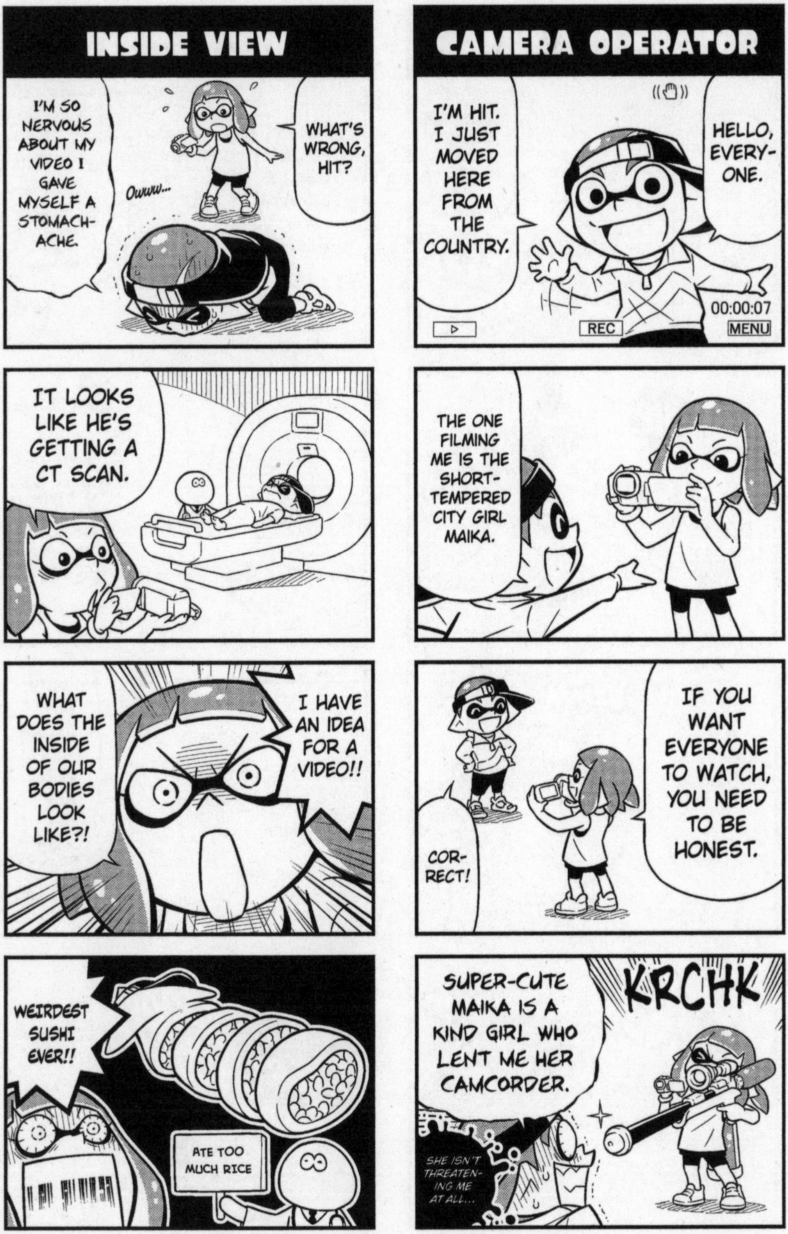
CAMERA OPERATOR
HELLO, EVERY-ONE.
I'M HIT. I JUST MOVED HERE FROM THE COUNTRY.
00:00:07
REC
MENU
THE ONE FILMING ME IS THE SHORT-TEMPERED CITY GIRL MAIKA.
IF YOU WANT EVERYONE TO WATCH, YOU NEED TO BE HONEST.
COR-RECT!
KRCHK
SUPER-CUTE MAIKA IS A KIND GIRL WHO LENT ME HER CAMCORDER.
SHE ISN'T THREATEN-ING ME AT ALL...
INSIDE VIEW
WHAT'S WRONG, HIT?
Owww...
I'M SO NERVOUS ABOUT MY VIDEO I GAVE MYSELF A STOMACH-ACHE.
IT LOOKS LIKE HE'S GETTING A CT SCAN.
I HAVE AN IDEA FOR A VIDEO!!
WHAT DOES THE INSIDE OF OUR BODIES LOOK LIKE?!
WEIRDEST SUSHI EVER!!
ATE TOO MUCH RICE

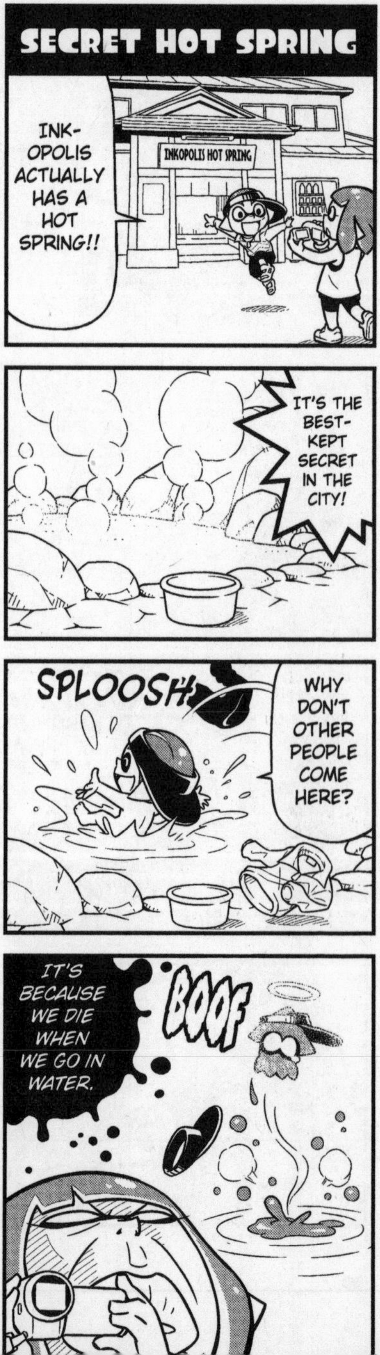
SECRET HOT SPRING
INKOPOLIS HOT SPRING
INK-OPOLIS ACTUALLY HAS A HOT SPRING!!
IT'S THE BEST-KEPT SECRET IN THE CITY!
WHY DON'T OTHER PEOPLE COME HERE?
SPLOOSH
BOOF
IT'S BECAUSE WE DIE WHEN WE GO IN WATER.

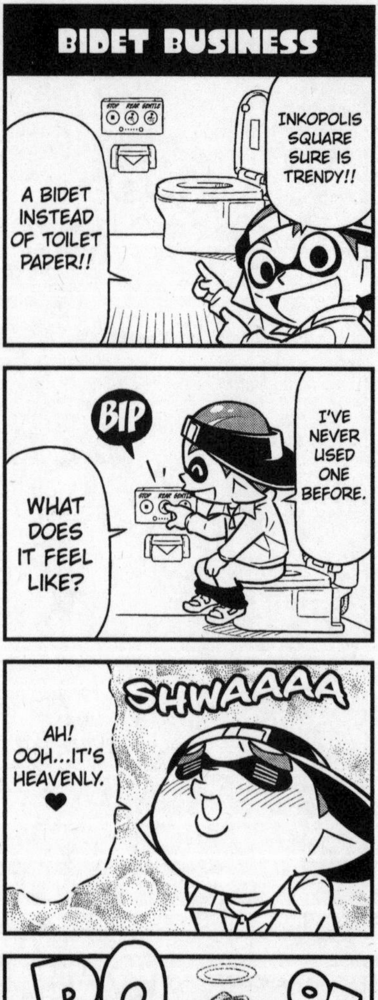
BIDET BUSINESS
INKOPOLIS SQUARE SURE IS TRENDY!!
STOP REAR GENTLE
A BIDET INSTEAD OF TOILET PAPER!!
I'VE NEVER USED ONE BEFORE.
BIP
WHAT DOES IT FEEL LIKE?
SHWAAAA
AH! OOH...IT'S HEAVENLY. ♥
BO OF
STOP REAR GENTLE

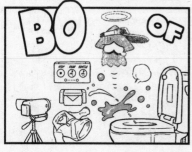

FANCY CLOTHES

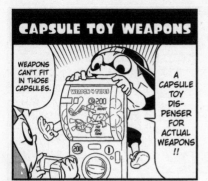

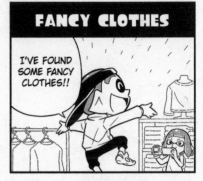

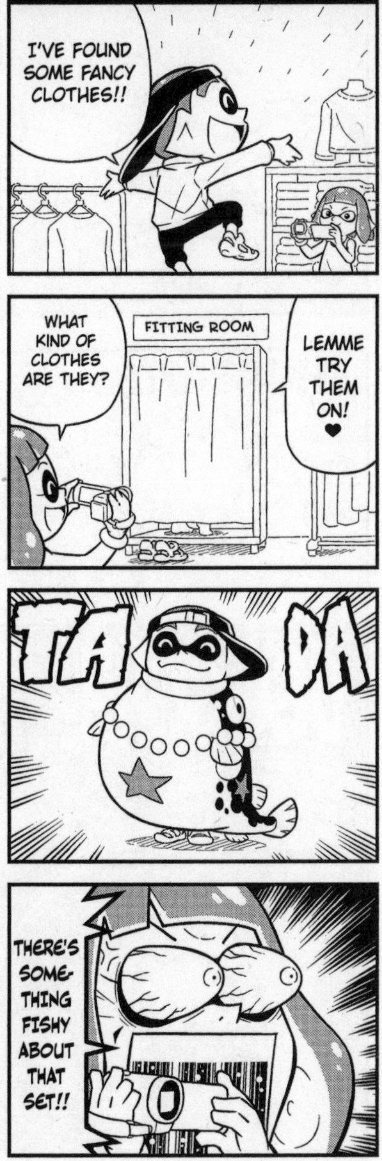
I'VE FOUND SOME FANCY CLOTHES!!
LEMME TRY THEM ON! ♥
FITTING ROOM
WHAT KIND OF CLOTHES ARE THEY?
TA DA
THERE'S SOME-THING FISHY ABOUT THAT SET!!

CAPSULE TOY WEAPONS

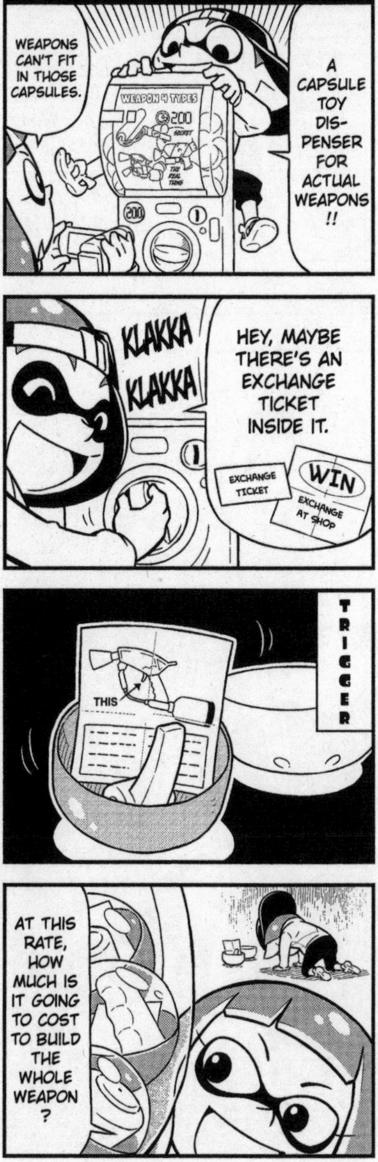
A CAPSULE TOY DIS-PENSER FOR ACTUAL WEAPONS!!
WEAPON 4 TYPES
200
SECRET
THE REAL THING
200
WEAPONS CAN'T FIT IN THOSE CAPSULES.
HEY, MAYBE THERE'S AN EXCHANGE TICKET INSIDE IT.
KLAKKA KLAKKA
WIN
EXCHANGE AT SHOP
EXCHANGE TICKET
TRIGGER
THIS
AT THIS RATE, HOW MUCH IS IT GOING TO COST TO BUILD THE WHOLE WEAPON?

PRIZE DUALIES

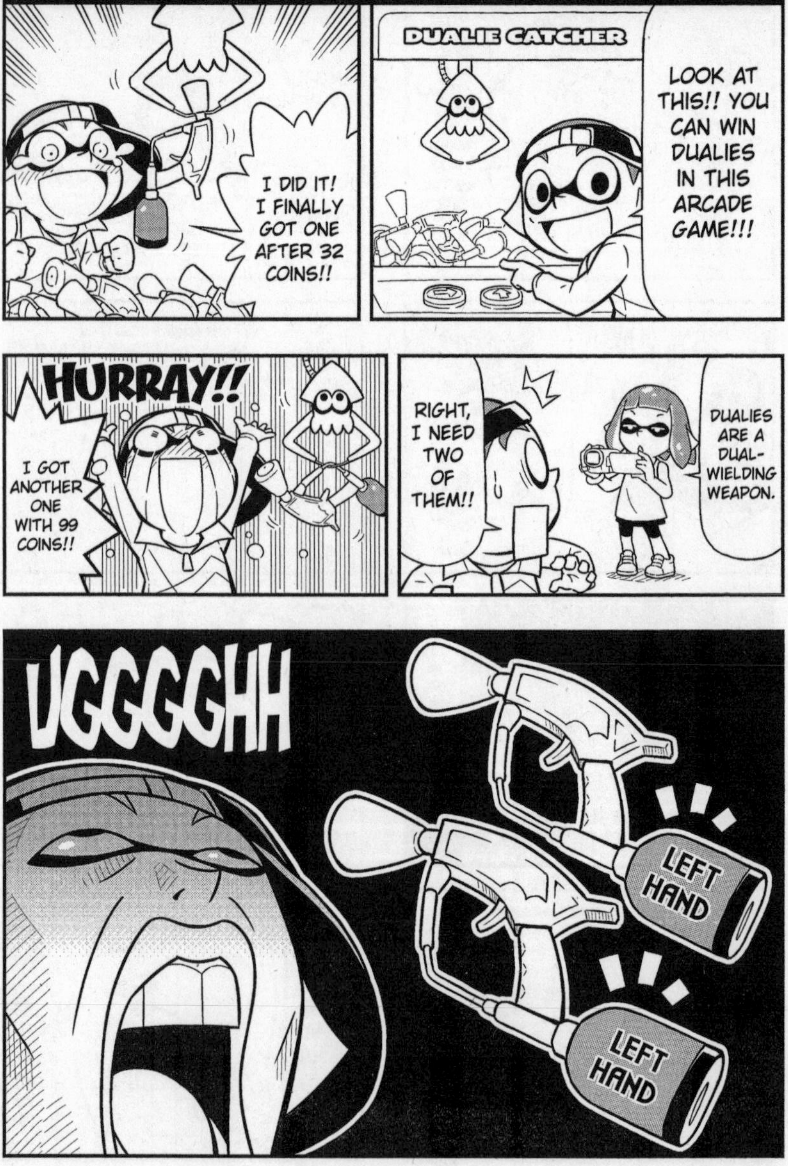
DUALIE CATCHER
LOOK AT THIS!! YOU CAN WIN DUALIES IN THIS ARCADE GAME!!!
I DID IT! I FINALLY GOT ONE AFTER 32 COINS!!
DUALIES ARE A DUAL-WIELDING WEAPON.
RIGHT, I NEED TWO OF THEM!!
HURRAY!!
I GOT ANOTHER ONE WITH 99 COINS!!
LEFT HAND
LEFT HAND
UGGGGHH

NEW PLAY MODE

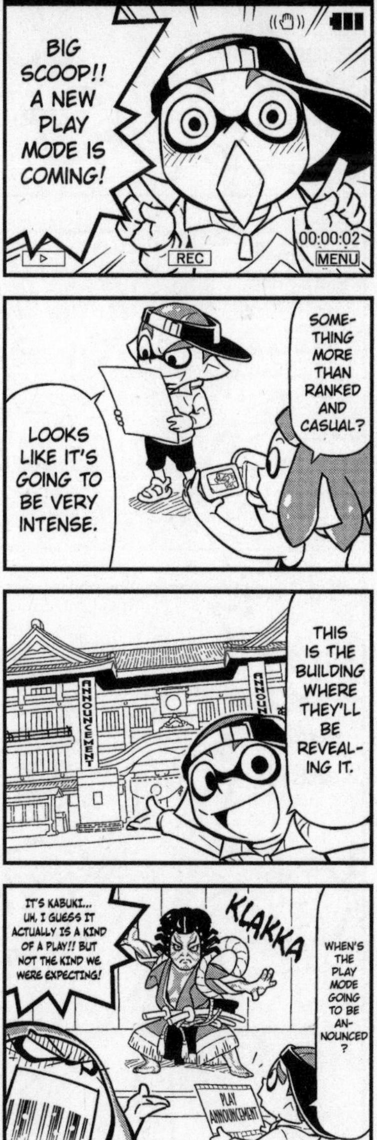
BIG SCOOP!! A NEW PLAY MODE IS COMING!
00:00:02
REC
MENU
SOMETHING MORE THAN RANKED AND CASUAL?
LOOKS LIKE IT'S GOING TO BE VERY INTENSE.
THIS IS THE BUILDING WHERE THEY'LL BE REVEALING IT.
ANNOUNCEMENT
KLAKKA
WHEN'S THE PLAY MODE GOING TO BE ANNOUNCED?
IT'S KABUKI... UH, I GUESS IT ACTUALLY IS A KIND OF A PLAY!! BUT NOT THE KIND WE WERE EXPECTING!
PLAY ANNOUNCEMENT

NEW WEAPON

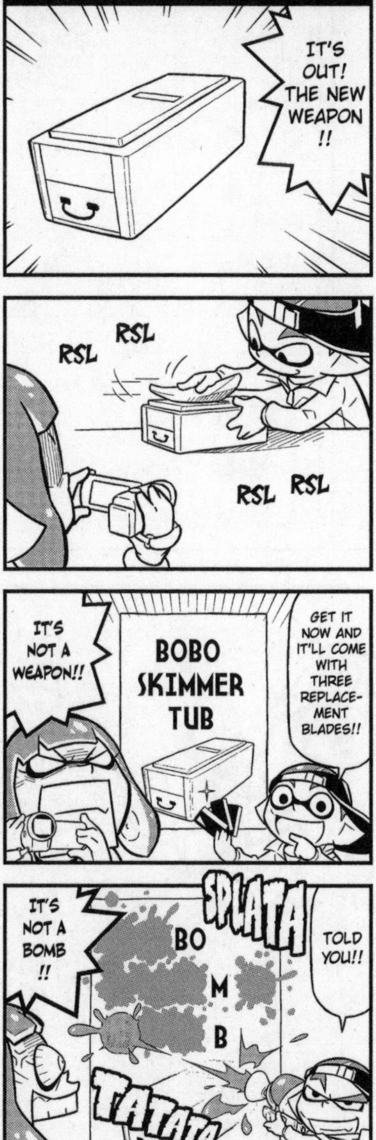
IT'S OUT! THE NEW WEAPON!!
RSL
RSL
RSL
RSL
GET IT NOW AND IT'LL COME WITH THREE REPLACEMENT BLADES!!
BOBO SKIMMER TUB
IT'S NOT A WEAPON!!
SPLATA
TOLD YOU!!
BOMB
IT'S NOT A BOMB!!
TATATA

SPECIAL WEAPON

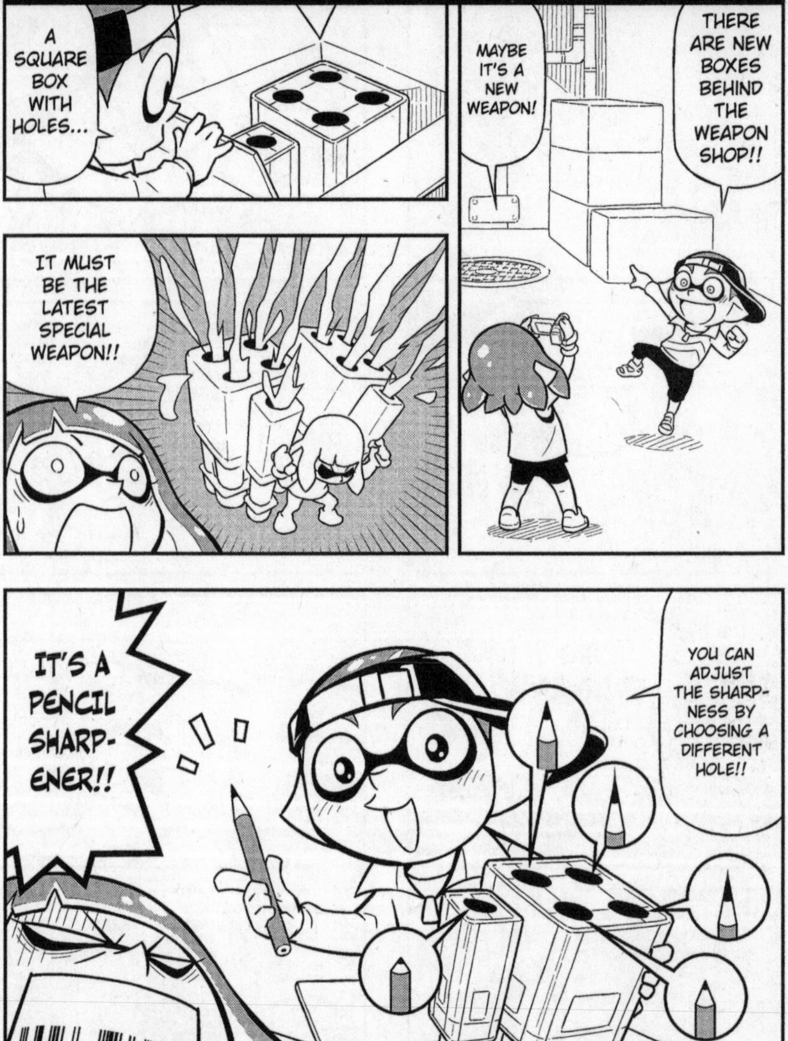
THERE ARE NEW BOXES BEHIND THE WEAPON SHOP!!
MAYBE IT'S A NEW WEAPON!
A SQUARE BOX WITH HOLES...
IT MUST BE THE LATEST SPECIAL WEAPON!!
YOU CAN ADJUST THE SHARPNESS BY CHOOSING A DIFFERENT HOLE!!
IT'S A PENCIL SHARPENER!!

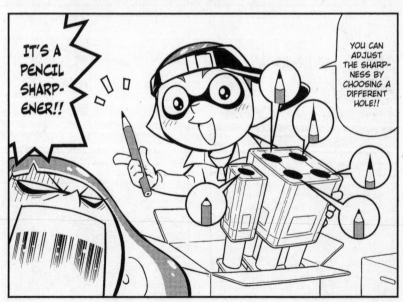

FIREFIGHTING

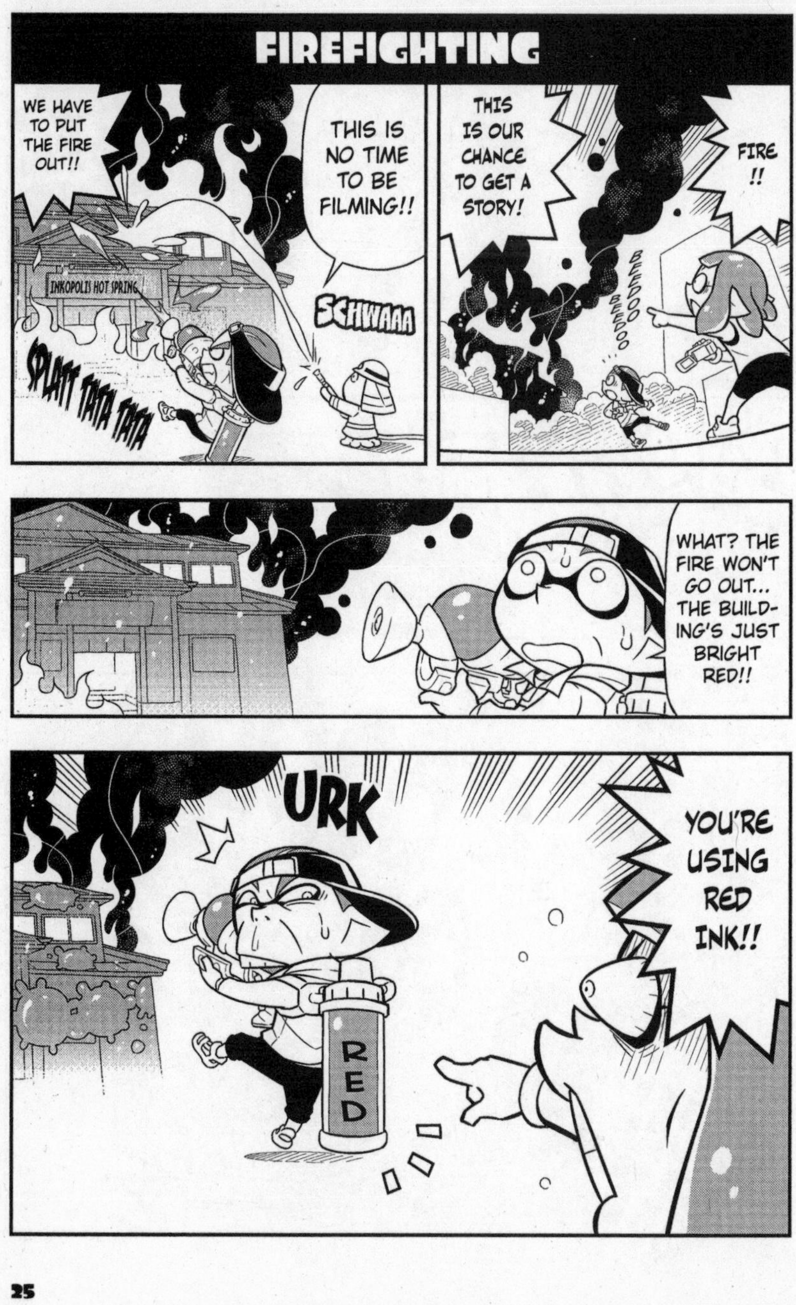
FIRE !!
THIS IS OUR CHANCE TO GET A STORY!
BEEDOO BEEDOO
THIS IS NO TIME TO BE FILMING!!
WE HAVE TO PUT THE FIRE OUT!!
INKOPOLIS HOT SPRING
SCHWAAA
SPLATT TATA TATA
WHAT? THE FIRE WON'T GO OUT... THE BUILDING'S JUST BRIGHT RED!!
YOU'RE USING RED INK!!
URK
RED

TENTA MISSILE HELP

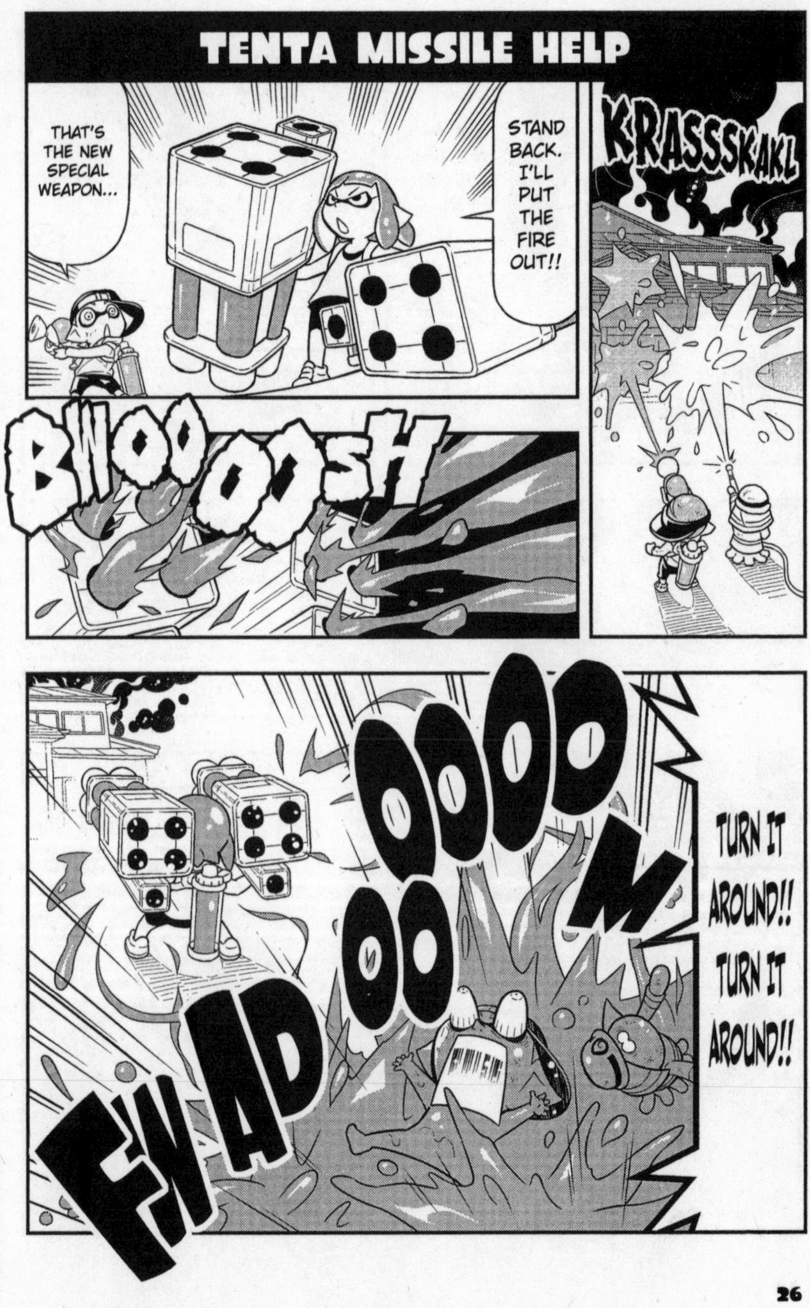
KRASSSKAKL
STAND BACK. I'LL PUT THE FIRE OUT!!
THAT'S THE NEW SPECIAL WEAPON...
BWOOOOSH
F'WADOOOOOOM
TURN IT AROUND!! TURN IT AROUND!!

FIRE RESCUE

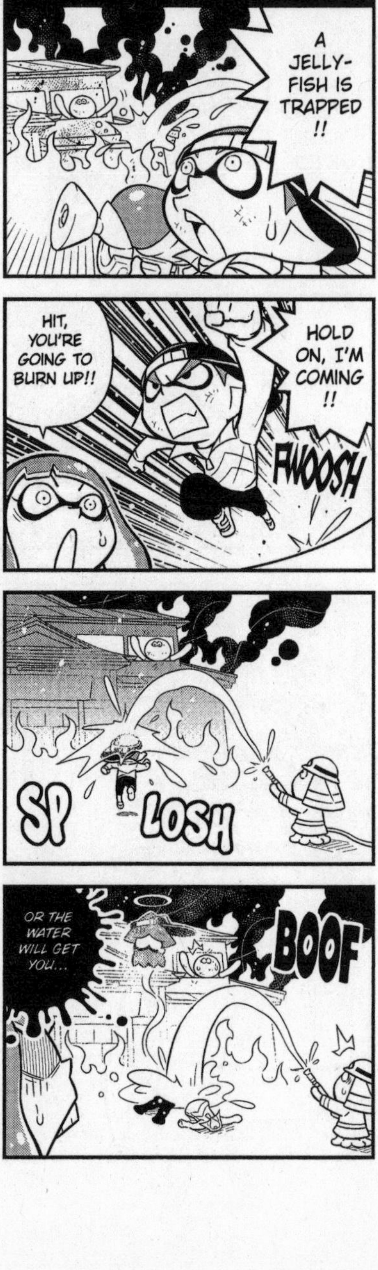
A JELLY-FISH IS TRAPPED!!
HOLD ON, I'M COMING!!
HIT, YOU'RE GOING TO BURN UP!!
FWOOSH
SP LOSH
BOOF
OR THE WATER WILL GET YOU...

TRANSFORMATION

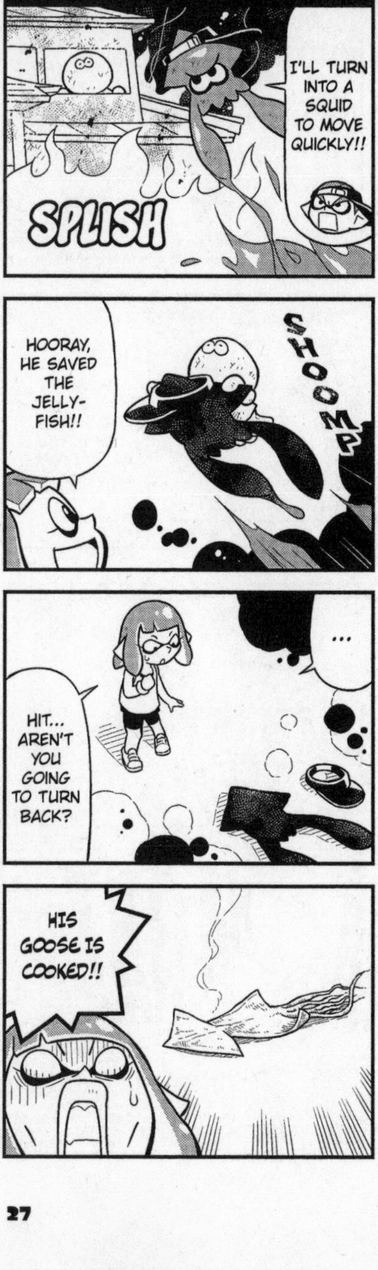
I'LL TURN INTO A SQUID TO MOVE QUICKLY!!
SPLISH
SHOOMP
HOORAY, HE SAVED THE JELLY-FISH!!
...
HIT... AREN'T YOU GOING TO TURN BACK?
HIS GOOSE IS COOKED!!

MR. POPULAR

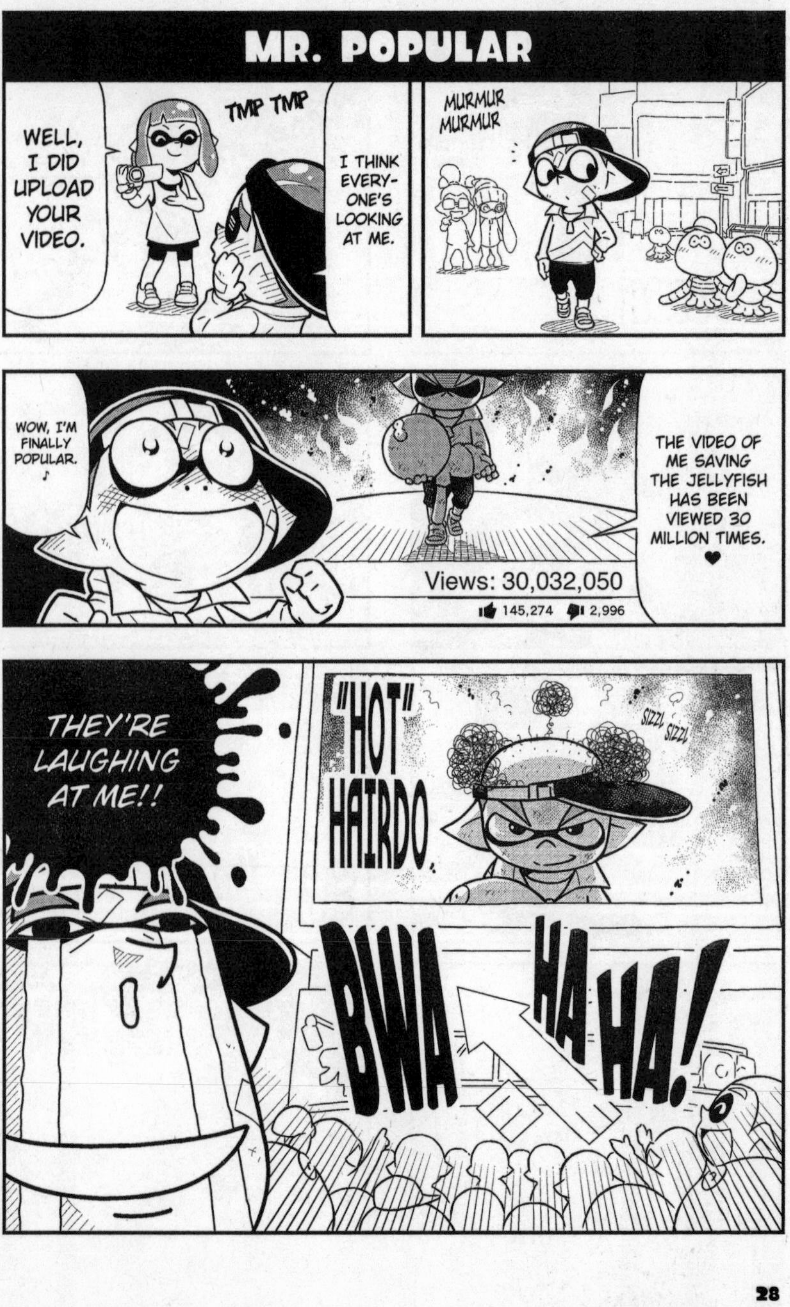
MURMUR MURMUR
I THINK EVERYONE'S LOOKING AT ME.
TMP TMP
WELL, I DID UPLOAD YOUR VIDEO.
THE VIDEO OF ME SAVING THE JELLYFISH HAS BEEN VIEWED 30 MILLION TIMES. ♥
Views: 30,032,050
145,274
2,996
WOW, I'M FINALLY POPULAR. ♪
SIZZL SIZZL
"HOT" HAIRDO
THEY'RE LAUGHING AT ME!!
BWA HA HA!

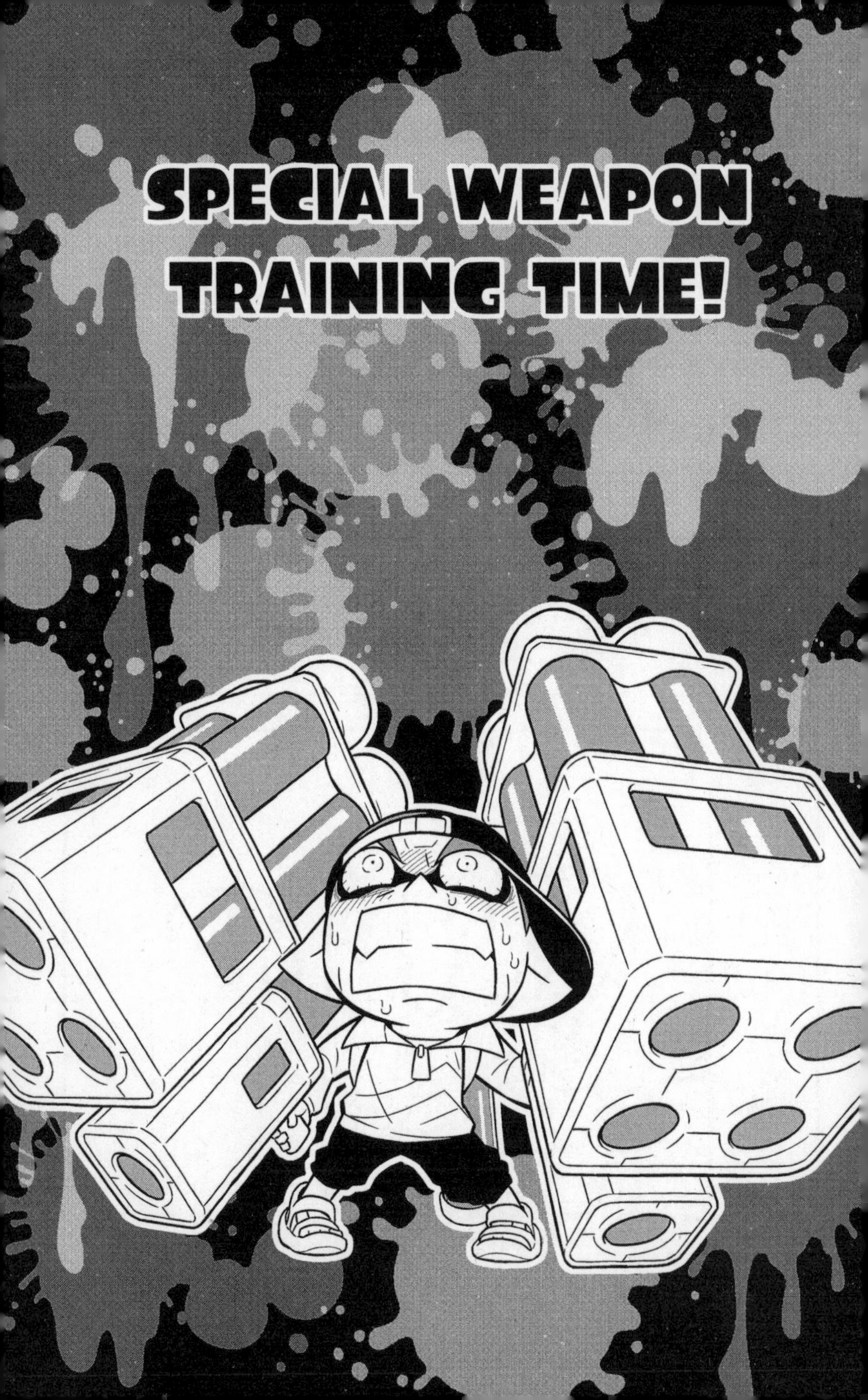
SPECIAL WEAPON
TRAINING TIME!

SPECIAL WEAPON

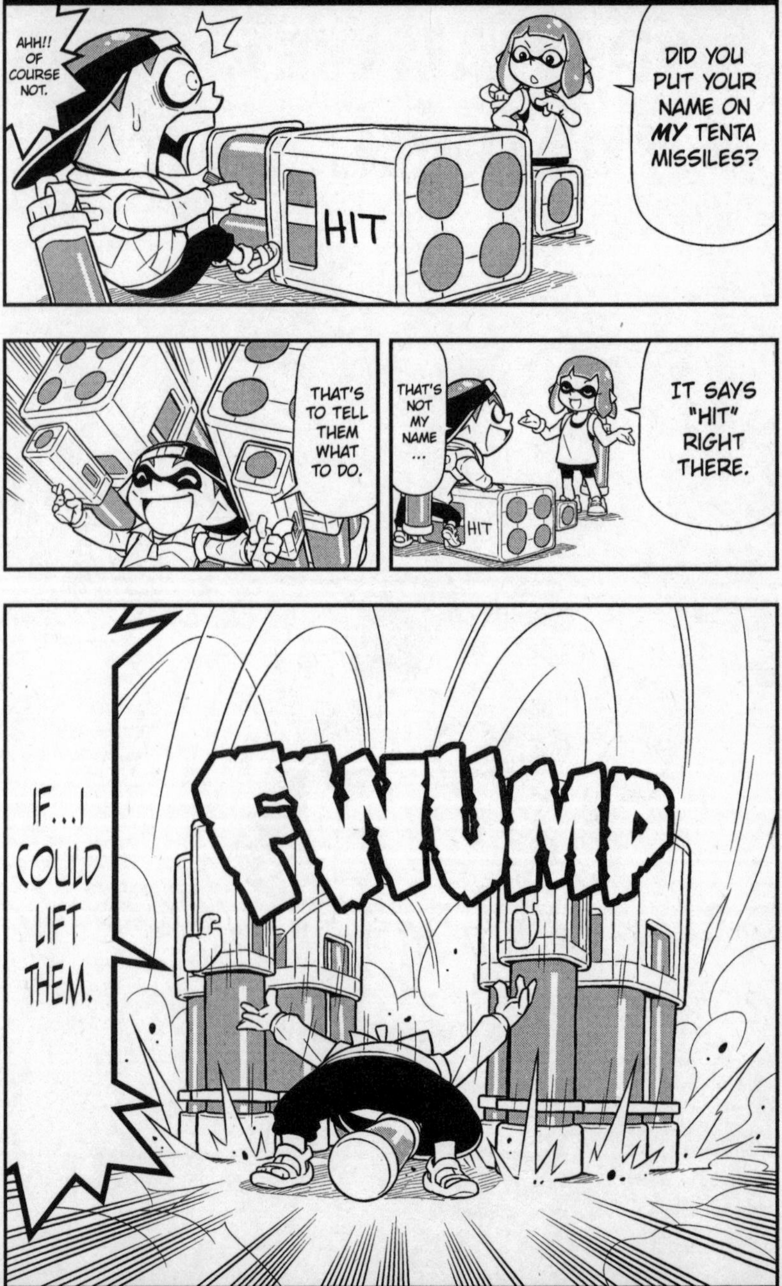
DID YOU PUT YOUR NAME ON MY TENTA MISSILES?
AHH!! OF COURSE NOT.
HIT
IT SAYS "HIT" RIGHT THERE.
THAT'S NOT MY NAME ...
HIT
THAT'S TO TELL THEM WHAT TO DO.
FNUMP
IF...I COULD LIFT THEM.

GYM

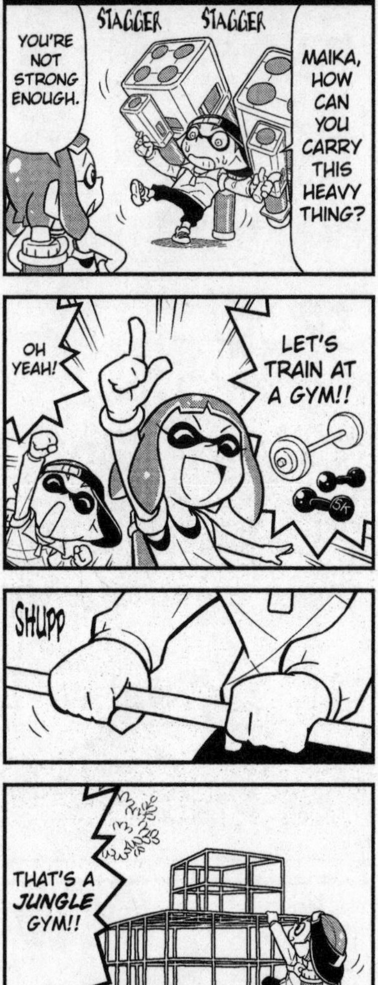
MAIKA, HOW CAN YOU CARRY THIS HEAVY THING?
STAGGER STAGGER
YOU'RE NOT STRONG ENOUGH.
LET'S TRAIN AT A GYM!!
OH YEAH!
5K
SHUPP
THAT'S A JUNGLE GYM!!

TRAINING WEAR

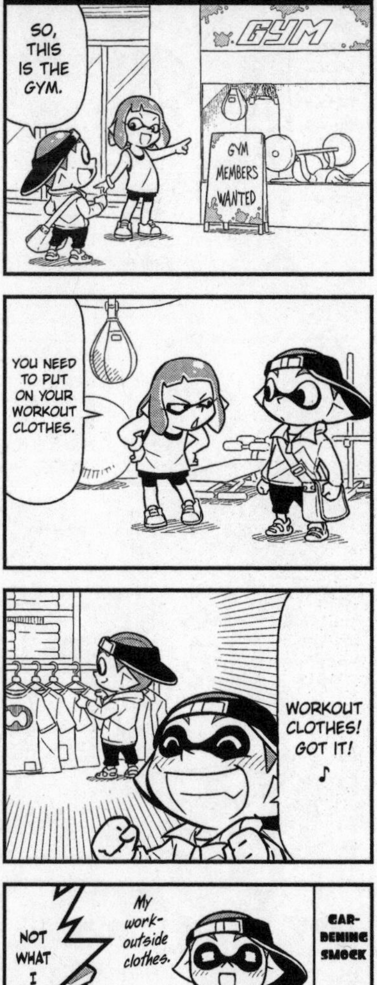
GYM
GYM MEMBERS WANTED
SO, THIS IS THE GYM.
YOU NEED TO PUT ON YOUR WORKOUT CLOTHES.
WORKOUT CLOTHES! GOT IT! ♪
GAR-DENING SMOCK
My work-outside clothes.
NOT WHAT I MEANT!!

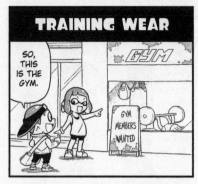

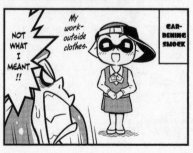

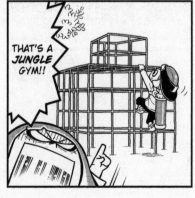

FILL UP

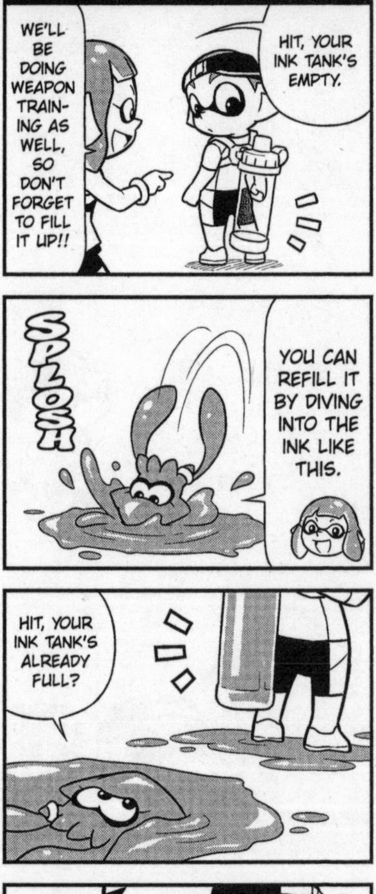
HIT, YOUR INK TANK'S EMPTY.
WE'LL BE DOING WEAPON TRAIN-ING AS WELL, SO DON'T FORGET TO FILL IT UP!!
YOU CAN REFILL IT BY DIVING INTO THE INK LIKE THIS.
SPLOSH
HIT, YOUR INK TANK'S ALREADY FULL?
ORANGE JUICE
WHAT? YOU CAN'T USE THAT!

PUSH-UPS

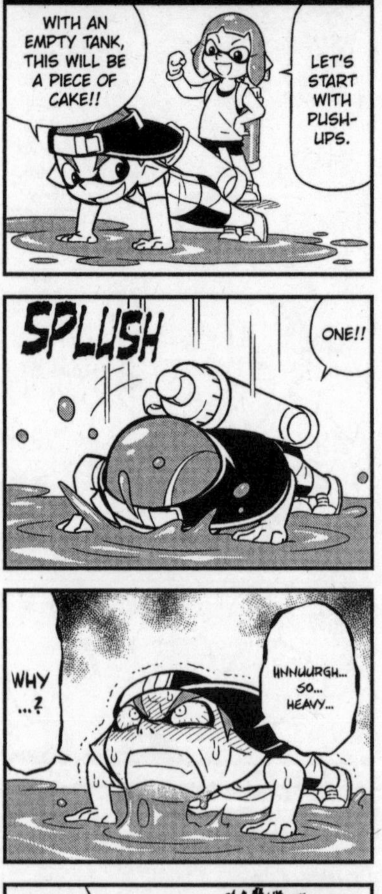
LET'S START WITH PUSH-UPS.
WITH AN EMPTY TANK, THIS WILL BE A PIECE OF CAKE!!
ONE!!
SPLUSH
UNNUURGH... SO... HEAVY...
WHY ...?
WHUMP
UM, YOU FILLED YOUR TANK BY GOING IN THE INK.

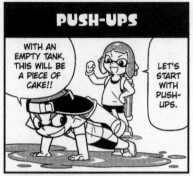

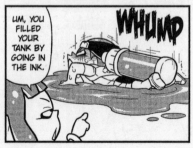

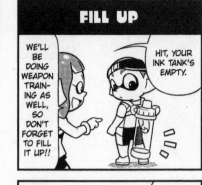

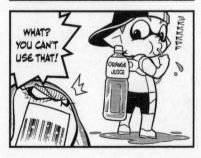

BULGING MUSCLES

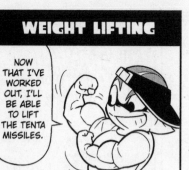

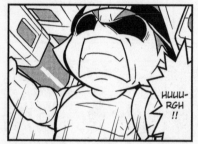

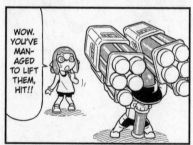

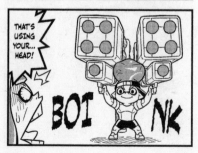

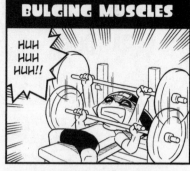

HUH HUH HUH!!
HUH HUH HUH!!
MAIKA, TAKE A LOOK AT MY MUSCLES.
PLUPP
HIS BRAIN ?!
The only muscle he DOESN'T work out.

WEIGHT LIFTING

NOW THAT I'VE WORKED OUT, I'LL BE ABLE TO LIFT THE TENTA MISSILES.
HUUU-RGH !!
WOW. YOU'VE MAN-AGED TO LIFT THEM, HIT!!
THAT'S USING YOUR... HEAD!
BOI NK

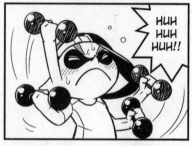

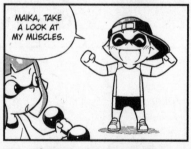

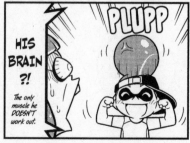

OUT OF INK

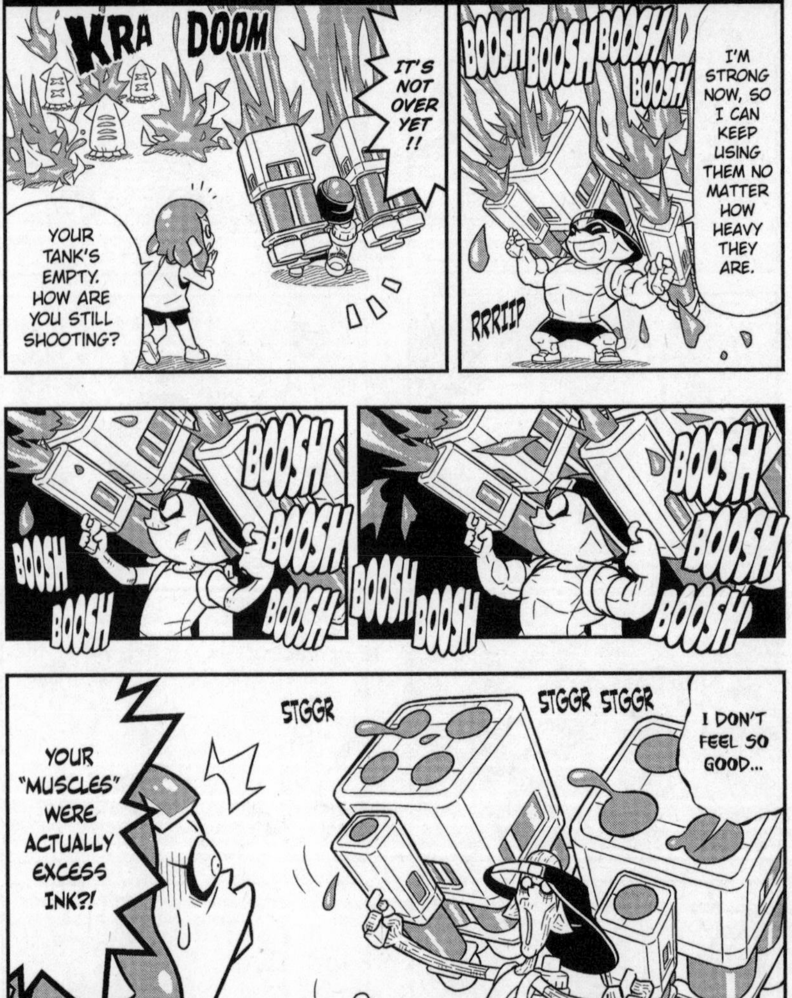

KRA
DOOM
YOUR TANK'S EMPTY. HOW ARE YOU STILL SHOOTING?
IT'S NOT OVER YET!!
BOOSH BOOSH BOOSH BOOSH
I'M STRONG NOW, SO I CAN KEEP USING THEM NO MATTER HOW HEAVY THEY ARE.
RRRIIP
BOOSH BOOSH BOOSH BOOSH BOOSH
BOOSH BOOSH BOOSH BOOSH BOOSH
STGGR
STGGR STGGR
I DON'T FEEL SO GOOD...
YOUR "MUSCLES" WERE ACTUALLY EXCESS INK?!
WOBBLE

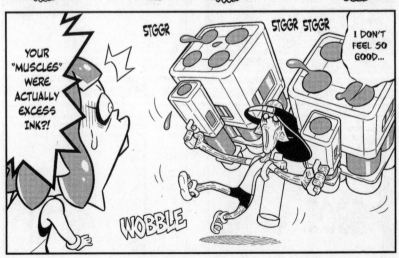

BURST BOMB TRAINING

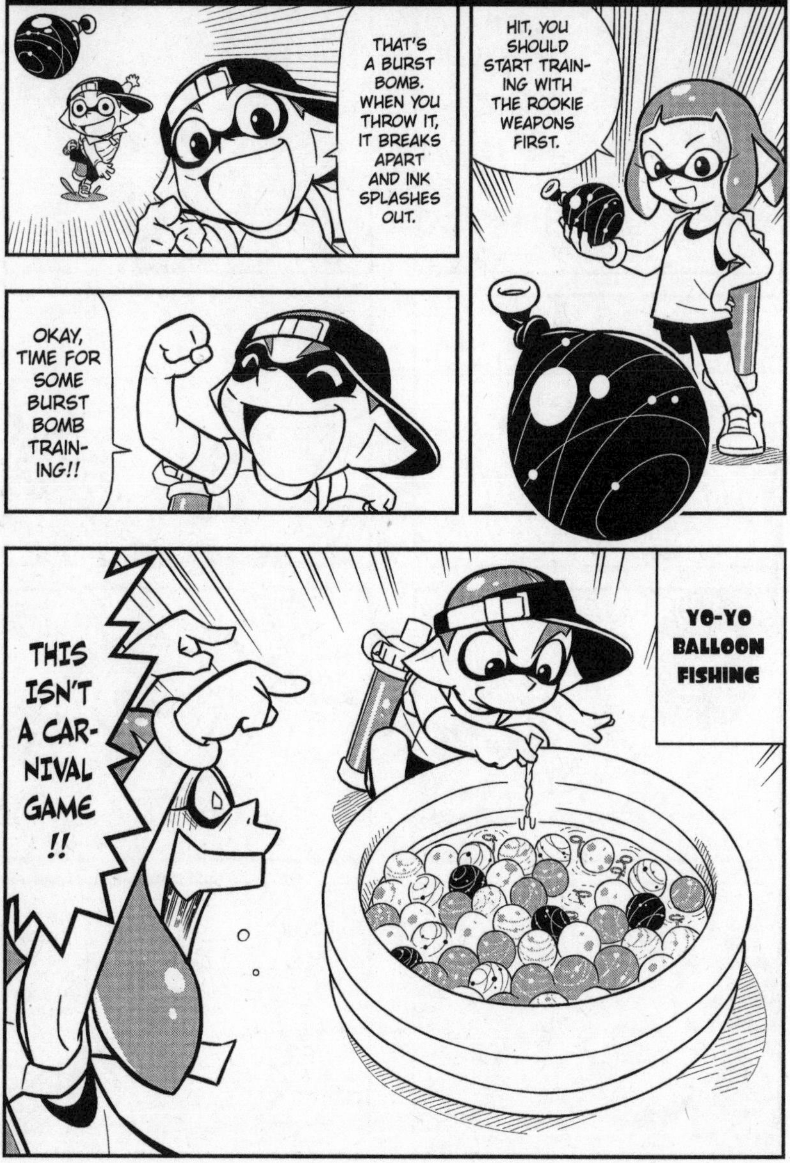

HIT, YOU SHOULD START TRAINING WITH THE ROOKIE WEAPONS FIRST.
THAT'S A BURST BOMB. WHEN YOU THROW IT, IT BREAKS APART AND INK SPLASHES OUT.
OKAY, TIME FOR SOME BURST BOMB TRAINING!!
YO-YO BALLOON FISHING
THIS ISN'T A CARNIVAL GAME!!

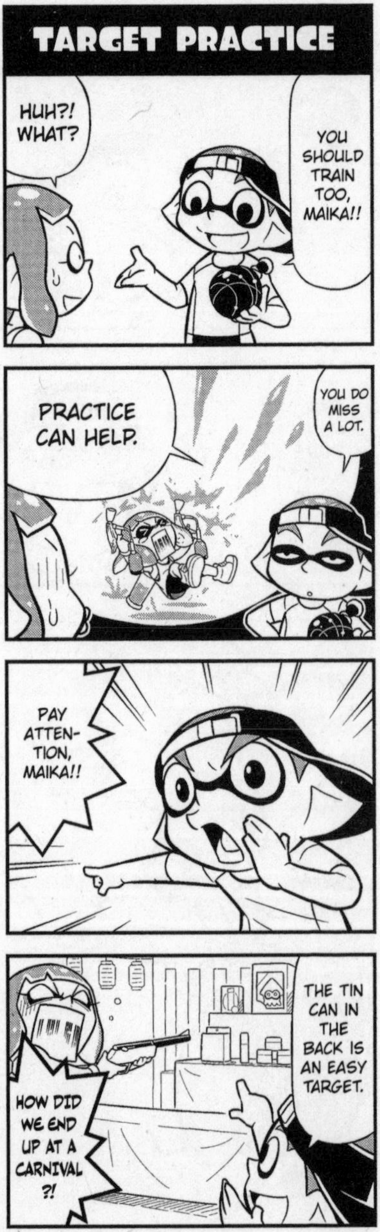
TARGET PRACTICE
YOU SHOULD TRAIN TOO, MAIKA!!
HUH?! WHAT?
YOU DO MISS A LOT.
PRACTICE CAN HELP.
PAY ATTENTION, MAIKA!!
THE TIN CAN IN THE BACK IS AN EASY TARGET.
HOW DID WE END UP AT A CARNIVAL?!

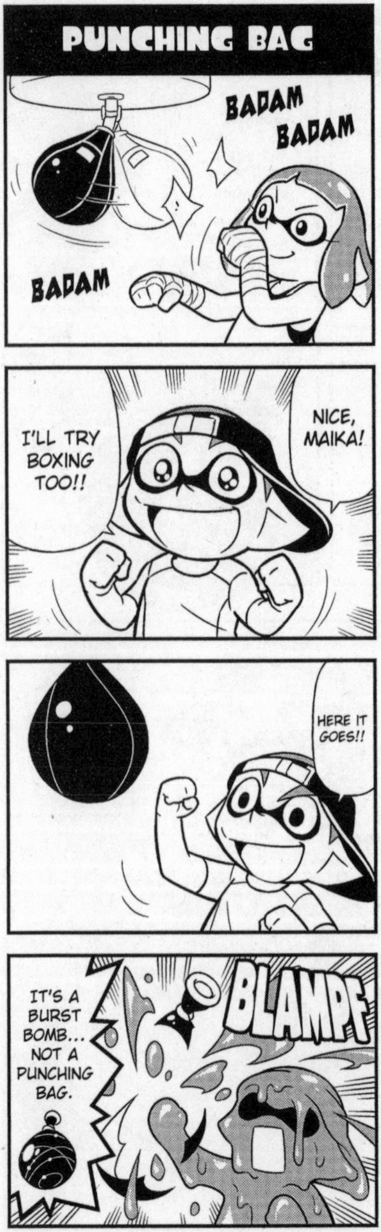
PUNCHING BAG
BADAM
BADAM
BADAM
NICE, MAIKA!
I'LL TRY BOXING TOO!!
HERE IT GOES!!
BLAMPF
IT'S A BURST BOMB... NOT A PUNCHING BAG.

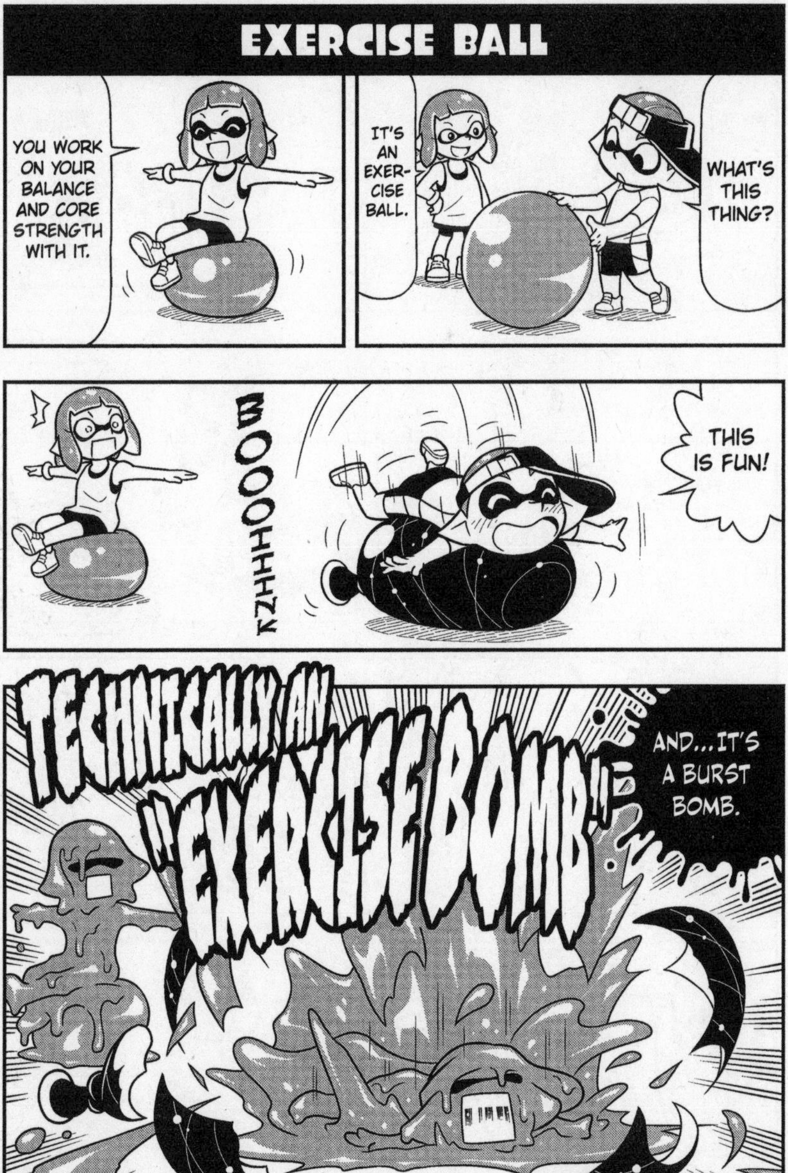
EXERCISE BALL
WHAT'S THIS THING?
IT'S AN EXER-CISE BALL.
YOU WORK ON YOUR BALANCE AND CORE STRENGTH WITH IT.
THIS IS FUN!
BOOOIIINK
AND...IT'S A BURST BOMB.
TECHNICALLY AN "EXERCISE BOMB"!

TURF WAR

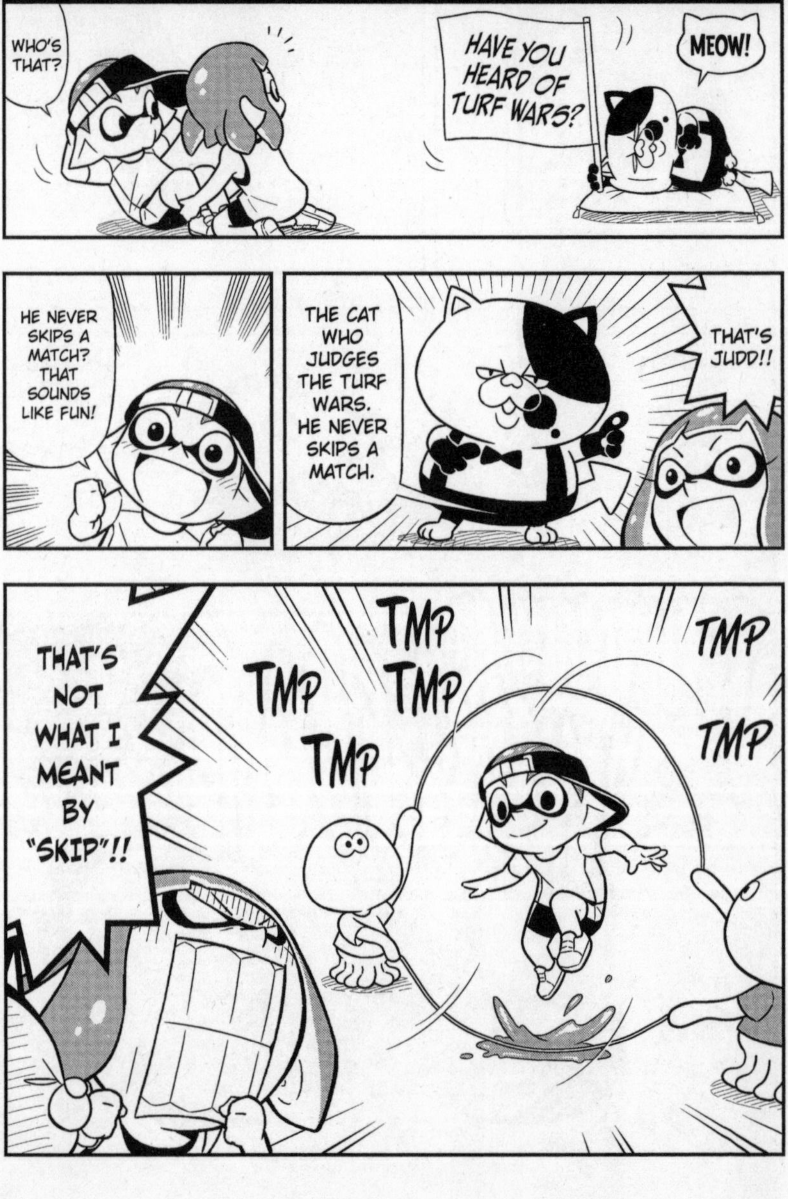

MEOW!
HAVE YOU HEARD OF TURF WARS?
WHO'S THAT?
THAT'S JUDD!!
THE CAT WHO JUDGES THE TURF WARS. HE NEVER SKIPS A MATCH.
HE NEVER SKIPS A MATCH? THAT SOUNDS LIKE FUN!
TMP
TMP
TMP
TMP
TMP
TMP
THAT'S NOT WHAT I MEANT BY "SKIP"!!

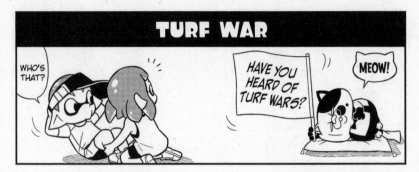

I'M READY!!

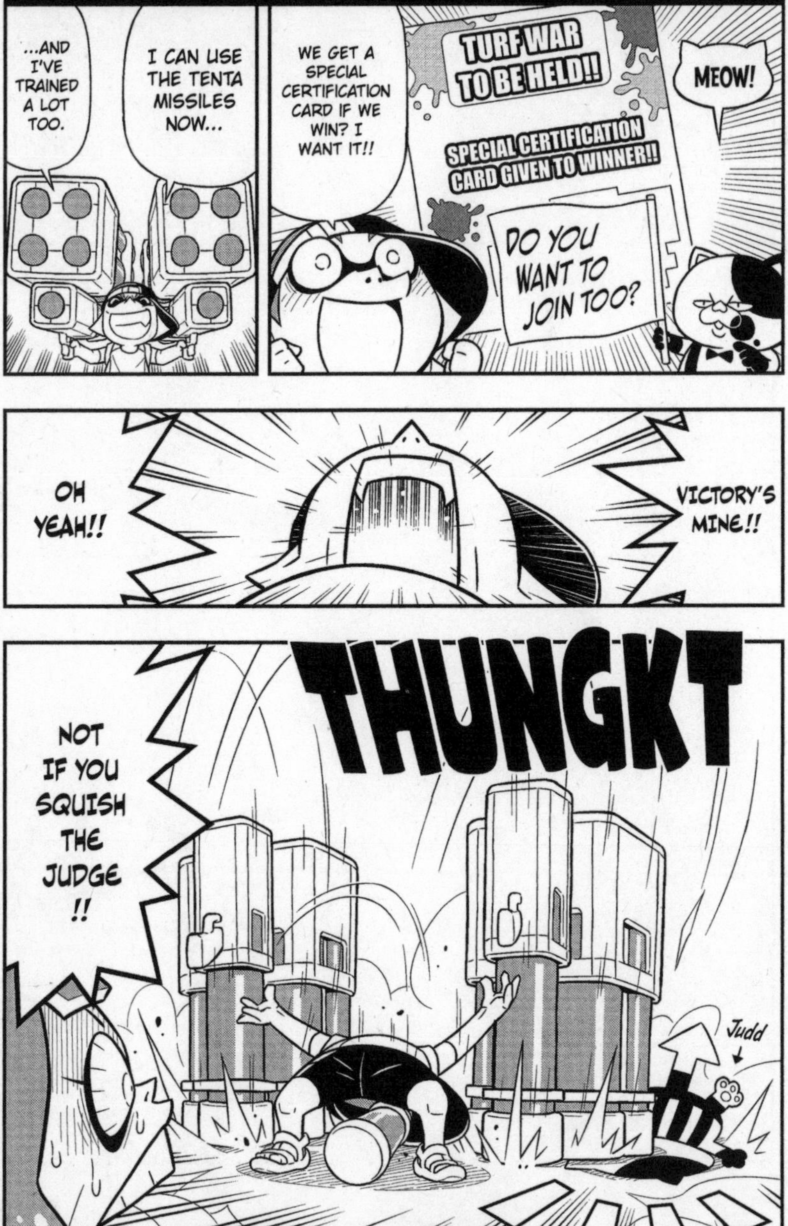
MEOW!
TURF WAR TO BE HELD!!
SPECIAL CERTIFICATION CARD GIVEN TO WINNER!!
WE GET A SPECIAL CERTIFICATION CARD IF WE WIN? I WANT IT!!
DO YOU WANT TO JOIN TOO?
I CAN USE THE TENTA MISSILES NOW...
...AND I'VE TRAINED A LOT TOO.
VICTORY'S MINE!!
OH YEAH!!
THUNGKT
NOT IF YOU SQUISH THE JUDGE!!
Judd

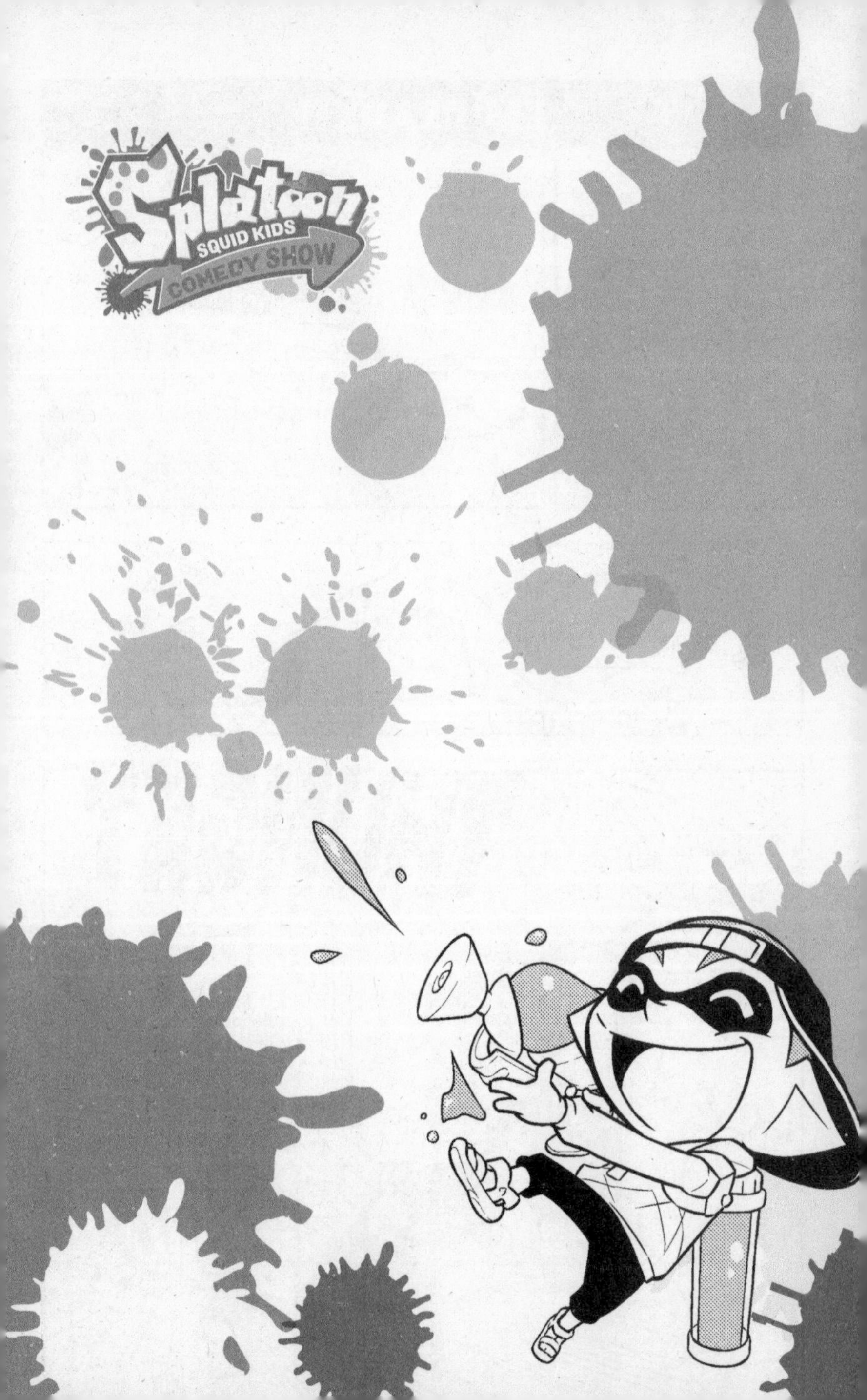
Splatoon
SQUID KIDS
COMEDY SHOW

TIME TO GET THE SPECIAL CERTIFICATION CARD!

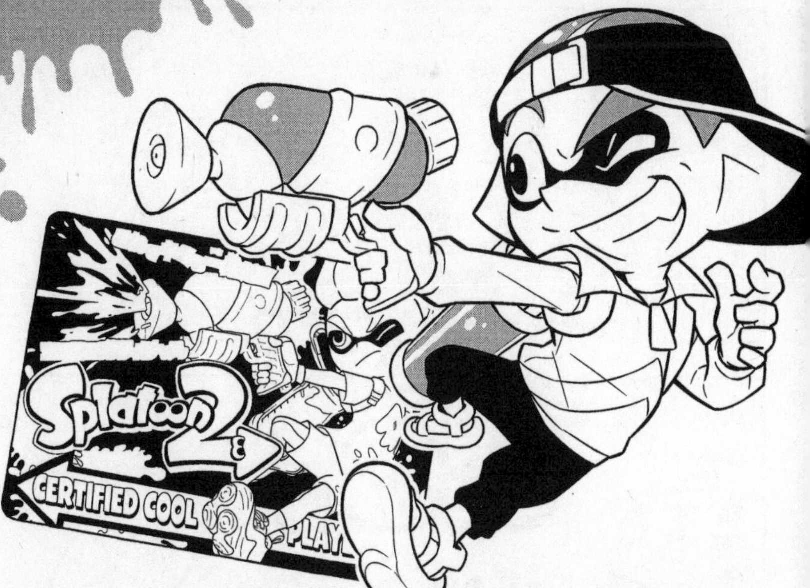
Splatoon 2
CERTIFIED COOL

MY FIRST TURF WAR

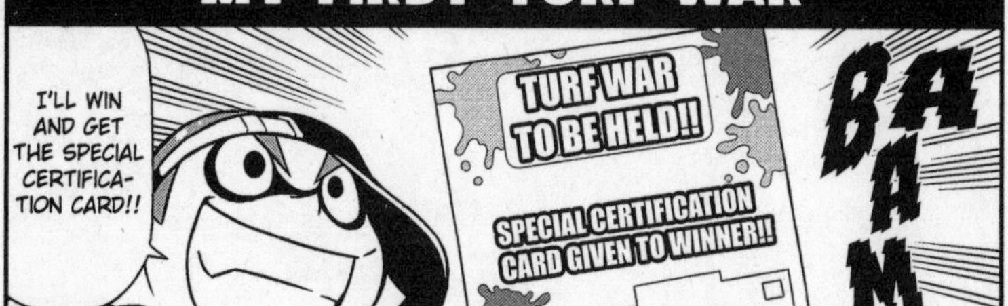
BAAM
TURF WAR TO BE HELD!!
SPECIAL CERTIFICATION CARD GIVEN TO WINNER!!
I'LL WIN AND GET THE SPECIAL CERTIFICATION CARD!!

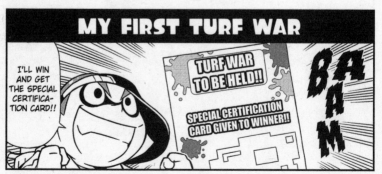

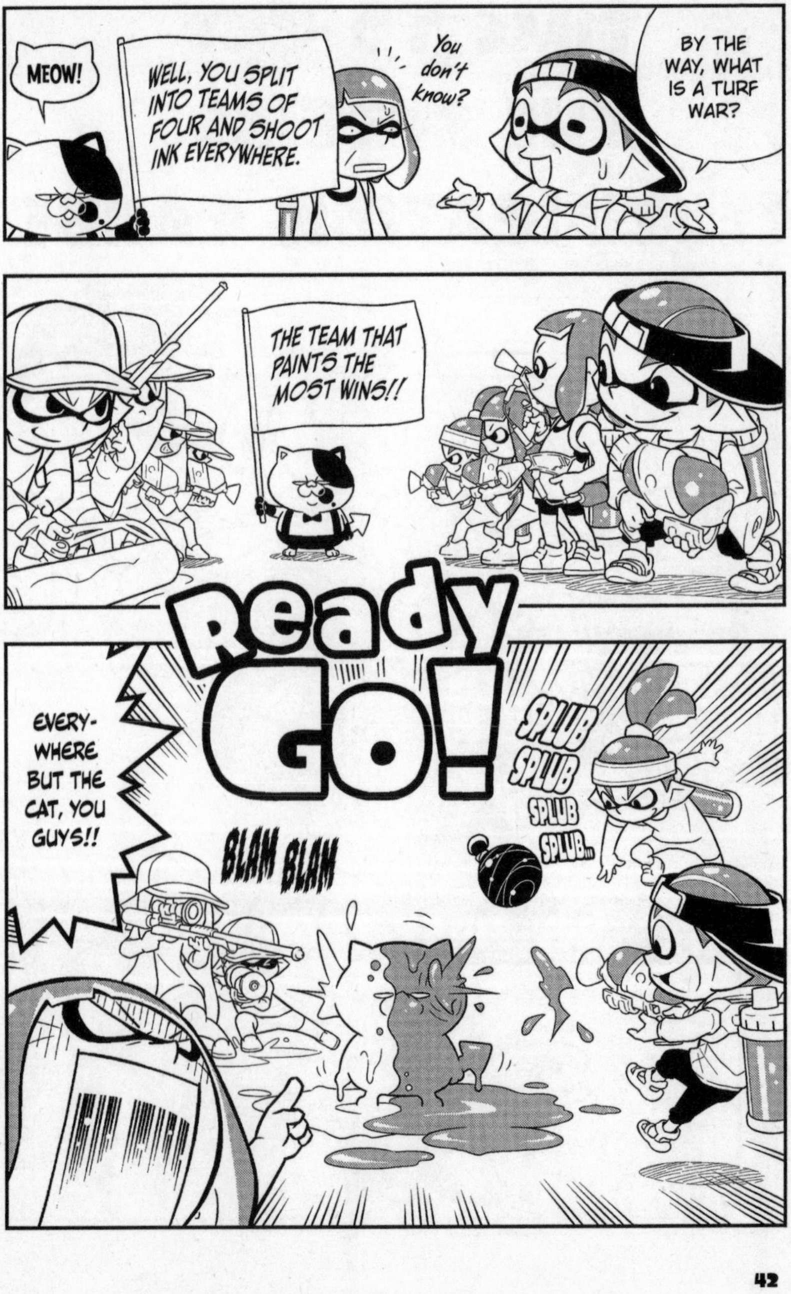
BY THE WAY, WHAT IS A TURF WAR?
You don't know?
WELL, YOU SPLIT INTO TEAMS OF FOUR AND SHOOT INK EVERYWHERE.
MEOW!
THE TEAM THAT PAINTS THE MOST WINS!!
Ready GO!
SPLUB SPLUB SPLUB SPLUB...
EVERY-WHERE BUT THE CAT, YOU GUYS!!
BLAM BLAM

HIDING

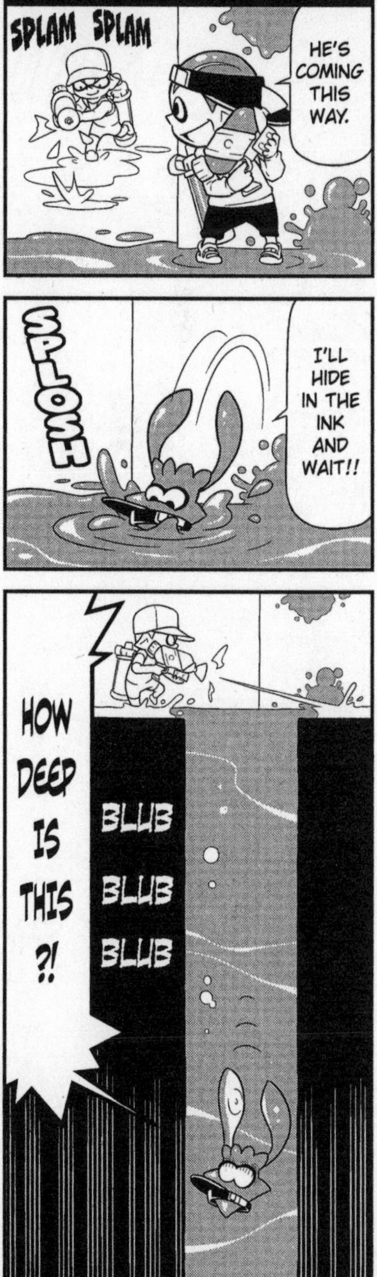
SPLAM SPLAM
HE'S COMING THIS WAY.
SPLOSH
I'LL HIDE IN THE INK AND WAIT!!
HOW DEEP IS THIS ?!
BLUB
BLUB
BLUB

TAKEOFF

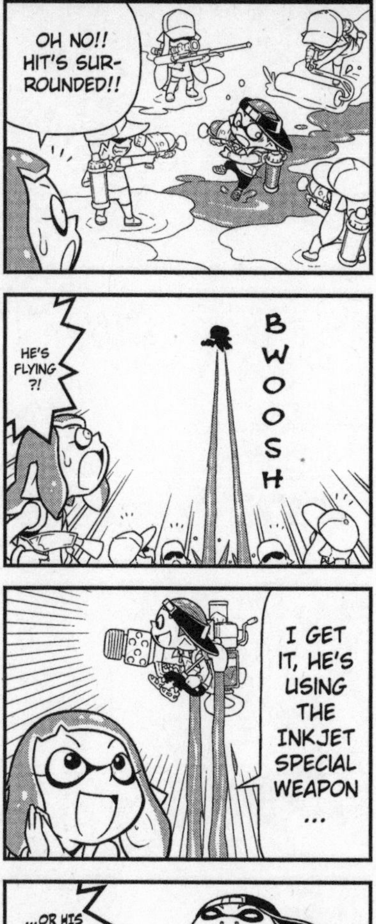
OH NO!! HIT'S SUR-ROUNDED!!
BWOOSH
HE'S FLYING ?!
I GET IT, HE'S USING THE INKJET SPECIAL WEAPON ...
...OR HIS REALLY RUNNY NOSE.

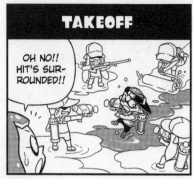

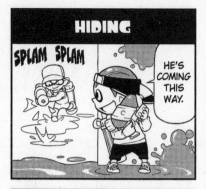

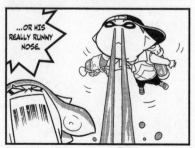

SWINGING ROLLER

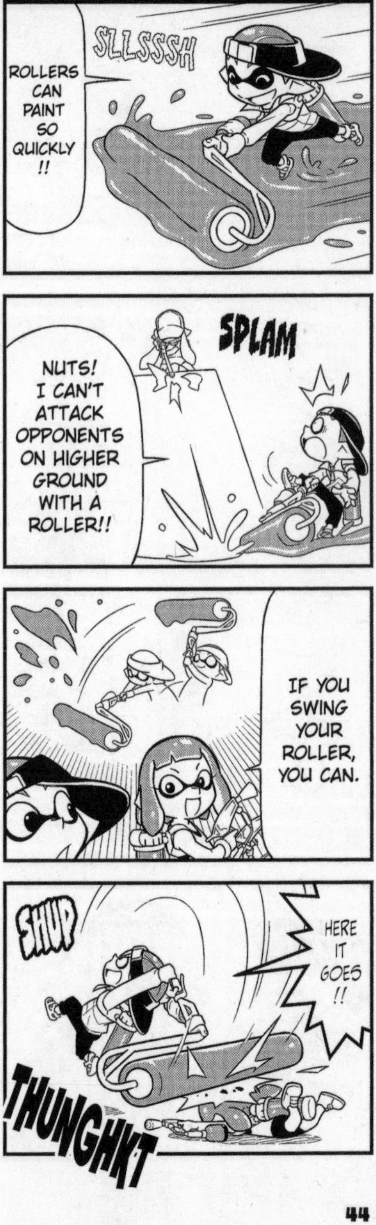
SLLSSSH
ROLLERS CAN PAINT SO QUICKLY!!
NUTS! I CAN'T ATTACK OPPONENTS ON HIGHER GROUND WITH A ROLLER!!
SPLAM
IF YOU SWING YOUR ROLLER, YOU CAN.
HERE IT GOES!!
SHUP
THUNGHKT

WATCH OUT!

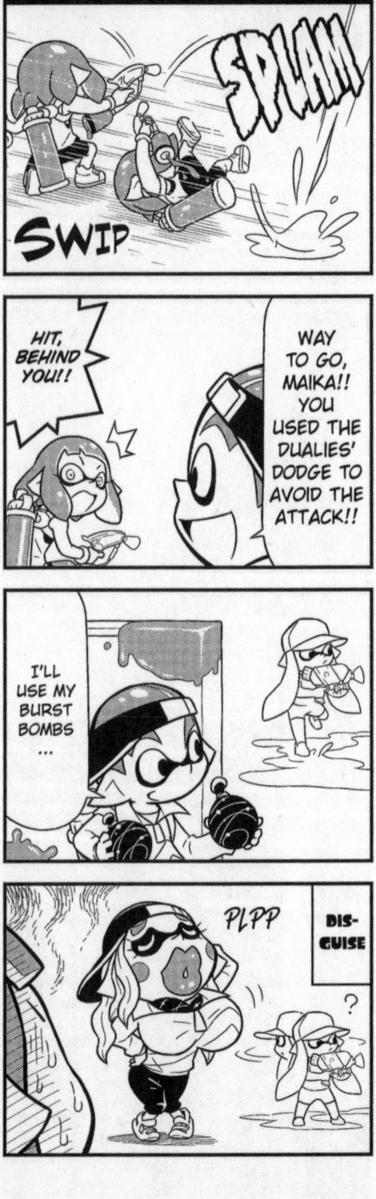
SPLAM
SWIP
WAY TO GO, MAIKA!! YOU USED THE DUALIES' DODGE TO AVOID THE ATTACK!!
HIT, BEHIND YOU!!
I'LL USE MY BURST BOMBS...
DIS-GUISE
PLPP
?

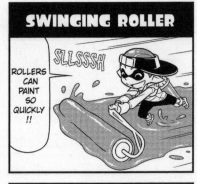

SPECIAL CARD

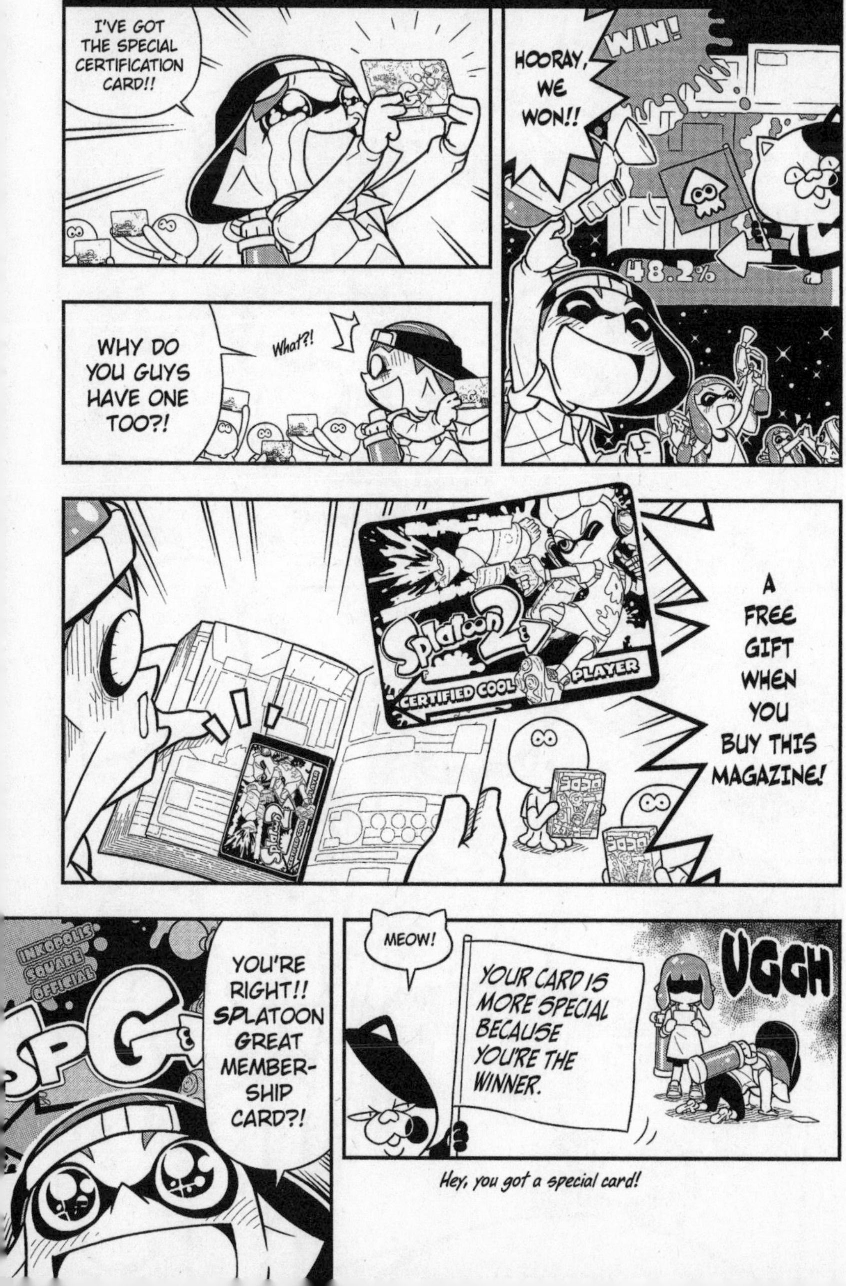
WIN!
HOORAY, WE WON!!
48.2%
I'VE GOT THE SPECIAL CERTIFICATION CARD!!
What?!
WHY DO YOU GUYS HAVE ONE TOO?!
A FREE GIFT WHEN YOU BUY THIS MAGAZINE!
Splatoon 2
CERTIFIED COOL PLAYER
MEOW!
YOUR CARD IS MORE SPECIAL BECAUSE YOU'RE THE WINNER.
UGGH
INKOPOLIS SQUARE OFFICIAL
SPG
YOU'RE RIGHT!! SPLATOON GREAT MEMBERSHIP CARD?!

Hey, you got a special card!

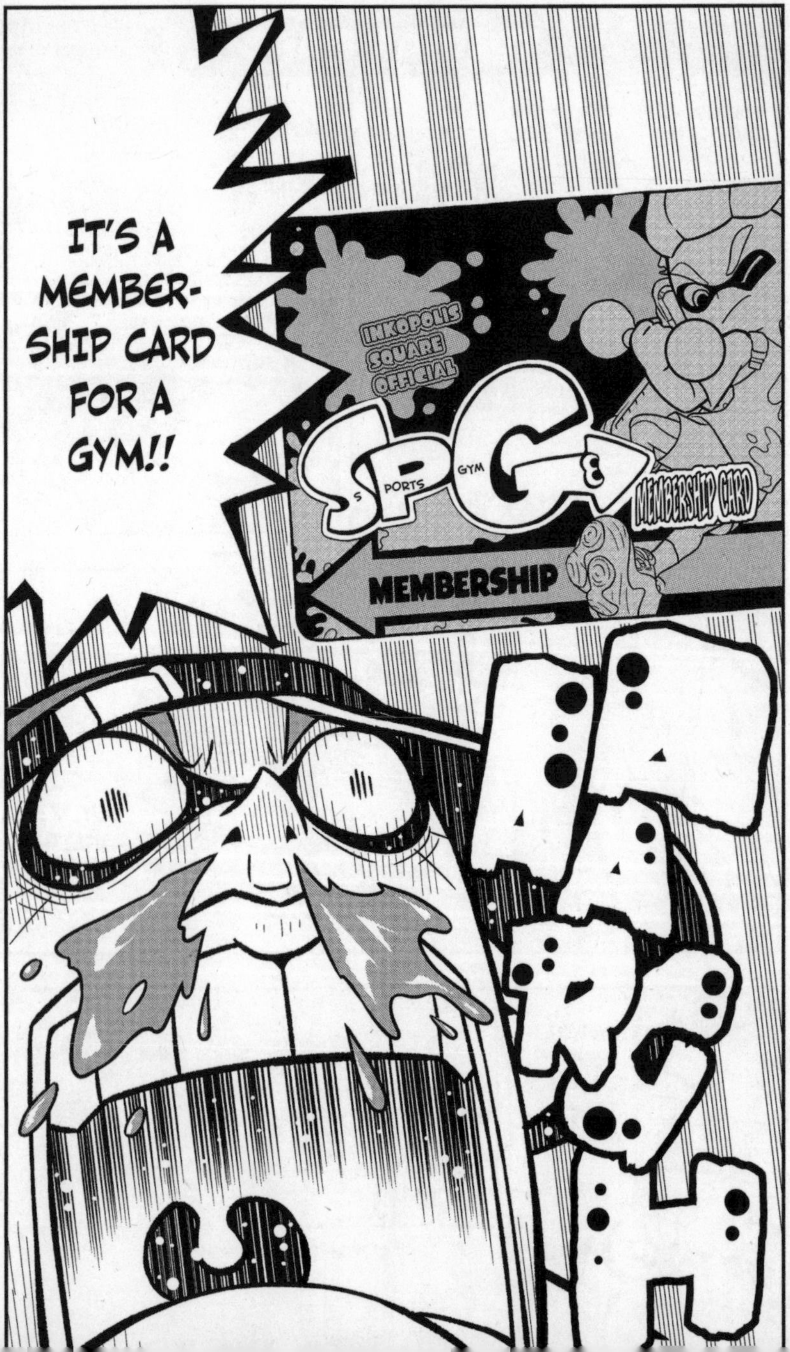
IT'S A MEMBER-SHIP CARD FOR A GYM!!
INKOPOLIS SQUARE OFFICIAL
SPORTS GYM
SPG
MEMBERSHIP CARD
MEMBERSHIP
AAARGH

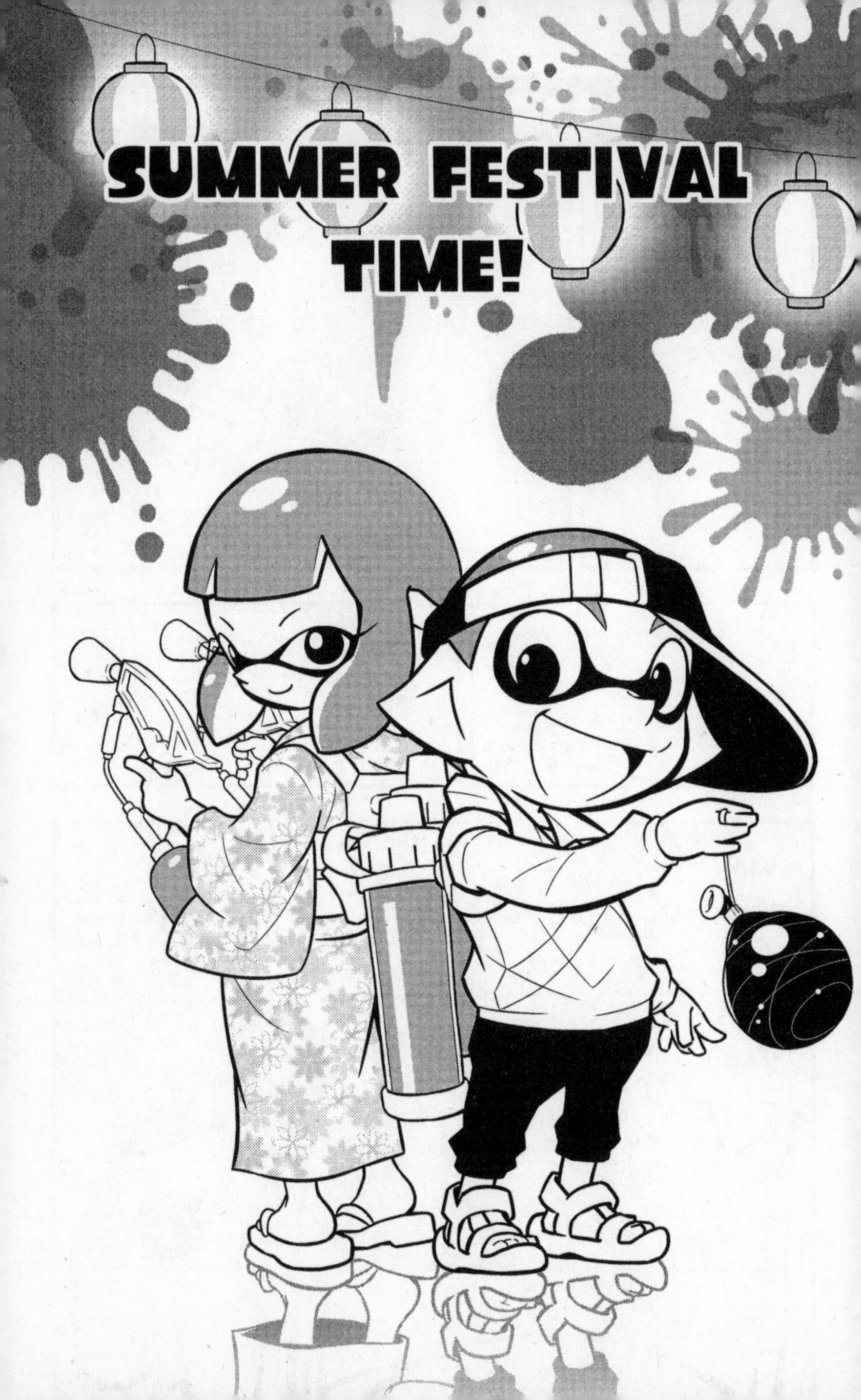
SUMMER FESTIVAL TIME!

MEETING AT THE SUMMER FESTIVAL

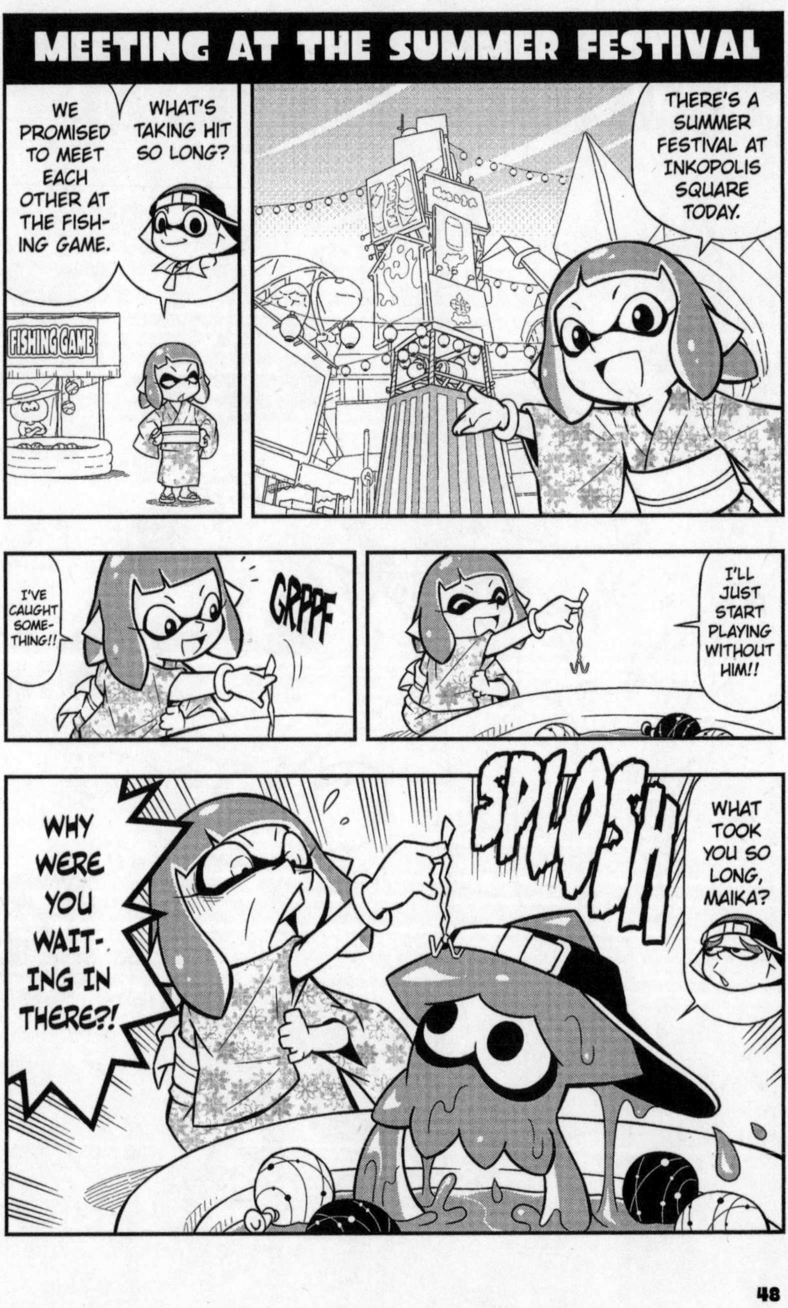
THERE'S A SUMMER FESTIVAL AT INKOPOLIS SQUARE TODAY.
WHAT'S TAKING HIT SO LONG?
WE PROMISED TO MEET EACH OTHER AT THE FISHING GAME.
FISHING GAME
I'LL JUST START PLAYING WITHOUT HIM!!
I'VE CAUGHT SOMETHING!!
GRPPF
WHAT TOOK YOU SO LONG, MAIKA?
SPLOSH
WHY WERE YOU WAITING IN THERE?!

MASK

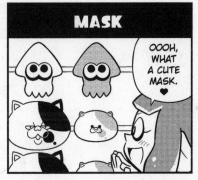

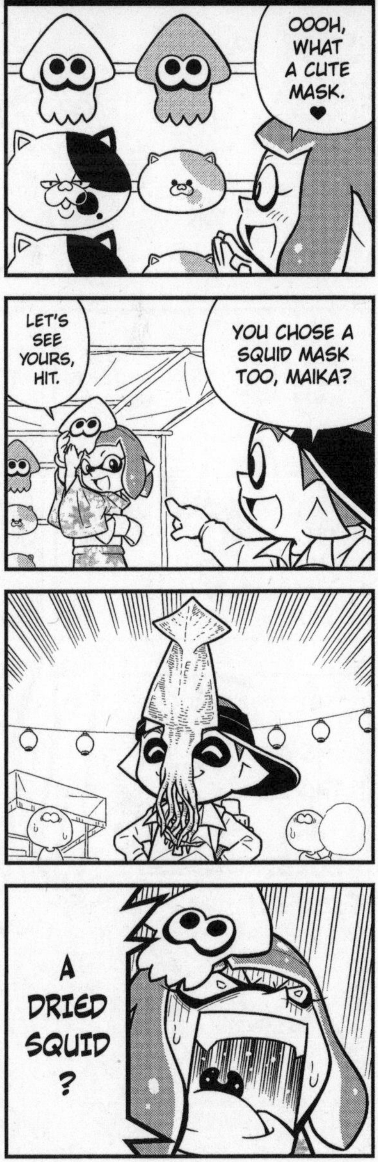
OOOH, WHAT A CUTE MASK. ♥
YOU CHOSE A SQUID MASK TOO, MAIKA?
LET'S SEE YOURS, HIT.
A DRIED SQUID ?

CREPE STALL

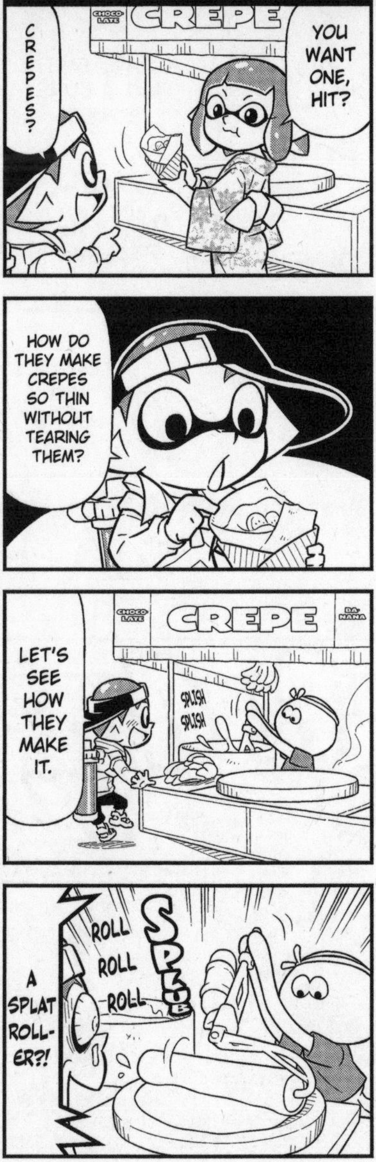
CHOCO-LATE
CREPE
YOU WANT ONE, HIT?
CREPES?
HOW DO THEY MAKE CREPES SO THIN WITHOUT TEARING THEM?
CHOCO-LATE
CREPE
BA-NANA
SPLISH
SPLISH
LET'S SEE HOW THEY MAKE IT.
SPLUB
ROLL
ROLL
ROLL
A SPLAT ROLL-ER?!

BROKEN BULB

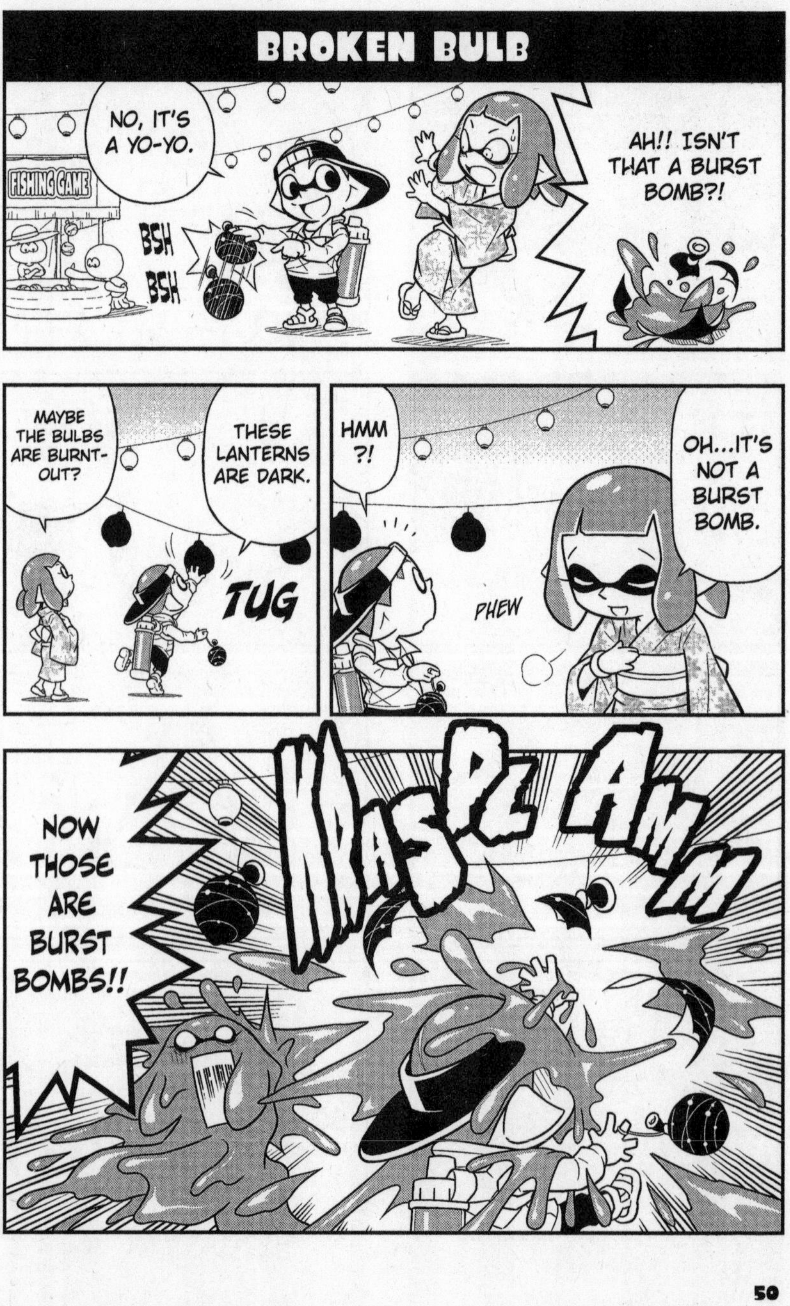
AH!! ISN'T THAT A BURST BOMB?!
NO, IT'S A YO-YO.
FISHING GAME
BSH
BSH
OH...IT'S NOT A BURST BOMB.
HMM ?!
PHEW
THESE LANTERNS ARE DARK.
MAYBE THE BULBS ARE BURNT-OUT?
TUG
KRASPLAMM
NOW THOSE ARE BURST BOMBS!!

OCTOPUS DUMPLINGS

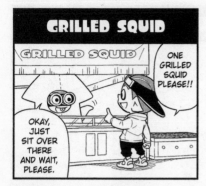

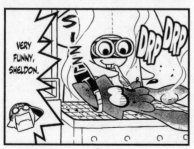

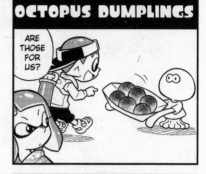

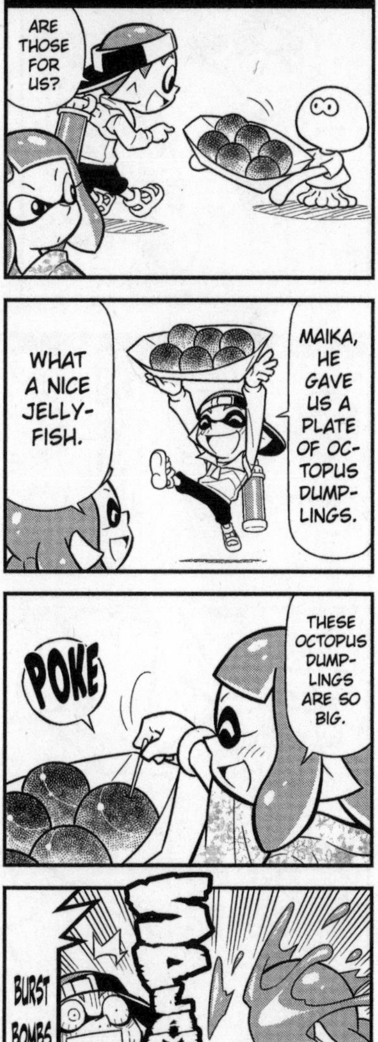
ARE THOSE FOR US?
MAIKA, HE GAVE US A PLATE OF OC-TOPUS DUMP-LINGS.
WHAT A NICE JELLY-FISH.
THESE OCTOPUS DUMP-LINGS ARE SO BIG.
POKE
SPLAT
BURST BOMBS !!

GRILLED SQUID

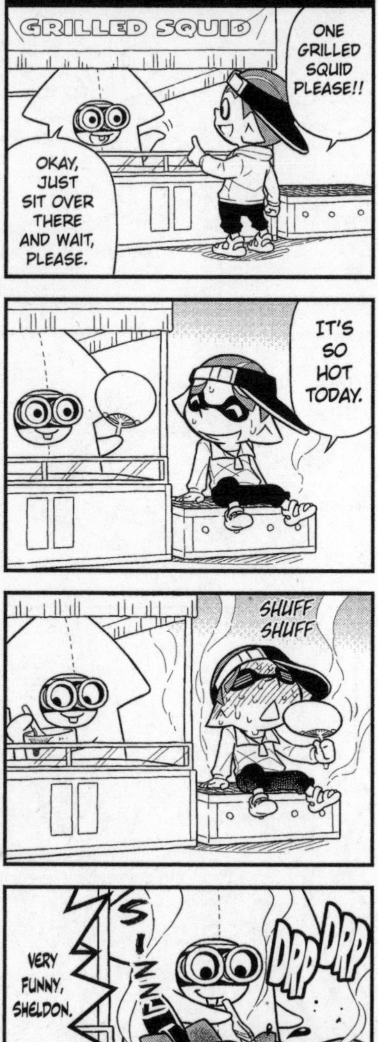
GRILLED SQUID
ONE GRILLED SQUID PLEASE!!
OKAY, JUST SIT OVER THERE AND WAIT, PLEASE.
IT'S SO HOT TODAY.
SHUFF SHUFF
DRP DRP
VERY FUNNY, SHELDON.

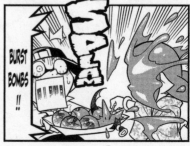

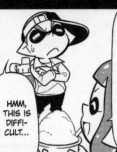

SHAVED ICE

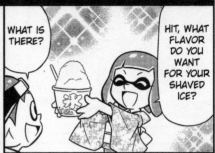

HIT, WHAT FLAVOR DO YOU WANT FOR YOUR SHAVED ICE?
WHAT IS THERE?
STRAW-BERRY, MELON, LEMON, PINEAPPLE, PEACH, GREEN TEA, BLUE-BERRY...
HMM, THIS IS DIFFI-CULT...
I'LL HAVE THEM ALL!!
STRAWBERRY
MELON
LEMON
PINEAPPLE
PEACH
GREEN TEA
COMING UP!!
KWADOOM
TOO MUCH... WAY TOO MUCH!!
TENTA MISSILES

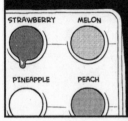

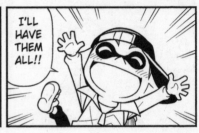

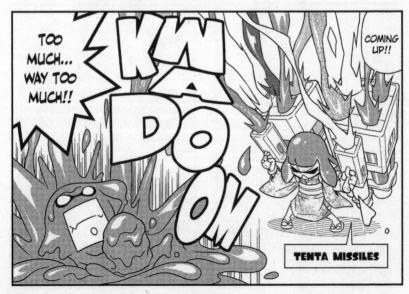

SHOOTING GALLERY PRIZE

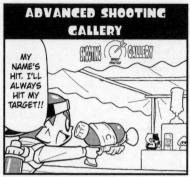

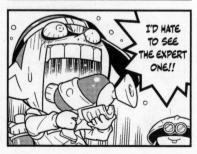

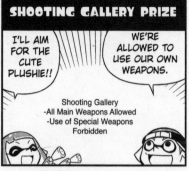

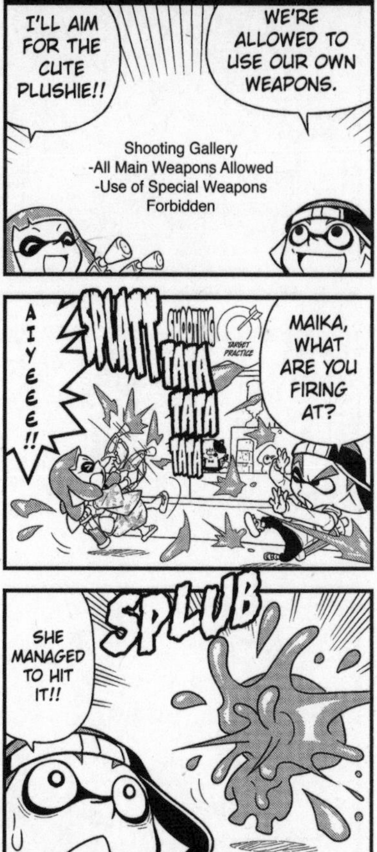
WE'RE ALLOWED TO USE OUR OWN WEAPONS.
I'LL AIM FOR THE CUTE PLUSHIE!!
Shooting Gallery
-All Main Weapons Allowed
-Use of Special Weapons Forbidden
MAIKA, WHAT ARE YOU FIRING AT?
SHOOTING
TARGET PRACTICE
SPLATT
TATA TATA TATA
AIYEEEE!!
SPLUB
SHE MANAGED TO HIT IT!!
I'M NOT A PRIZE...
SHOOTING
TARGET PRACTICE
SORRY, SHELDON!!

ADVANCED SHOOTING GALLERY

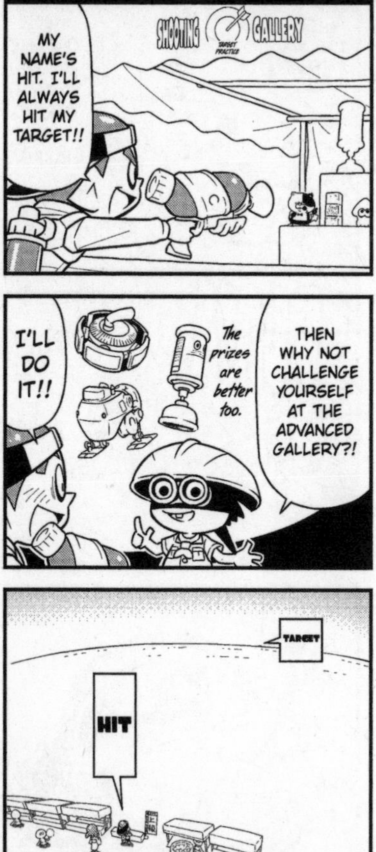
SHOOTING GALLERY
TARGET PRACTICE
MY NAME'S HIT. I'LL ALWAYS HIT MY TARGET!!
THEN WHY NOT CHALLENGE YOURSELF AT THE ADVANCED GALLERY?!
The prizes are better too.
I'LL DO IT!!
TARGET
HIT
I'D HATE TO SEE THE EXPERT ONE!!

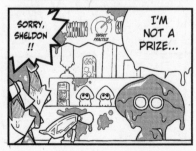

SUB WEAPON PRIZE

HIT, THERE'S A SUB WEAPON AMONG THE PRIZES!!
YEAH, I'LL AIM AT THAT ONE!!
SPLAM
I GOT IT!!
IT HASN'T FALLEN DOWN, SO THAT DOESN'T COUNT.
SUCTION BOMB
NO FAIR!!

I GOT THE ROBOT!

SPLAM
I GOT SOMETHING!!
A WALKING ROBOT!!
TMP
TMP
TMP
HOW CUTE. ❤ IT'S FOLLOWING ME AROUND.
TMP
TMP
TMP
KRA
SPLAM
AUTO-BOMB

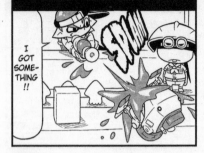

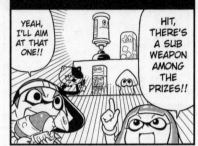

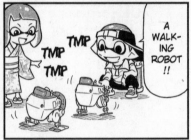

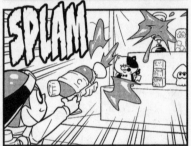

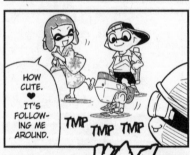

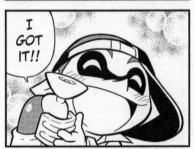

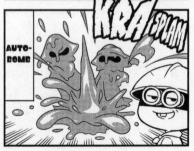

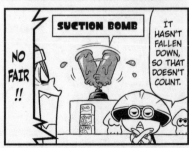

THE OFFENSIVE POWER OF THE DUALIES

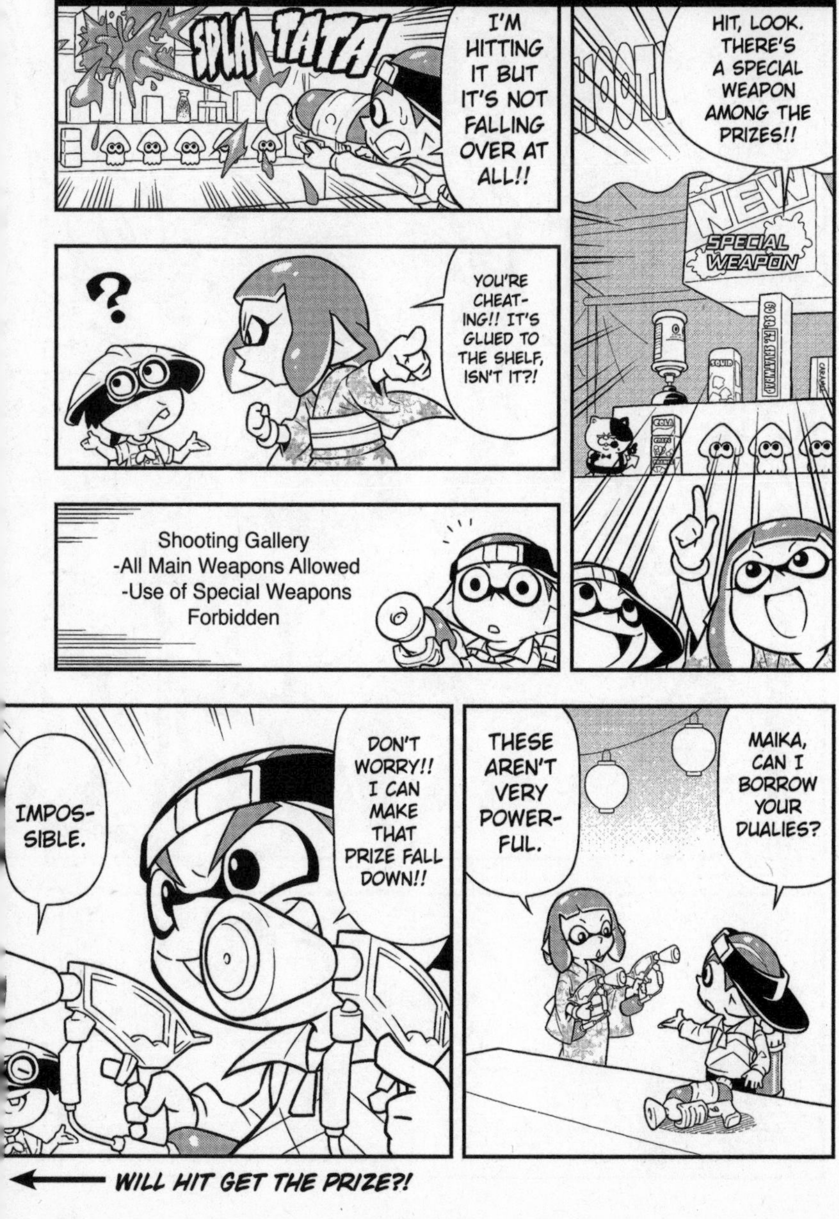
HIT, LOOK. THERE'S A SPECIAL WEAPON AMONG THE PRIZES!!
NEW
SPECIAL WEAPON
SQUID
COLA
SPLA TATA
I'M HITTING IT BUT IT'S NOT FALLING OVER AT ALL!!
?
YOU'RE CHEAT-ING!! IT'S GLUED TO THE SHELF, ISN'T IT?!
Shooting Gallery
-All Main Weapons Allowed
-Use of Special Weapons Forbidden
MAIKA, CAN I BORROW YOUR DUALIES?
THESE AREN'T VERY POWER-FUL.
DON'T WORRY!! I CAN MAKE THAT PRIZE FALL DOWN!!
IMPOS-SIBLE.

← *WILL HIT GET THE PRIZE?!*

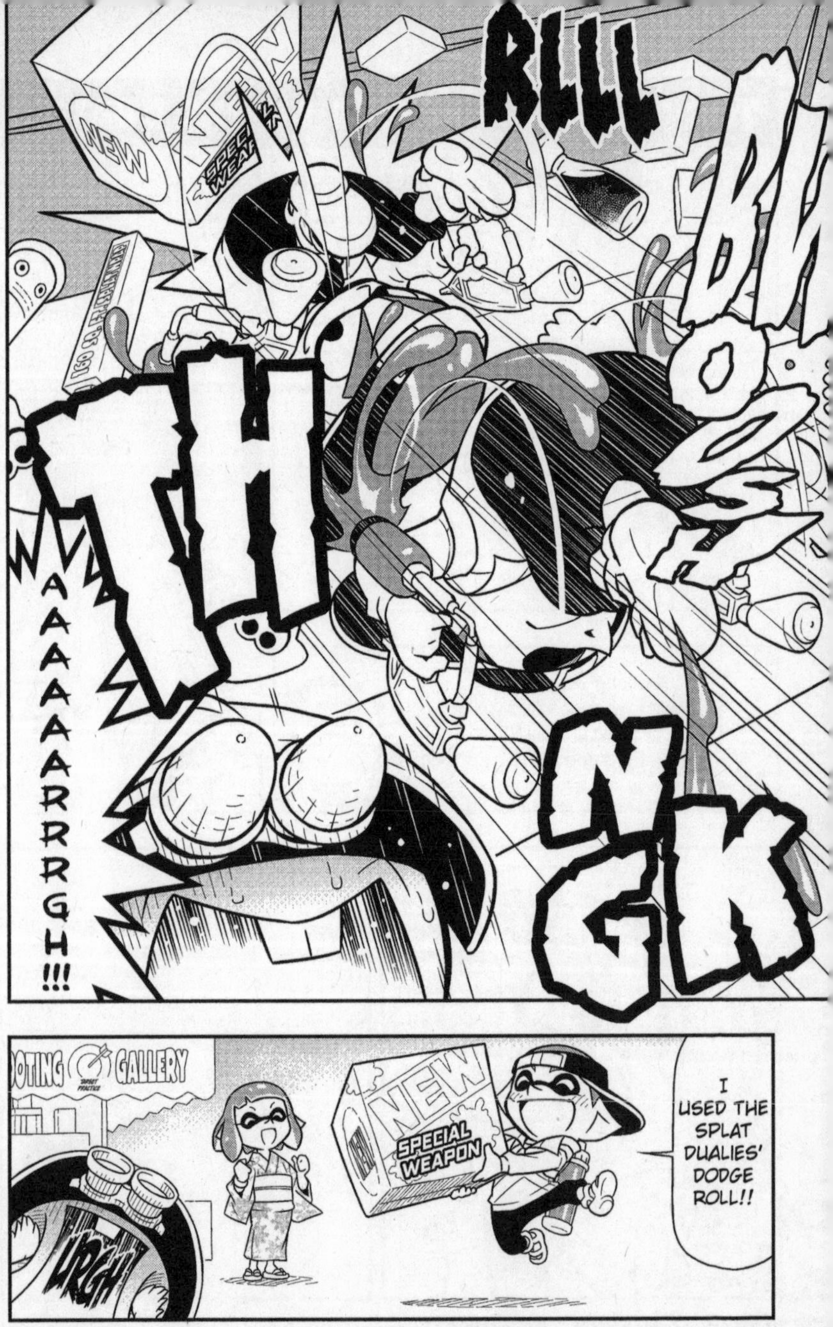
RLLL
NEW
SPECIAL WEAPON
AAAAAARRRGH!!!
TH
NGK
I USED THE SPLAT DUALIES' DODGE ROLL!!
NEW
SPECIAL WEAPON
SHOOTING GALLERY
URGH

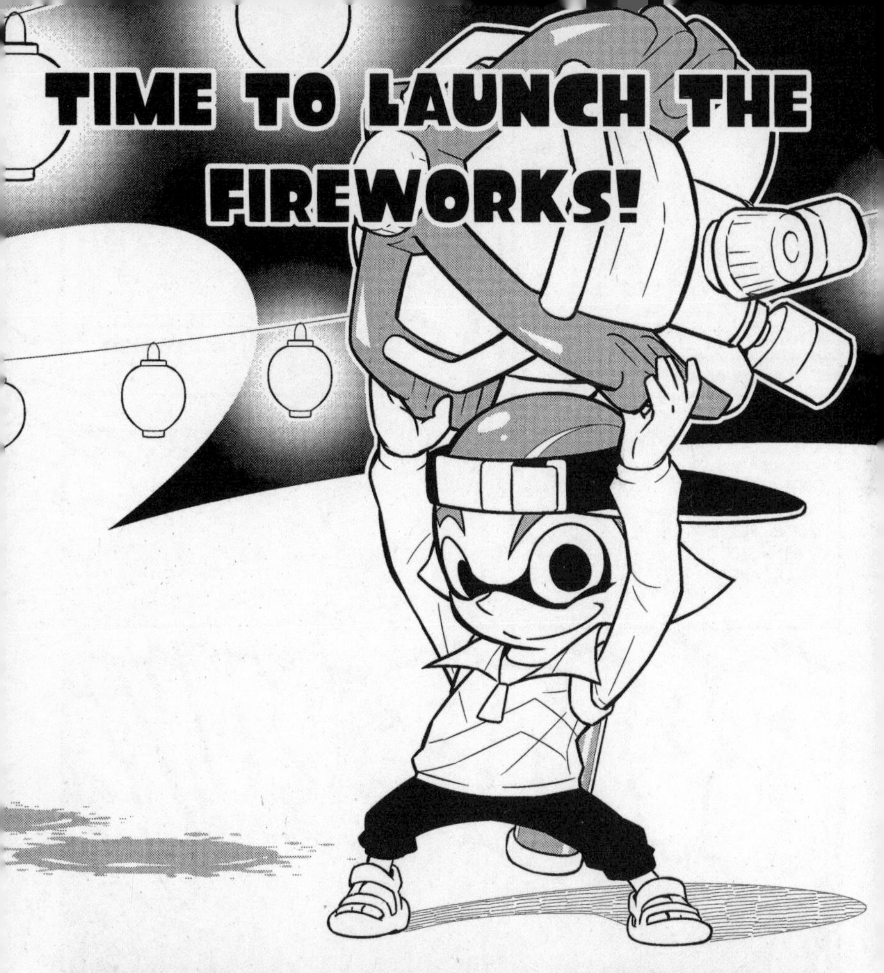
TIME TO LAUNCH THE FIREWORKS!

FESTIVAL DANCE

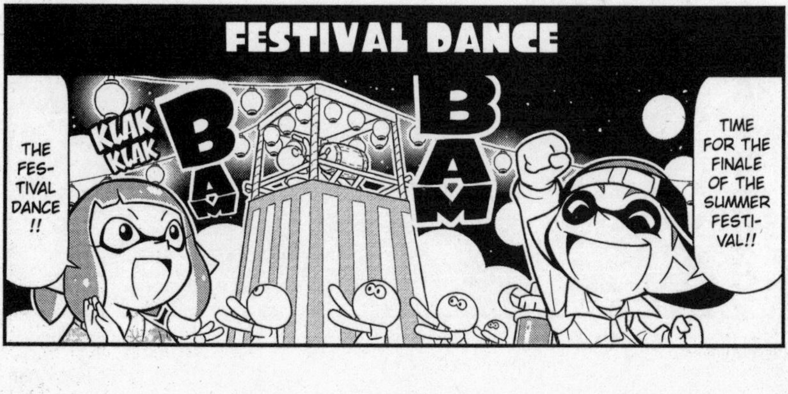
TIME FOR THE FINALE OF THE SUMMER FESTIVAL!!
BAM
BAM
KLAK KLAK
THE FESTIVAL DANCE!!

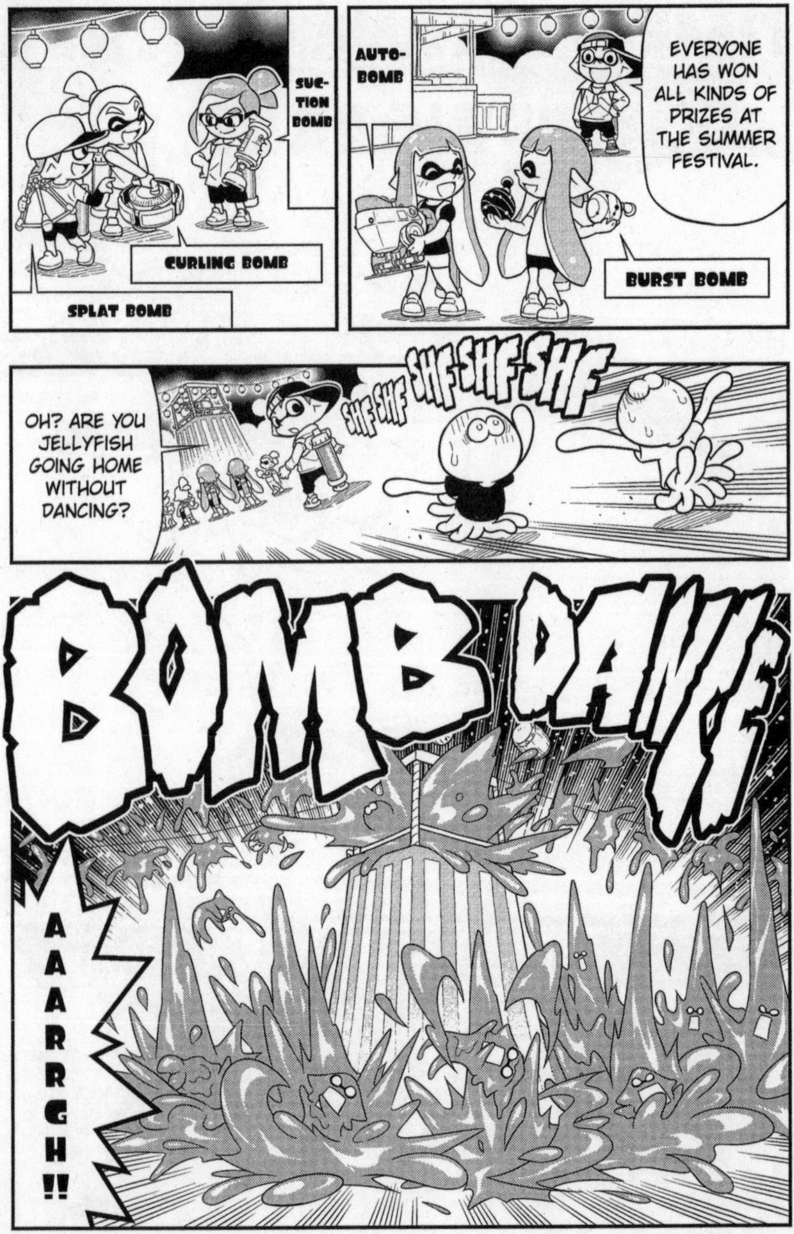
EVERYONE HAS WON ALL KINDS OF PRIZES AT THE SUMMER FESTIVAL.
AUTO-BOMB
BURST BOMB
SUC-TION BOMB
CURLING BOMB
SPLAT BOMB
SHF SHF SHF SHF SHF
OH? ARE YOU JELLYFISH GOING HOME WITHOUT DANCING?
BOMB DANCE
AAARRGH!!

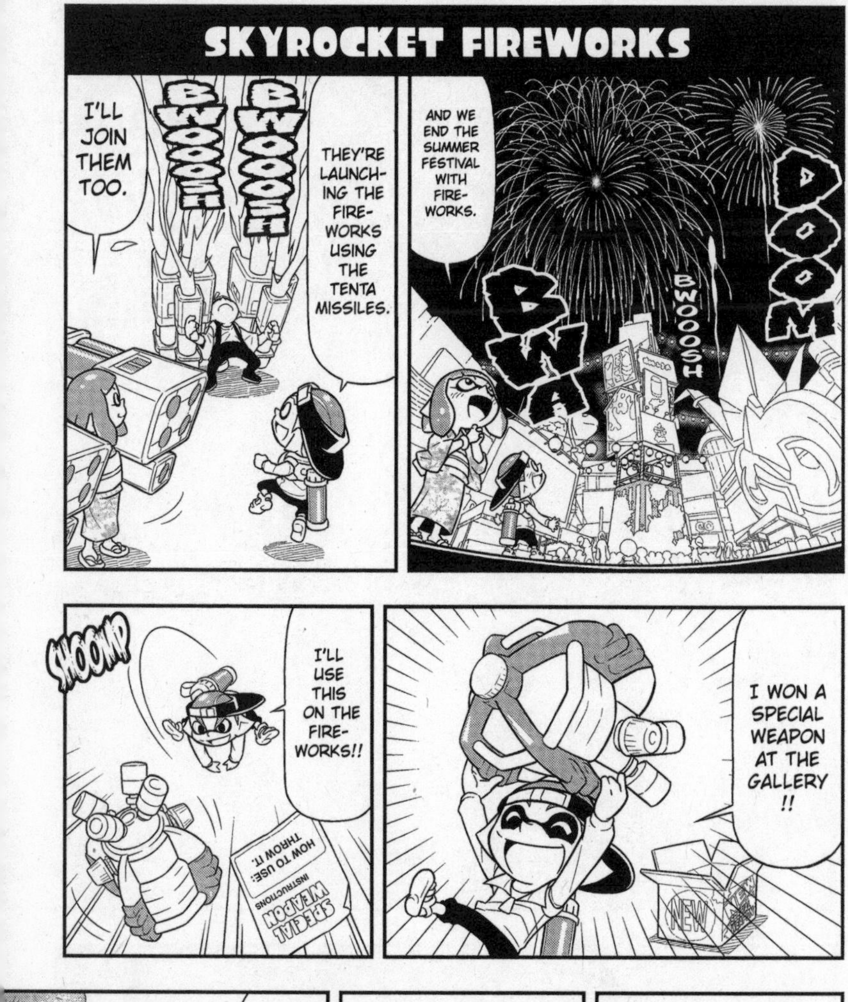
SKYROCKET FIREWORKS
DOOM
AND WE END THE SUMMER FESTIVAL WITH FIRE-WORKS.
BWOOOSH
BWA
THEY'RE LAUNCH-ING THE FIRE-WORKS USING THE TENTA MISSILES.
BWOOOSH!!
BWOOOSH!!
I'LL JOIN THEM TOO.
I WON A SPECIAL WEAPON AT THE GALLERY!!
NEW
I'LL USE THIS ON THE FIRE-WORKS!!
SHOOMP
SPECIAL WEAPON INSTRUCTIONS
HOW TO USE: THROW IT.
KLAK
RLL
RLL
RLL
FSSSH...
SMOKE'S COMING OUT OF IT... IS IT DEFECTIVE?
SHWOO
SHWOO

← WILL HIT GET THE PRIZE?!

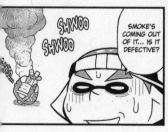

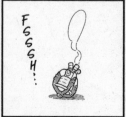

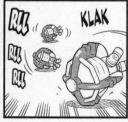

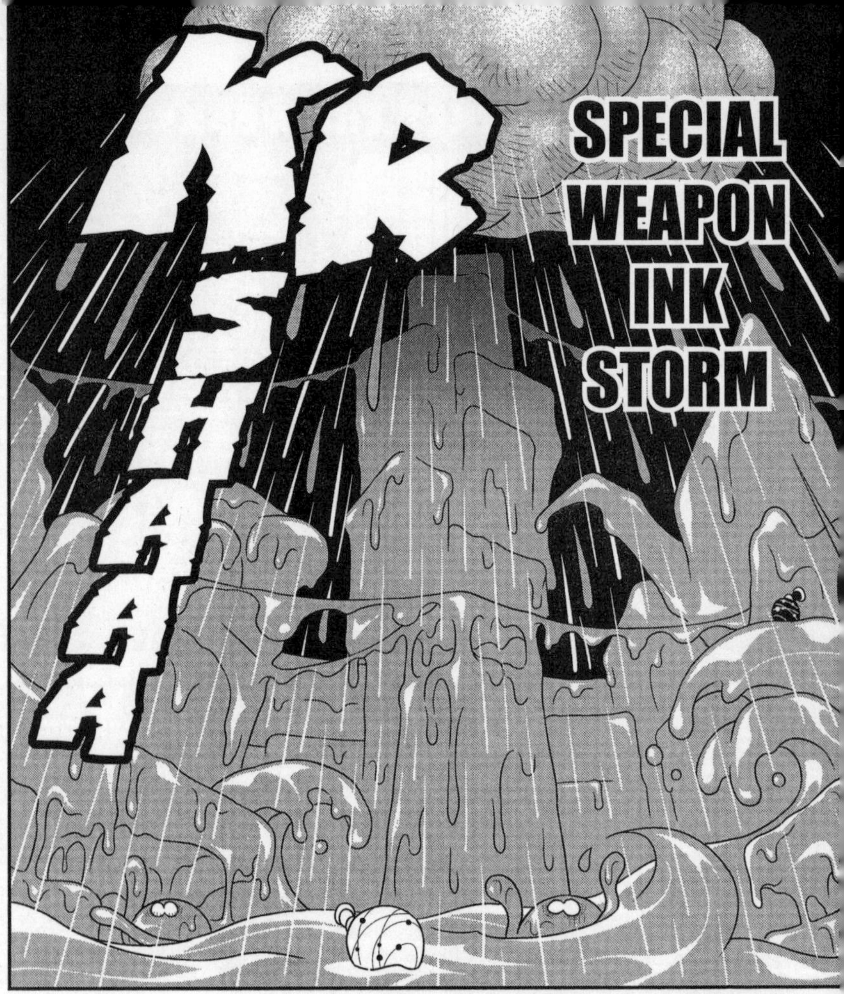
KRSHAAA
SPECIAL WEAPON INK STORM
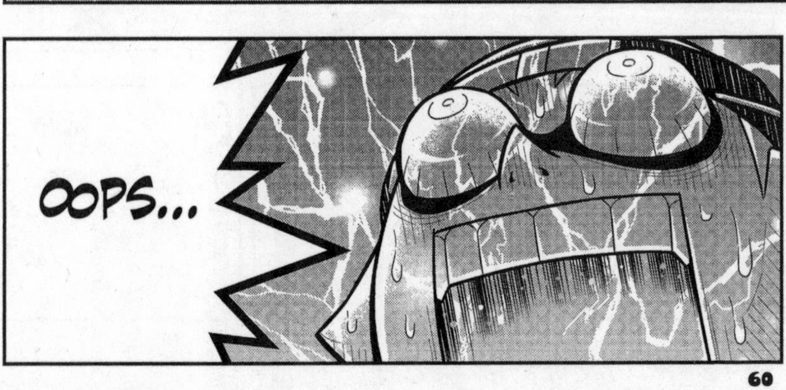
OOPS...

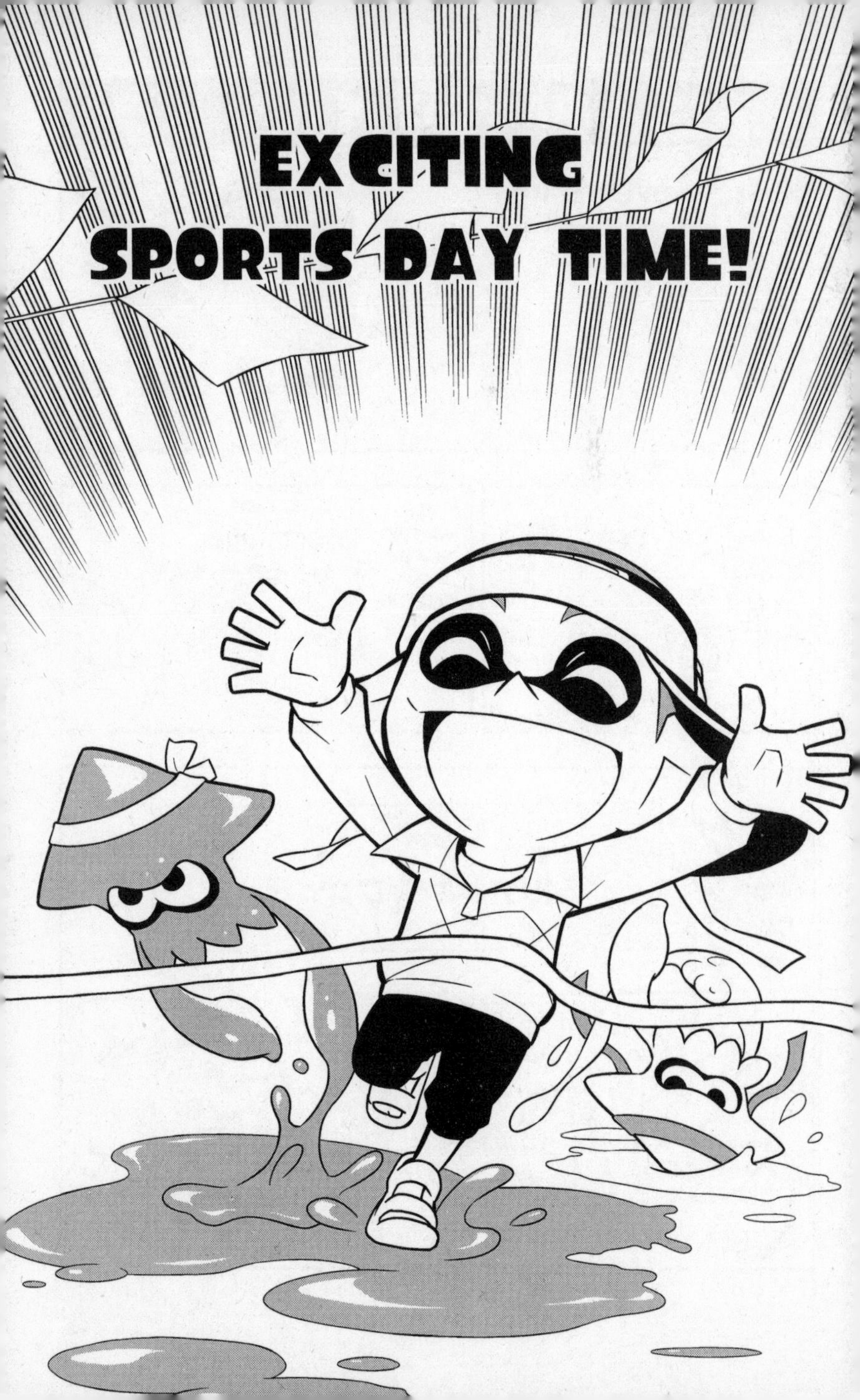
EXCITING SPORTS DAY TIME!

WHAT DAY IS IT?

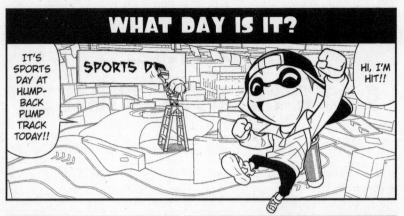

HI, I'M HIT!!
IT'S SPORTS DAY AT HUMP-BACK PUMP TRACK TODAY!!
SPORTS D
SPORTS DAY
THE WRITING IS A BIT SMALL. CAN YOU REWRITE IT?
YOU'RE RIGHT, MAIKA. I'LL CLEAN THE BOARD FIRST.
SPO T DAY
SPLATT TATA TATA
THANKS.
OOPS... I'M OUT OF INK.
SPO T DAY
SPOT DAY ?!

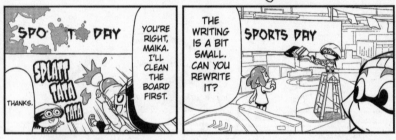

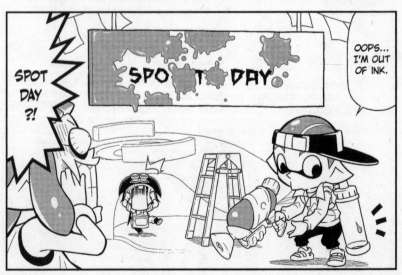

ONLY WAY TO STRETCH

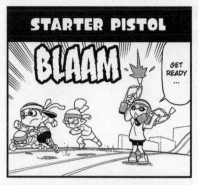

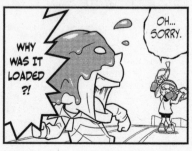

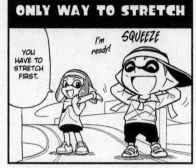

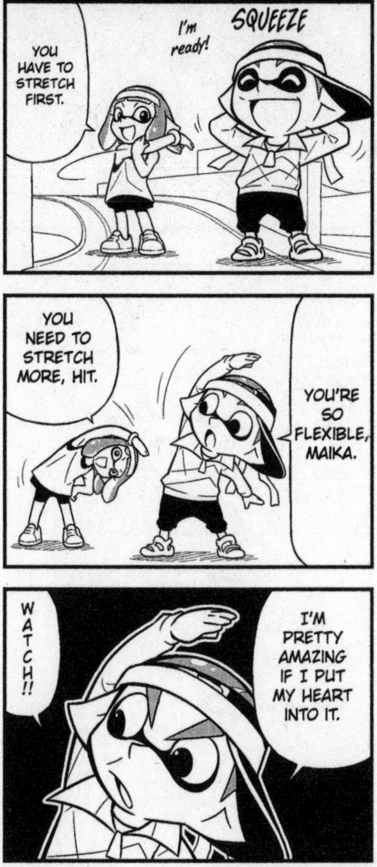
SQUEEZE
I'm ready!
YOU HAVE TO STRETCH FIRST.
YOU'RE SO FLEXIBLE, MAIKA.
YOU NEED TO STRETCH MORE, HIT.
I'M PRETTY AMAZING IF I PUT MY HEART INTO IT.
WATCH!!
SKWEEEE...
THAT'S CHEAT-ING!

STARTER PISTOL

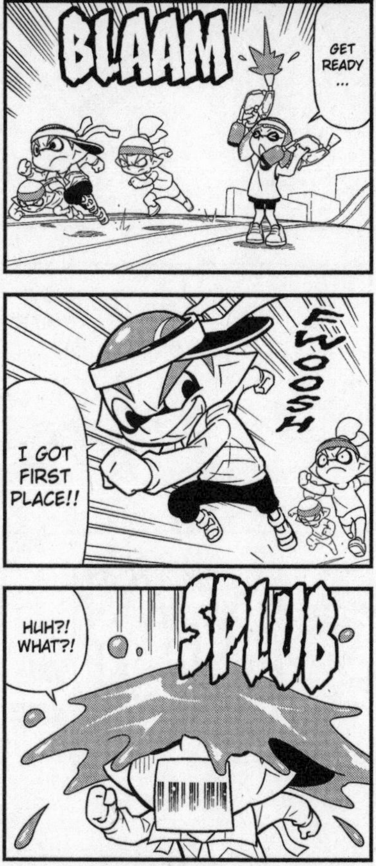
GET READY ...
BLAAM
FWOOSH
I GOT FIRST PLACE!!
SPLUB
HUH?! WHAT?!
OH... SORRY.
WHY WAS IT LOADED ?!

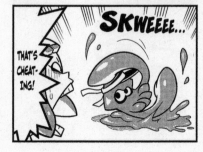

ROLL ON THROUGH

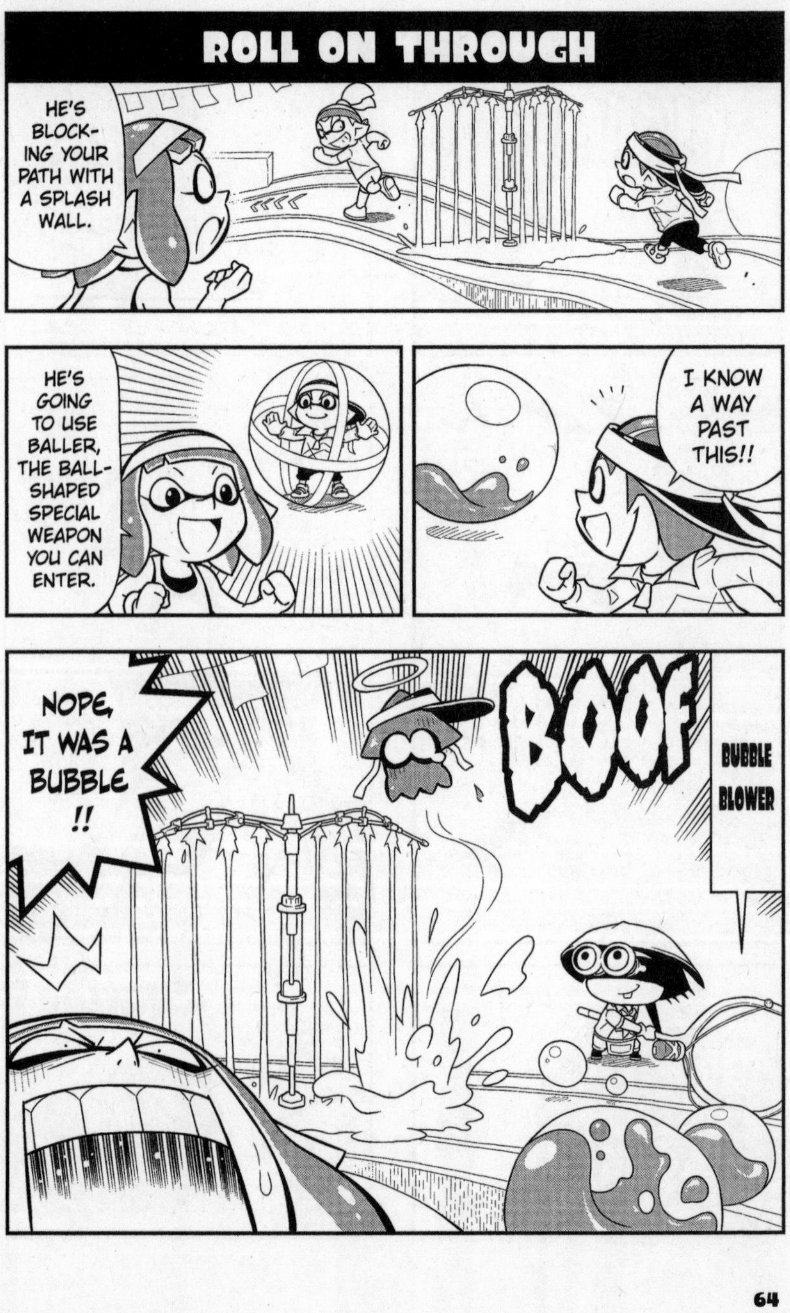
HE'S BLOCKING YOUR PATH WITH A SPLASH WALL.
I KNOW A WAY PAST THIS!!
HE'S GOING TO USE BALLER, THE BALL-SHAPED SPECIAL WEAPON YOU CAN ENTER.
BUBBLE BLOWER
BOOF
NOPE, IT WAS A BUBBLE!!

SLOW MOTION

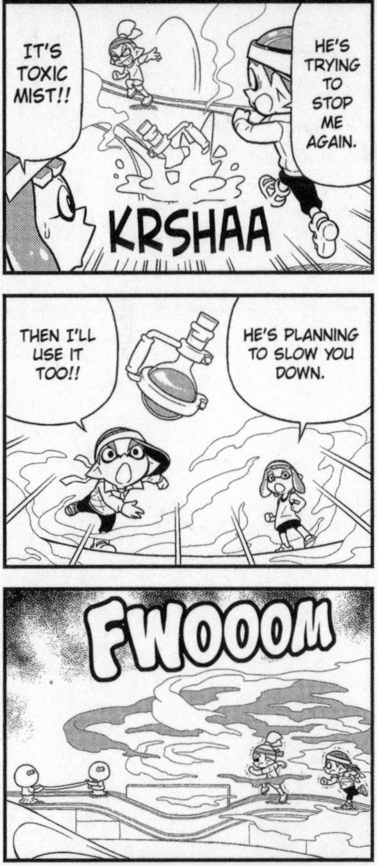
HE'S TRYING TO STOP ME AGAIN.
IT'S TOXIC MIST!!
KRSHAA
HE'S PLANNING TO SLOW YOU DOWN.
THEN I'LL USE IT TOO!!
FWOOOM
PLEASE TELL ME THIS GAME WILL END SOON!!

IT'S THE BALLER

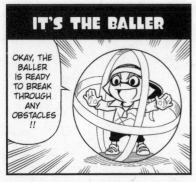

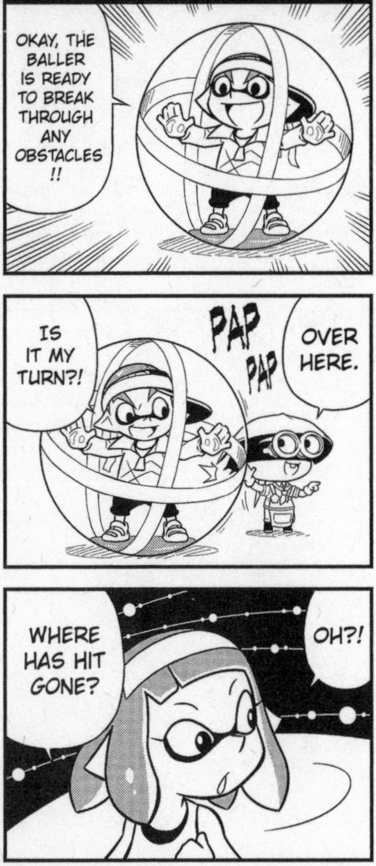
OKAY, THE BALLER IS READY TO BREAK THROUGH ANY OBSTACLES !!
OVER HERE.
PAP
PAP
IS IT MY TURN?!
OH?!
WHERE HAS HIT GONE?
HE'S BEING USED FOR THE GIANT BALL RACE!!
ROLL ROLL ROLL

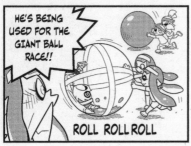

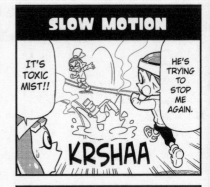

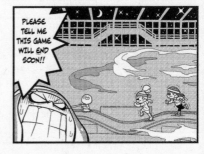

THE RIGHT WEAPON

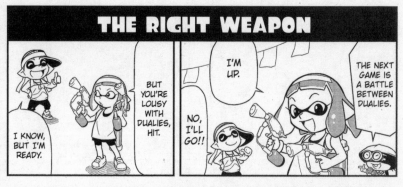

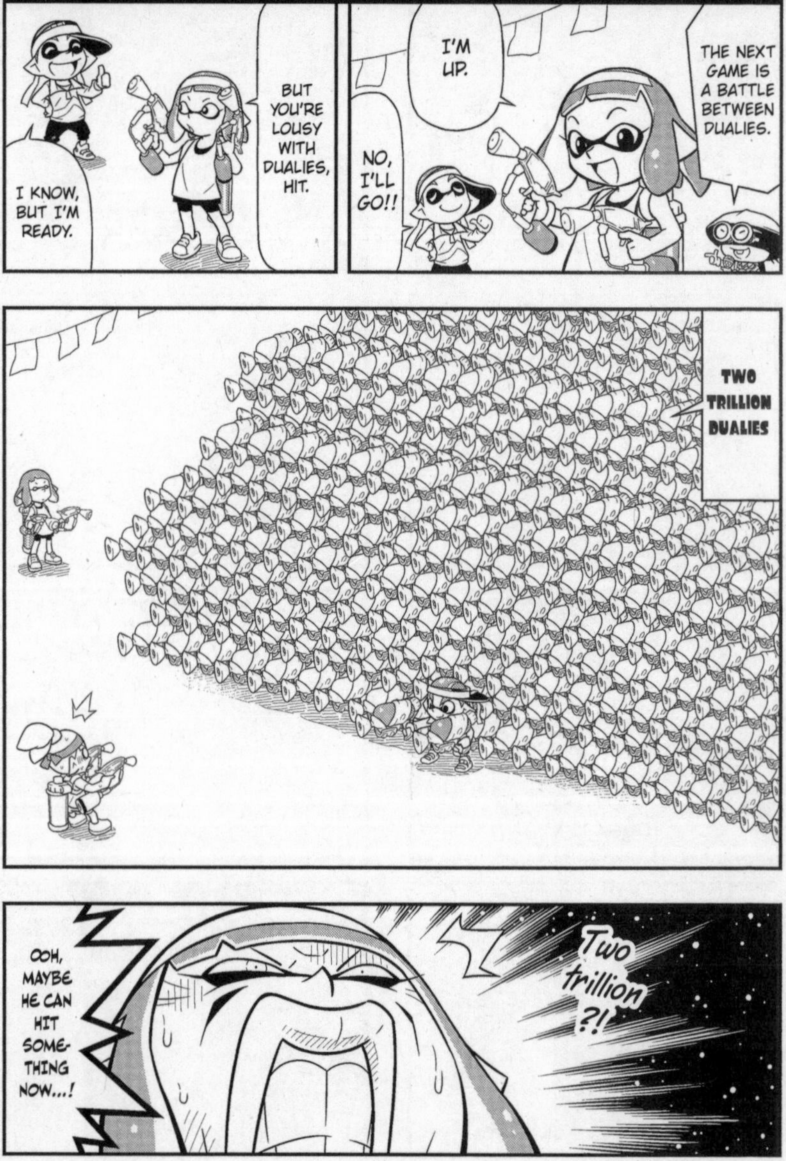
THE NEXT GAME IS A BATTLE BETWEEN DUALIES.
I'M UP.
NO, I'LL GO!!
BUT YOU'RE LOUSY WITH DUALIES, HIT.
I KNOW, BUT I'M READY.
TWO TRILLION DUALIES
Two trillion?!
OOH, MAYBE HE CAN HIT SOME-THING NOW...!

THREE-LEGGED RACE

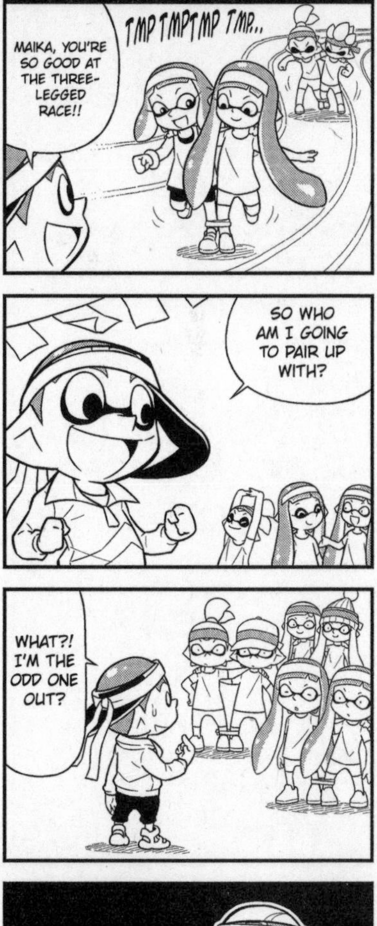
TMP TMPTMP TMP TMP...
MAIKA, YOU'RE SO GOOD AT THE THREE-LEGGED RACE!!
SO WHO AM I GOING TO PAIR UP WITH?
WHAT?! I'M THE ODD ONE OUT?
AUTO-BOMB

FINISH LINE

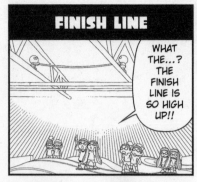

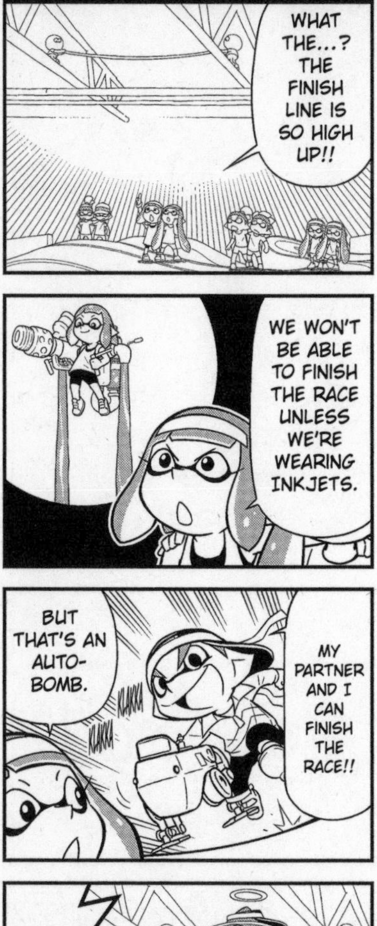
WHAT THE...? THE FINISH LINE IS SO HIGH UP!!
WE WON'T BE ABLE TO FINISH THE RACE UNLESS WE'RE WEARING INKJETS.
MY PARTNER AND I CAN FINISH THE RACE!!
KLAKKA
KLAKKA
BUT THAT'S AN AUTO-BOMB.
DOOM
KRA
AT LEAST HE CROSSED THE FINISH LINE!!

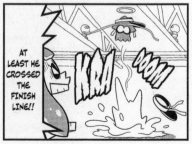

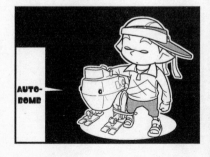

TUG-OF-WAR

NEXT IS THIS!
IT'S TUG-OF-WAR NEXT. WE DON'T NEED WEAPONS.
I KNOW. LET ME GET PREPARED.
THIS IS THE ROPE?
H-3 NOZZLENOSE
THE AUDIENCE IS GETTING COVERED IN INK!!
GRRRRP...

OBSTACLE COURSE

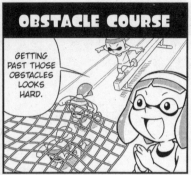

GETTING PAST THOSE OBSTACLES LOOKS HARD.
Heh heh heh heh...
I'VE COME UP WITH A SECRET PLAN.
I CAN MOVE QUICKLY IF I CHANGE INTO A SQUID!!
SWIP
I CAN SLIP THROUGH THE NET TOO!!
PLIP PLIP
YOU CAN'T MOVE QUICKLY BECAUSE THERE'S NO INK!!

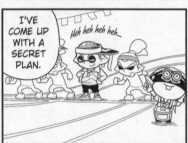

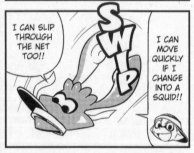

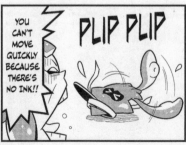

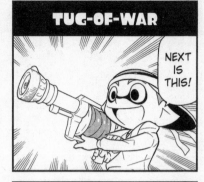

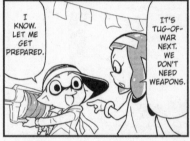

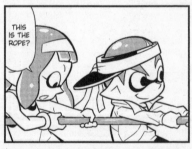

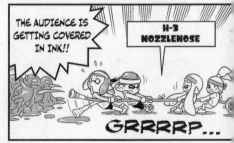

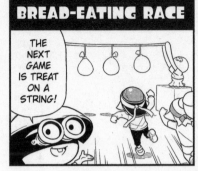

BREAD-EATING RACE

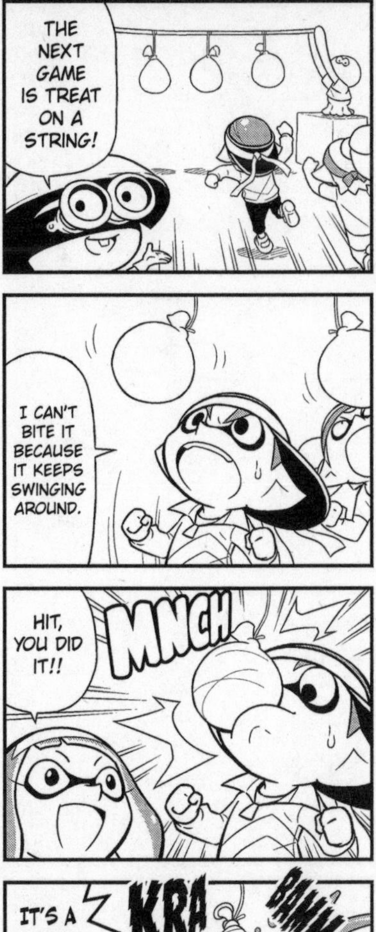
THE NEXT GAME IS TREAT ON A STRING!
I CAN'T BITE IT BECAUSE IT KEEPS SWINGING AROUND.
MNCH
HIT, YOU DID IT!!
KRA
BAMM
IT'S A BURST BOMB!!

BEANBAG TOSS

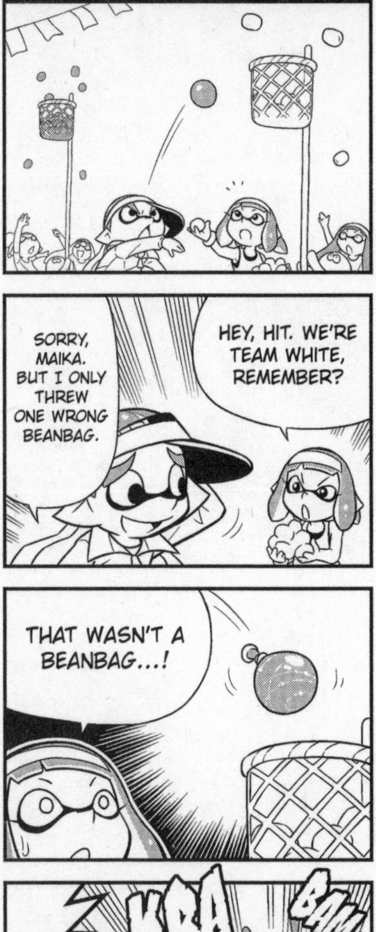
HEY, HIT. WE'RE TEAM WHITE, REMEMBER?
SORRY, MAIKA. BUT I ONLY THREW ONE WRONG BEANBAG.
THAT WASN'T A BEANBAG...!
KRA
BAM
AAAAH!
THAT WAS A BURST BOMB! AND IT'S ALL RED!!

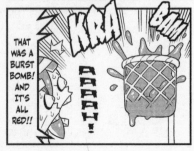

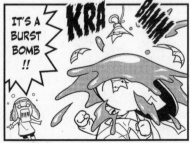

SCAVENGER HUNT

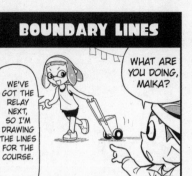

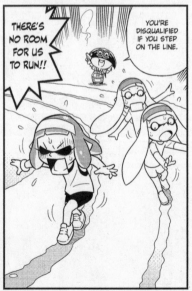

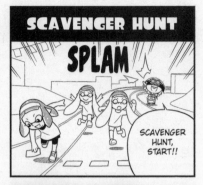

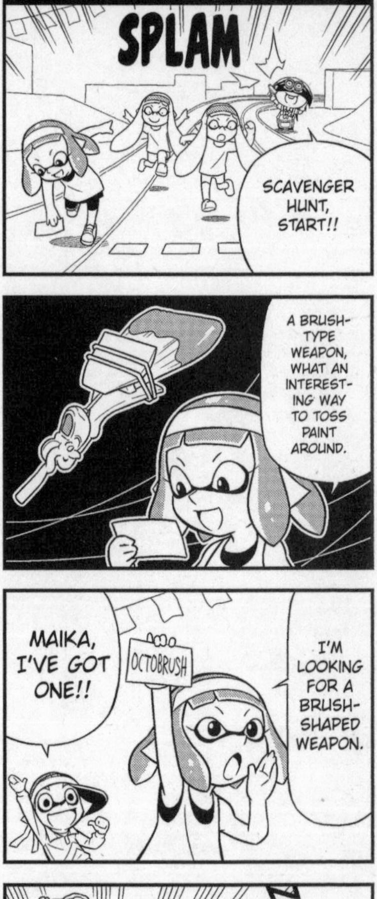
SPLAM
SCAVENGER HUNT, START!!
A BRUSH-TYPE WEAPON, WHAT AN INTERESTING WAY TO TOSS PAINT AROUND.
I'M LOOKING FOR A BRUSH-SHAPED WEAPON.
OCTOBRUSH
MAIKA, I'VE GOT ONE!!
I SAID TOSS PAINT NOT TOSS SALAD!

BOUNDARY LINES

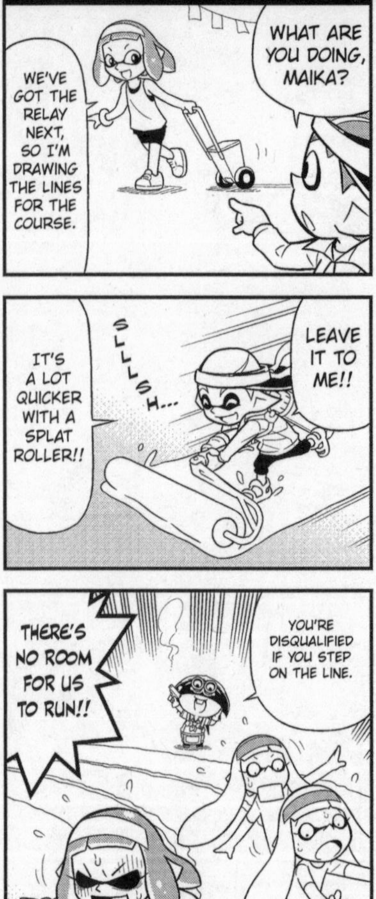
WHAT ARE YOU DOING, MAIKA?
WE'VE GOT THE RELAY NEXT, SO I'M DRAWING THE LINES FOR THE COURSE.
LEAVE IT TO ME!!
SLLLSH...
IT'S A LOT QUICKER WITH A SPLAT ROLLER!!
YOU'RE DISQUALIFIED IF YOU STEP ON THE LINE.
THERE'S NO ROOM FOR US TO RUN!!

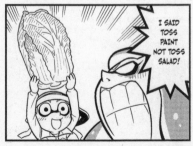

RELAY RACE

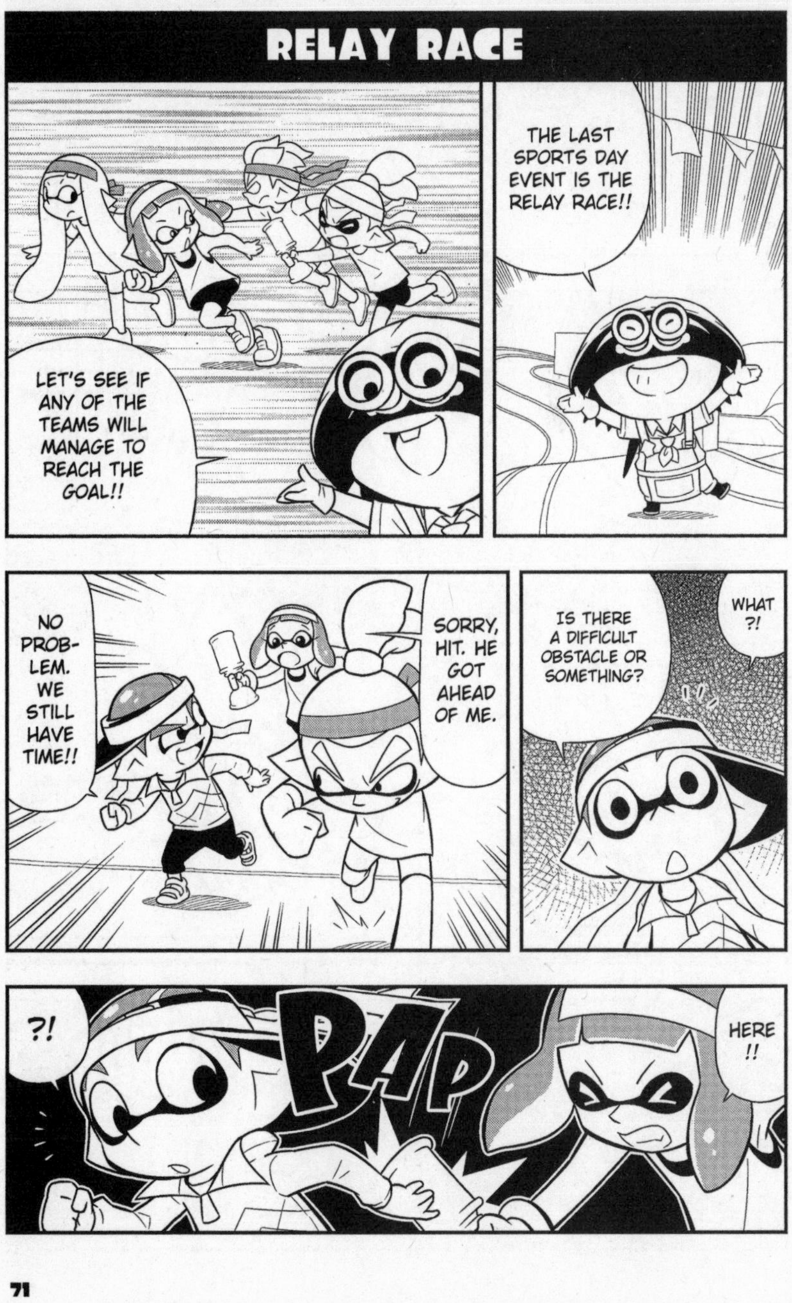
THE LAST SPORTS DAY EVENT IS THE RELAY RACE!!
LET'S SEE IF ANY OF THE TEAMS WILL MANAGE TO REACH THE GOAL!!
WHAT?!
IS THERE A DIFFICULT OBSTACLE OR SOMETHING?
SORRY, HIT. HE GOT AHEAD OF ME.
NO PROB-LEM. WE STILL HAVE TIME!!
HERE!!
PAP
?!

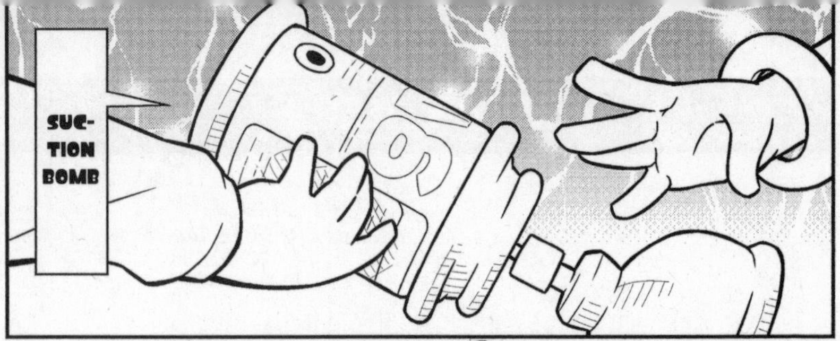
SUC-TION BOMB

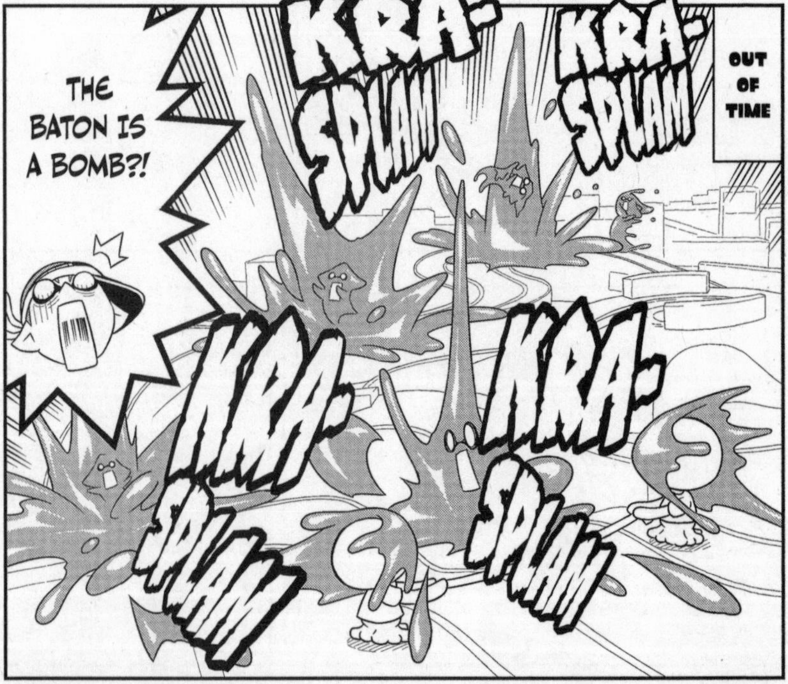
OUT OF TIME
KRA-SPLAM
KRA-SPLAM
THE BATON IS A BOMB?!
KRA-SPLAM
KRA-SPLAM

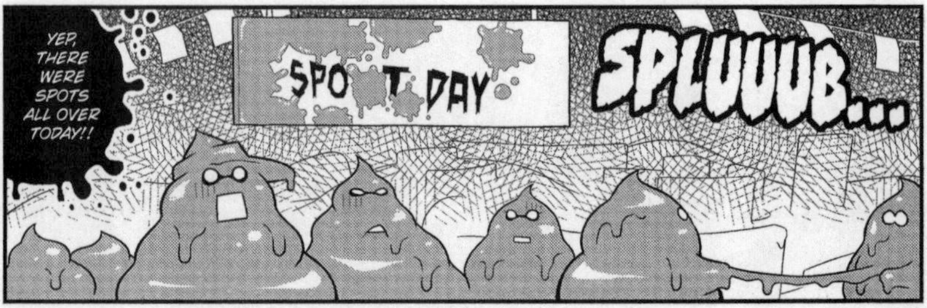
SPLUUUB...
SPO T DAY
YEP, THERE WERE SPOTS ALL OVER TODAY!!

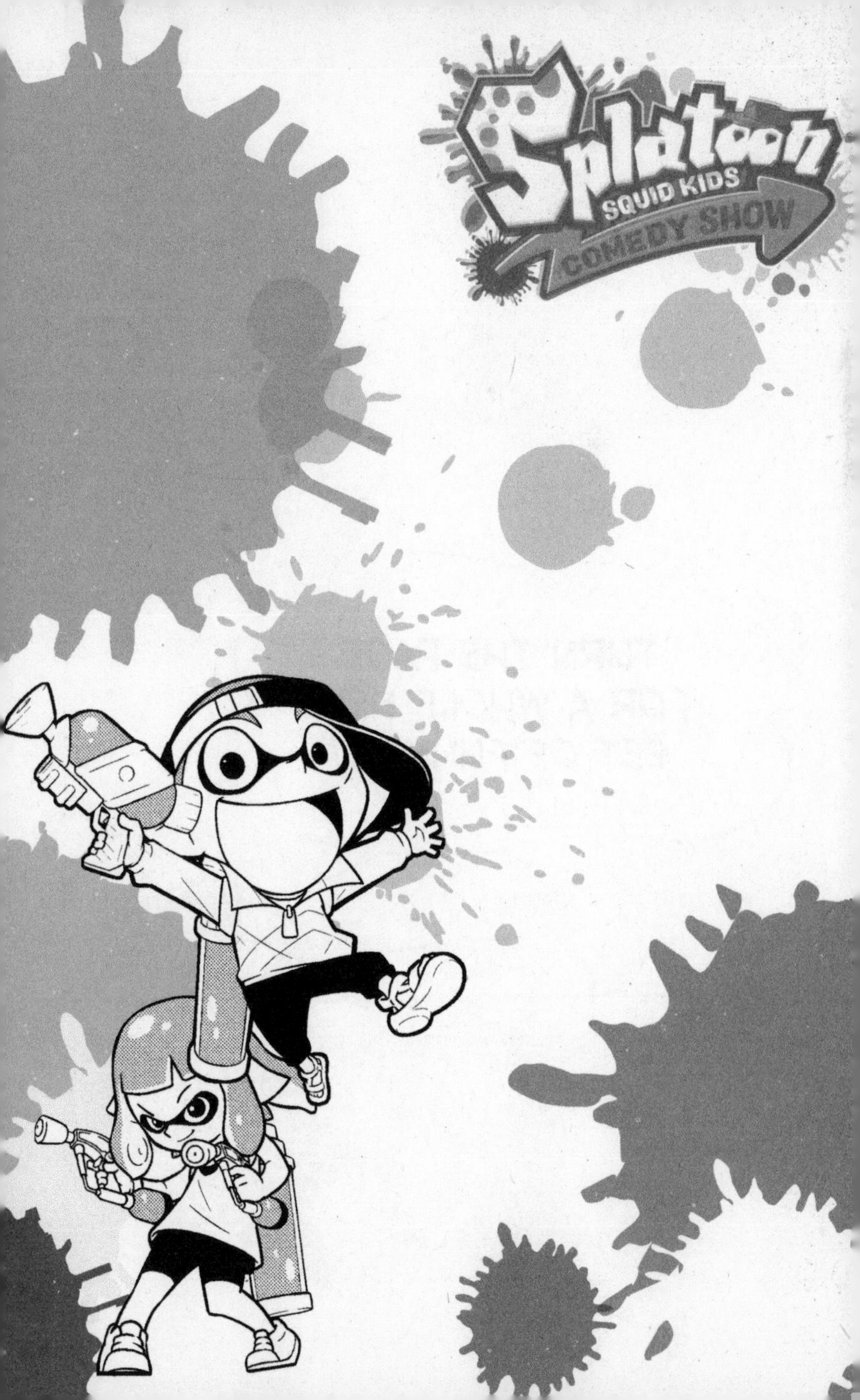
Splatoon
SQUID KIDS
COMEDY SHOW

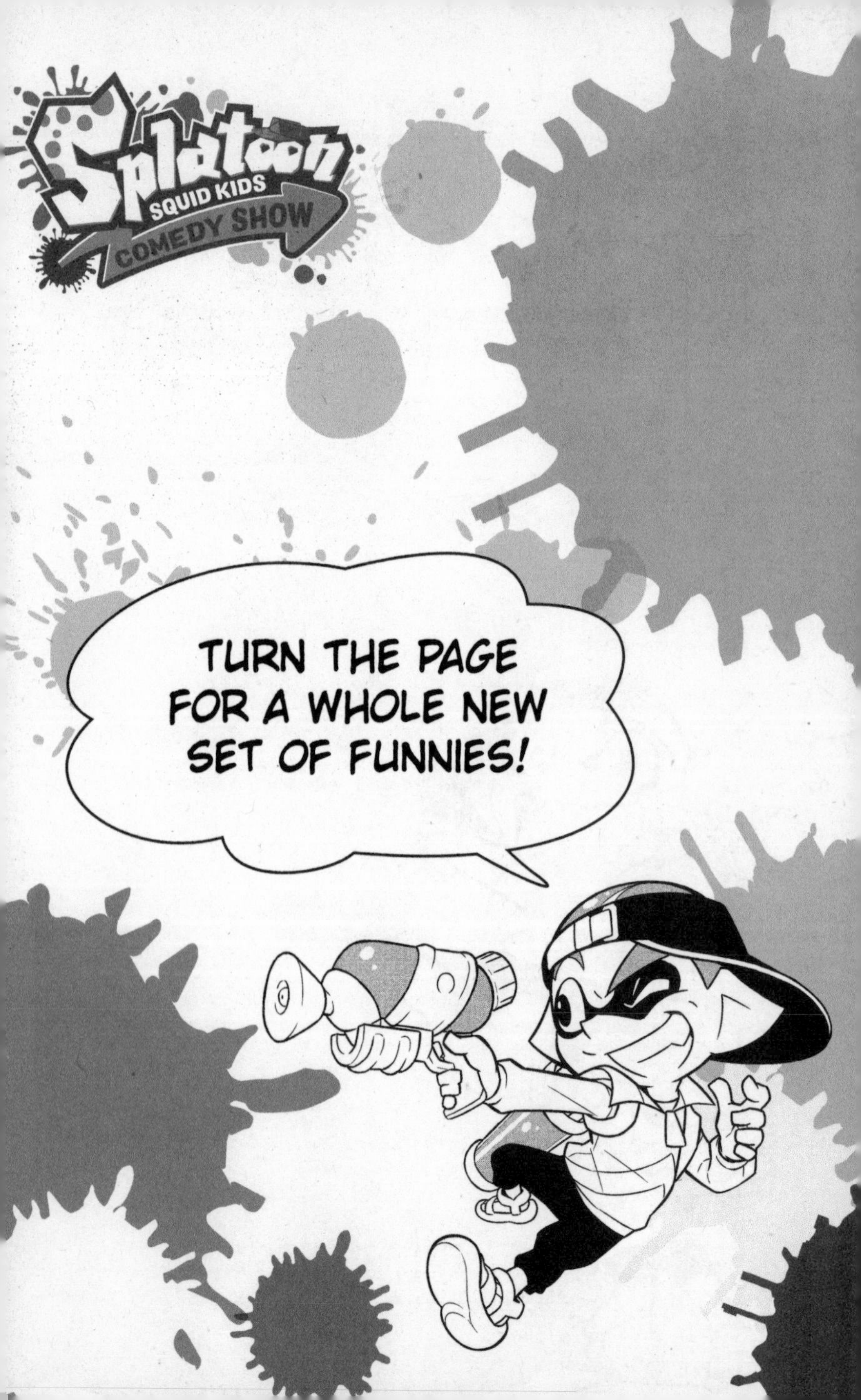
Splatoon
SQUID KIDS
COMEDY SHOW
TURN THE PAGE FOR A WHOLE NEW SET OF FUNNIES!

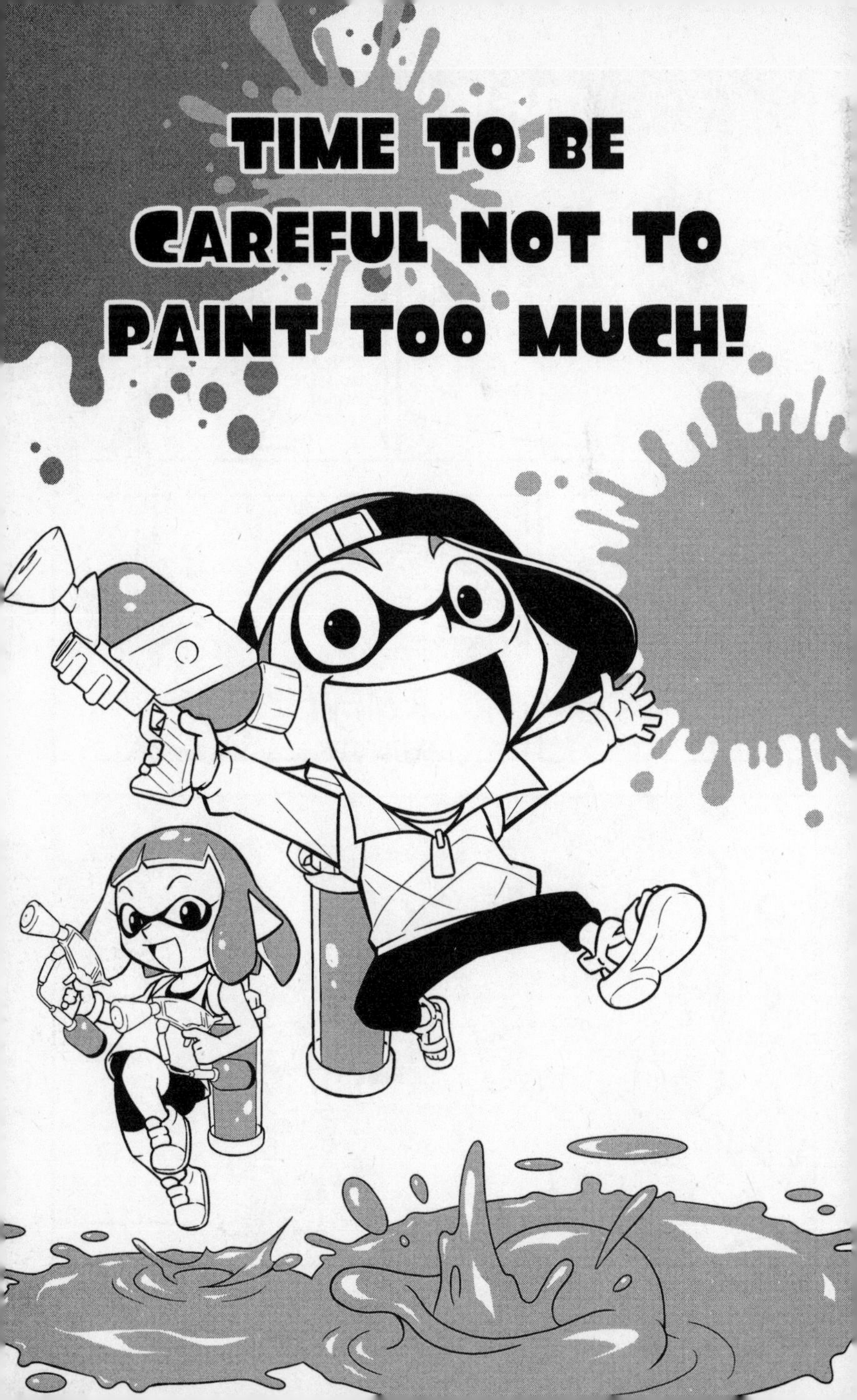
TIME TO BE
CAREFUL NOT TO
PAINT TOO MUCH!

SELF-INTRODUCTION

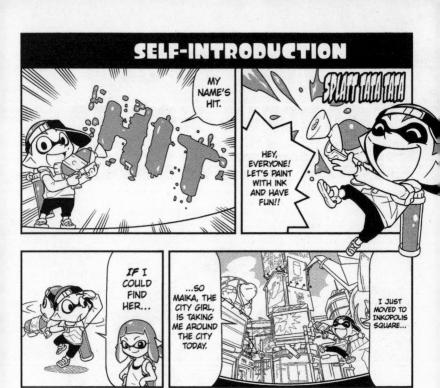

SPLATT TATA TATA
HEY, EVERYONE! LET'S PAINT WITH INK AND HAVE FUN!!
MY NAME'S HIT.
HIT
I JUST MOVED TO INKOPOLIS SQUARE...
...SO MAIKA, THE CITY GIRL, IS TAKING ME AROUND THE CITY TODAY.
IF I COULD FIND HER...
OVER HERE.
SORRY!!

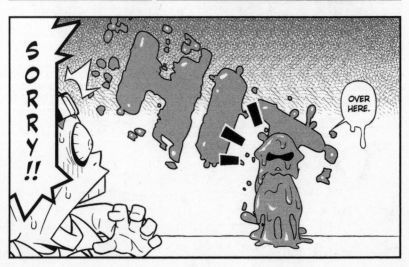

TURN INTO A SQUID

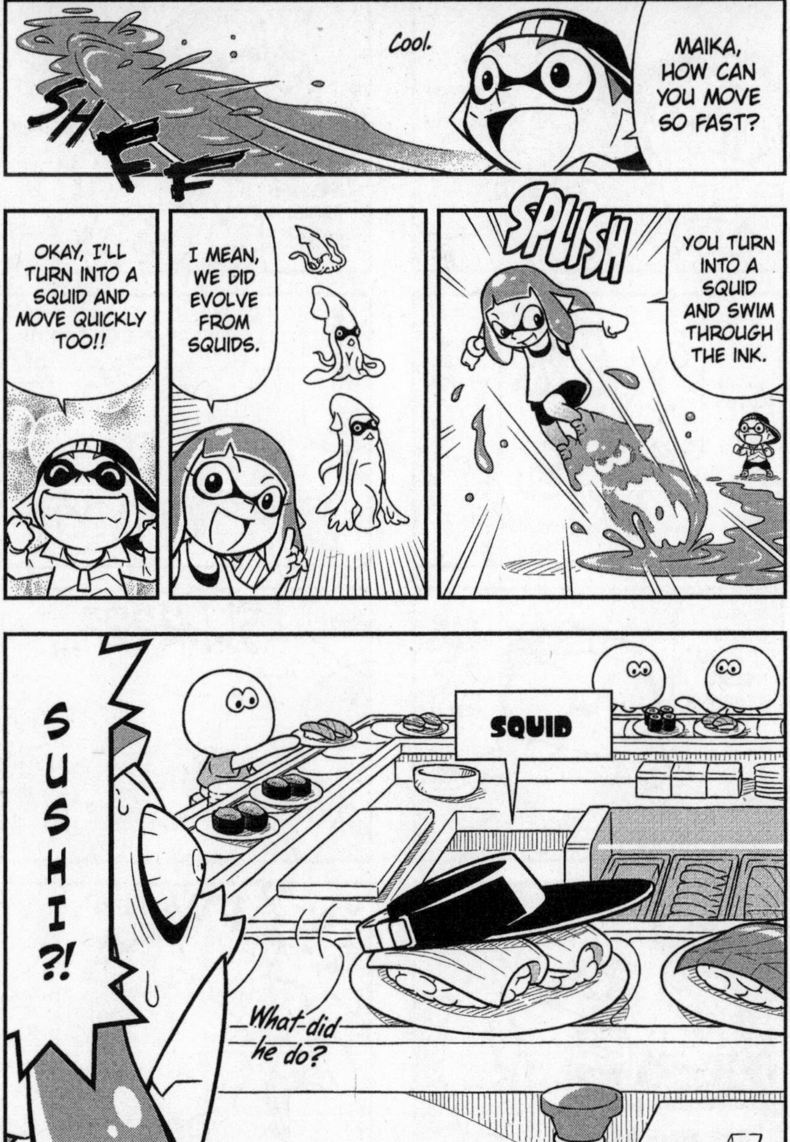
MAIKA, HOW CAN YOU MOVE SO FAST?
Cool.
SHFF
YOU TURN INTO A SQUID AND SWIM THROUGH THE INK.
SPLISH
I MEAN, WE DID EVOLVE FROM SQUIDS.
OKAY, I'LL TURN INTO A SQUID AND MOVE QUICKLY TOO!!
SQUID
SUSHI?!
What did he do?

INK REFILL

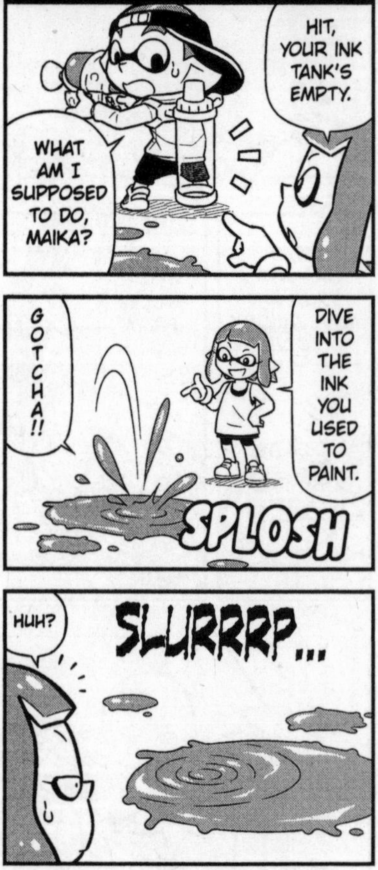
HIT, YOUR INK TANK'S EMPTY.
WHAT AM I SUPPOSED TO DO, MAIKA?
DIVE INTO THE INK YOU USED TO PAINT.
GOTCHA!!
SPLOSH
SLURRRP...
HUH?
FWUUMP
HOW'S THIS? ♥
YOU'RE NOT SUPPOSED TO DRINK IT!!

DUALIES

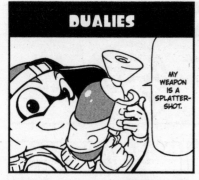

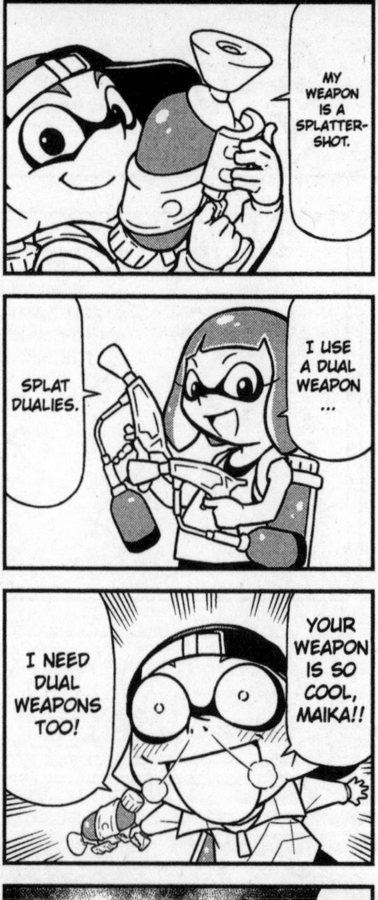
MY WEAPON IS A SPLATTER-SHOT.
I USE A DUAL WEAPON ...
SPLAT DUALIES.
YOUR WEAPON IS SO COOL, MAIKA!!
I NEED DUAL WEAPONS TOO!
WHO'S THAT?
THE WEAPON WITCH

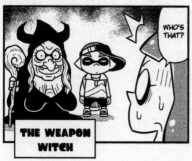

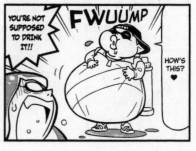

TWO ROLLERS

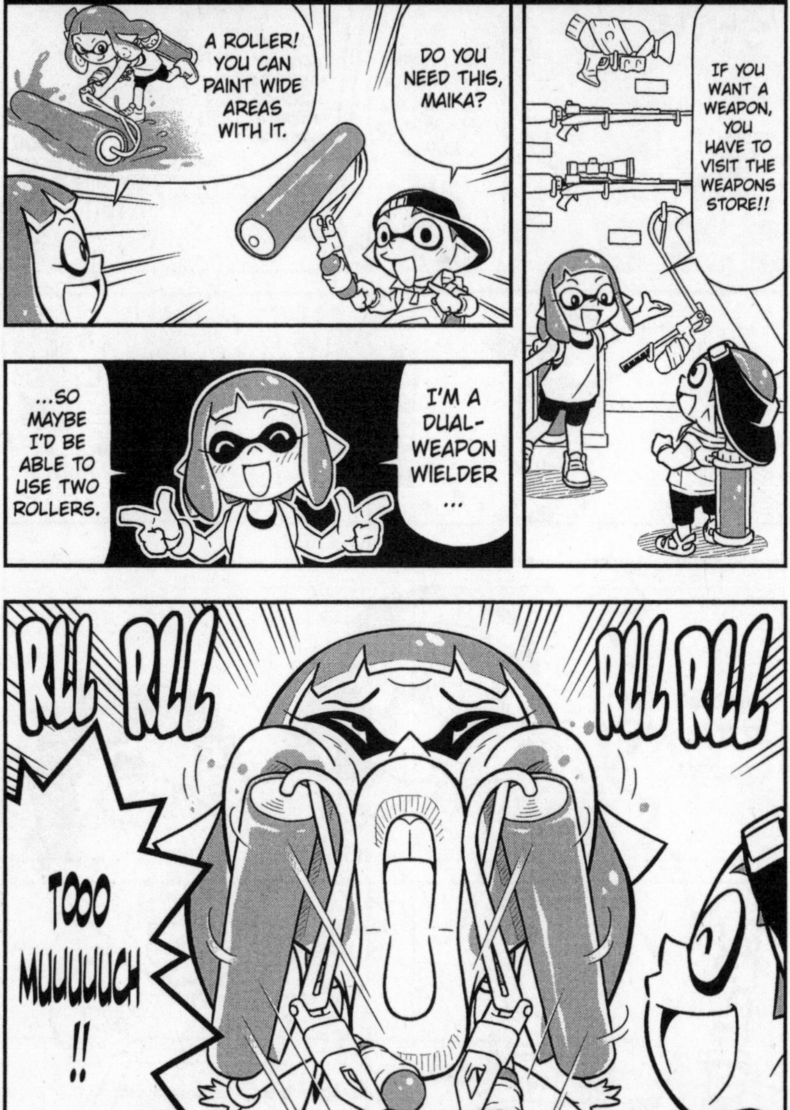
IF YOU WANT A WEAPON, YOU HAVE TO VISIT THE WEAPONS STORE!!
DO YOU NEED THIS, MAIKA?
A ROLLER! YOU CAN PAINT WIDE AREAS WITH IT.
I'M A DUAL-WEAPON WIELDER ...
...SO MAYBE I'D BE ABLE TO USE TWO ROLLERS.
RLL RLL
RLL RLL
TOOO MUUUUUCH !!

HOW FAR CAN YOU GO?

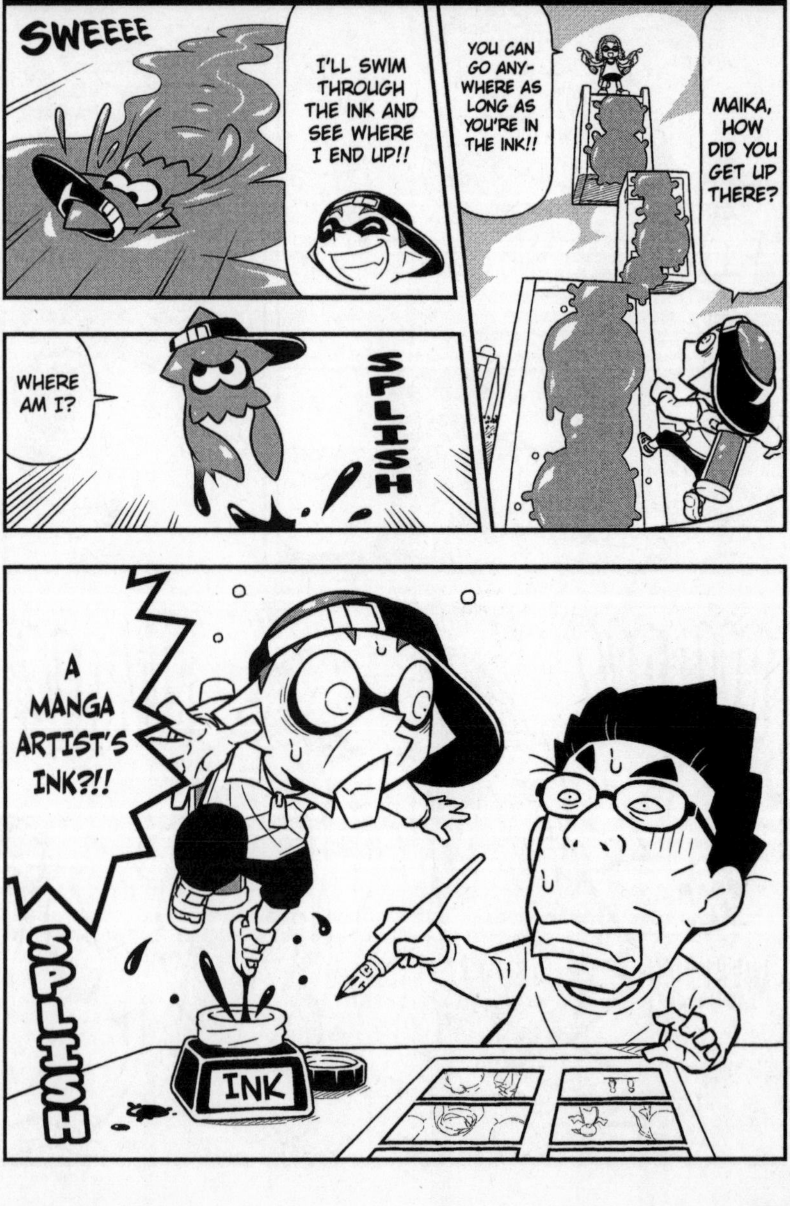
MAIKA, HOW DID YOU GET UP THERE?
YOU CAN GO ANY-WHERE AS LONG AS YOU'RE IN THE INK!!
I'LL SWIM THROUGH THE INK AND SEE WHERE I END UP!!
SWEEEE
SPLISH
WHERE AM I?
A MANGA ARTIST'S INK?!!
SPLISH
INK

FANCY COAT

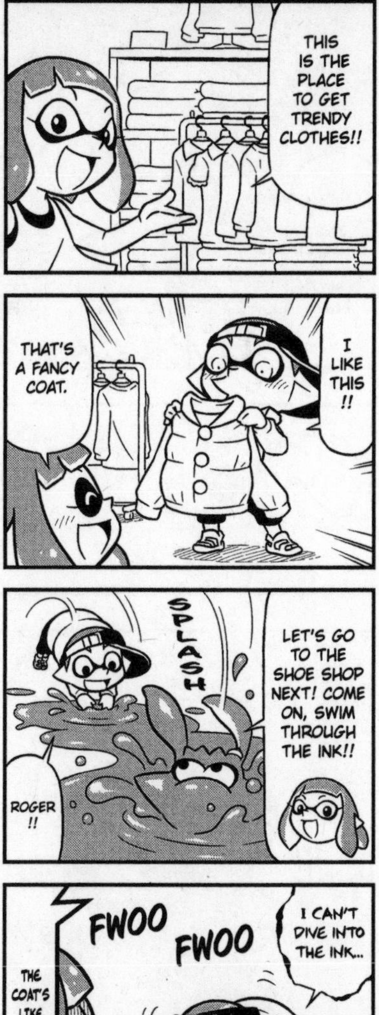
THIS IS THE PLACE TO GET TRENDY CLOTHES!!
I LIKE THIS!!
THAT'S A FANCY COAT.
LET'S GO TO THE SHOE SHOP NEXT! COME ON, SWIM THROUGH THE INK!!
SPLASH
ROGER!!
I CAN'T DIVE INTO THE INK...
FWOO FWOO
THE COAT'S LIKE A LIFE JACKET!!

BURST BOMB

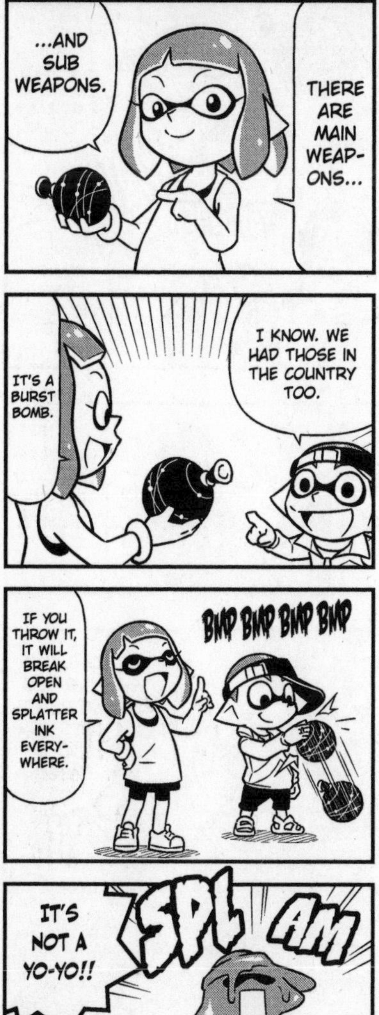
THERE ARE MAIN WEAPONS...
...AND SUB WEAPONS.
I KNOW. WE HAD THOSE IN THE COUNTRY TOO.
IT'S A BURST BOMB.
BMP BMP BMP BMP
IF YOU THROW IT, IT WILL BREAK OPEN AND SPLATTER INK EVERYWHERE.
SPLAM
IT'S NOT A YO-YO!!

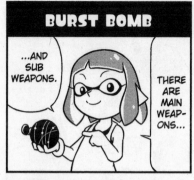

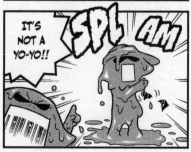

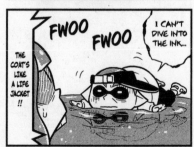

WEAPON TESTING

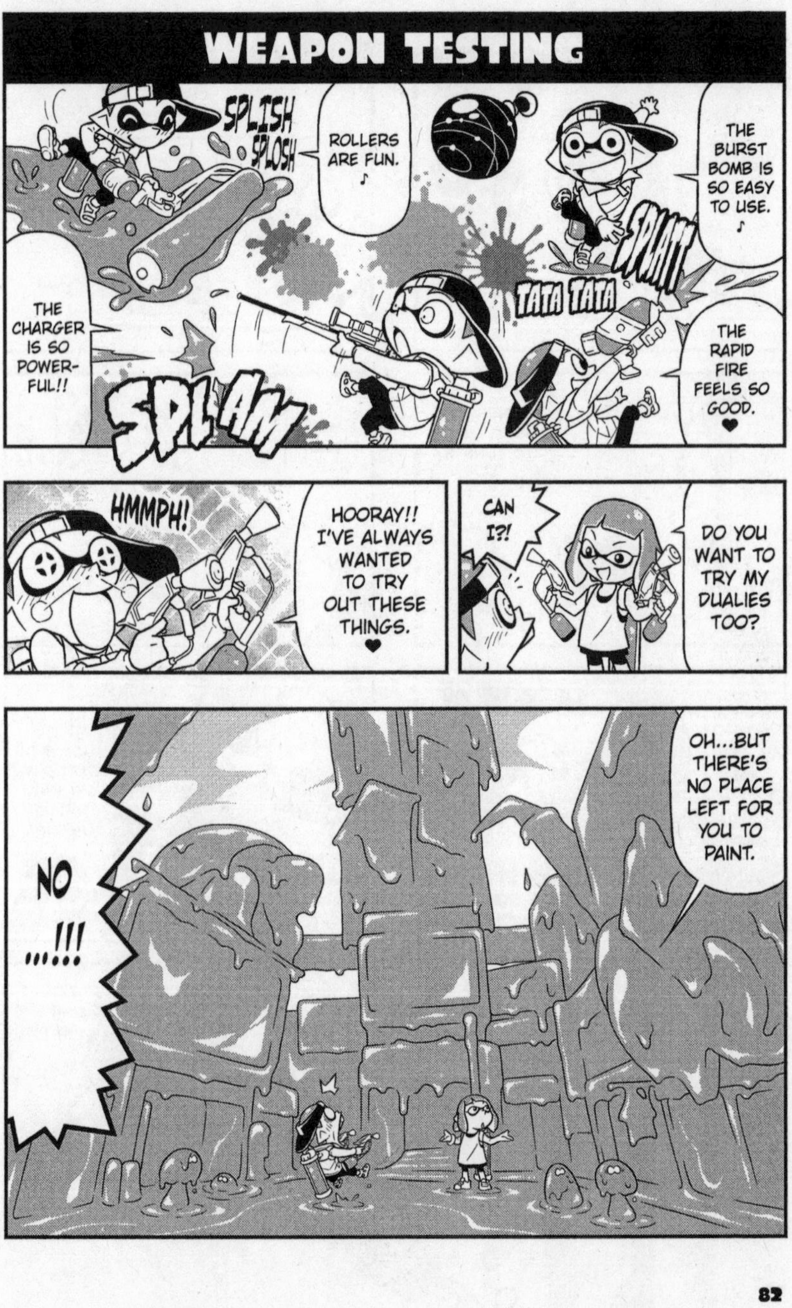
THE BURST BOMB IS SO EASY TO USE. ♪
SPLAT
ROLLERS ARE FUN. ♪
SPLISH SPLOSH
THE RAPID FIRE FEELS SO GOOD. ♥
TATA TATA
THE CHARGER IS SO POWER-FUL!!
SPLAM
DO YOU WANT TO TRY MY DUALIES TOO?
CAN I?!
HOORAY!! I'VE ALWAYS WANTED TO TRY OUT THESE THINGS. ♥
HMMPH!
OH...BUT THERE'S NO PLACE LEFT FOR YOU TO PAINT.
NO ......!!!

TIME TO USE THE INK IN A COOL WAY!

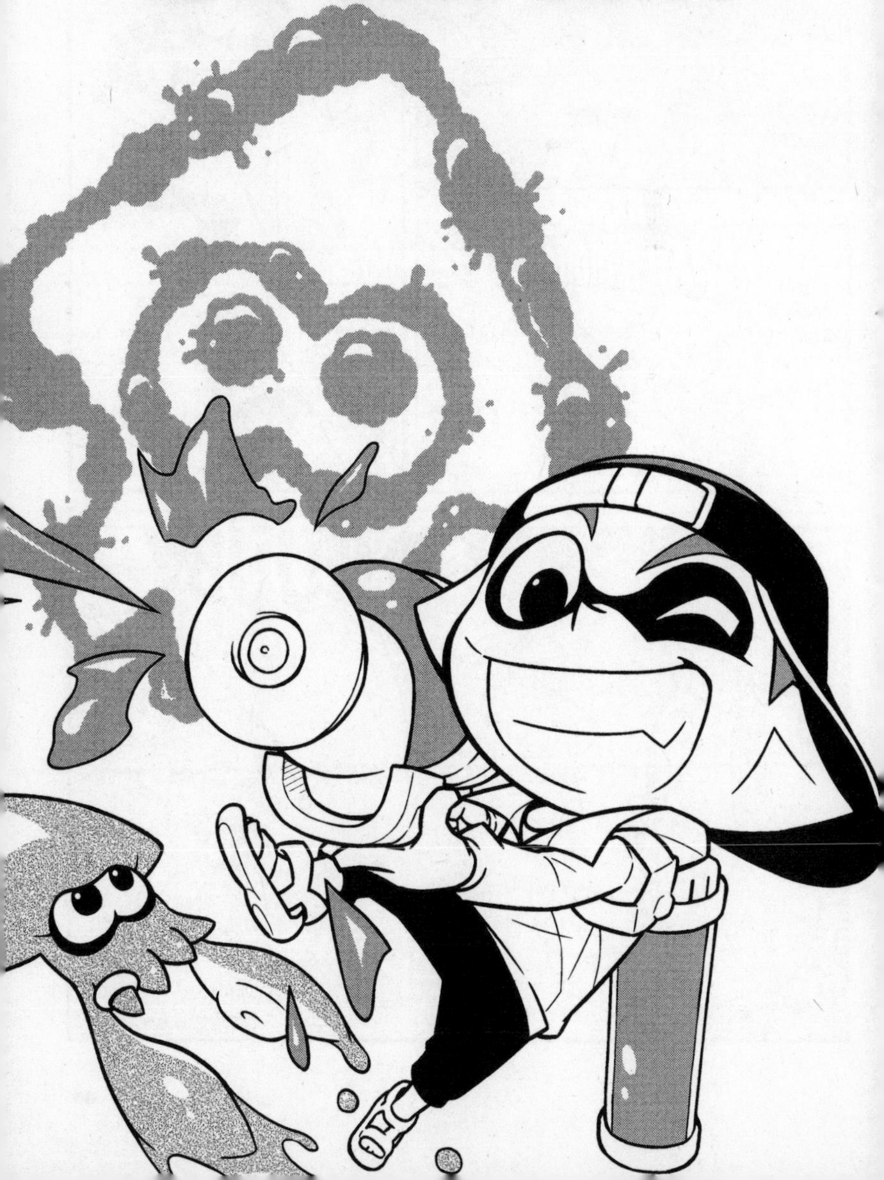

LOUSY AIM

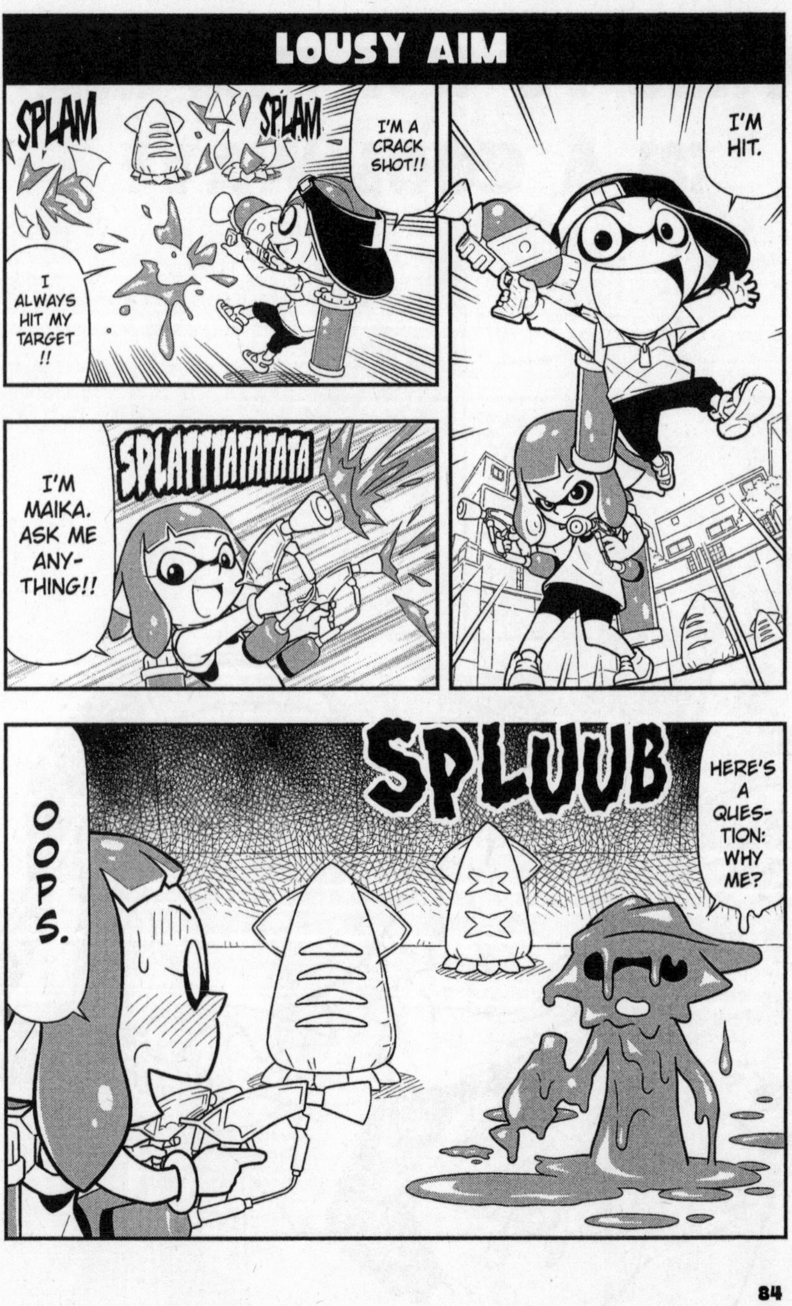
I'M HIT.
SPLAM
SPLAM
I'M A CRACK SHOT!!
I ALWAYS HIT MY TARGET!!
SPLATTTATATATA
I'M MAIKA. ASK ME ANY-THING!!
SPLUUB
HERE'S A QUES-TION: WHY ME?
OOPS.

SPARE INK

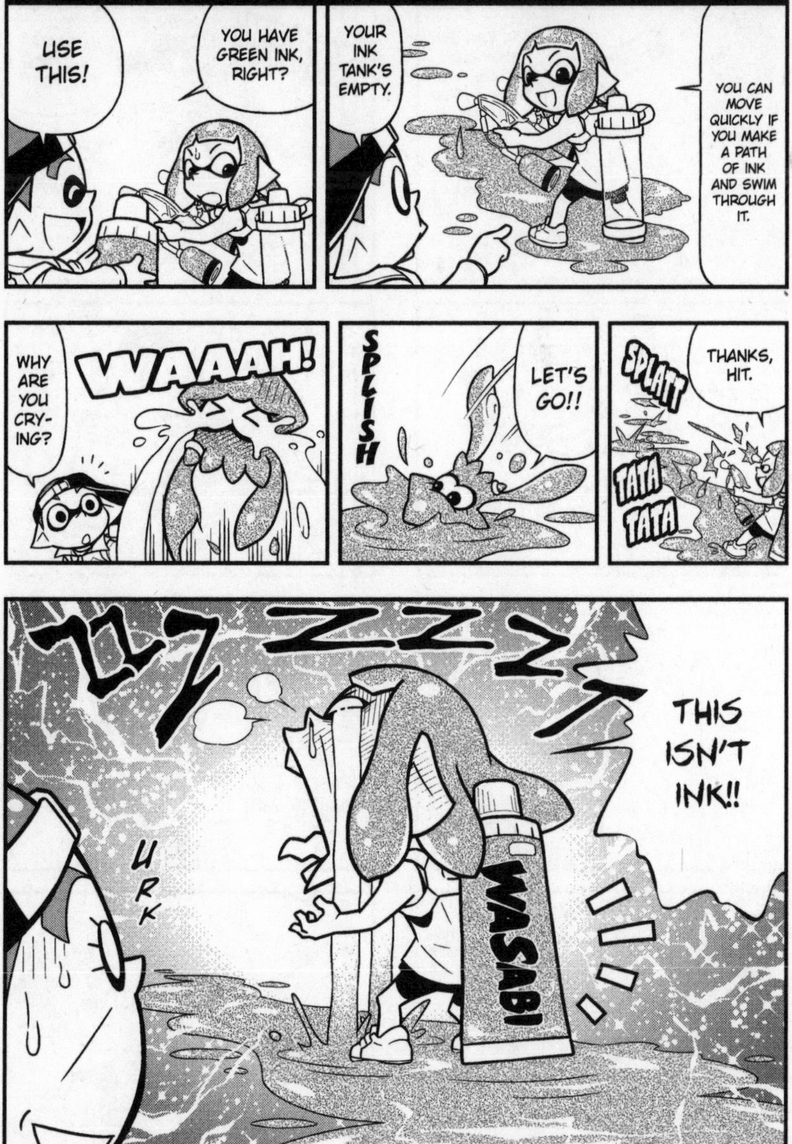

YOU CAN MOVE QUICKLY IF YOU MAKE A PATH OF INK AND SWIM THROUGH IT.
YOUR INK TANK'S EMPTY.
YOU HAVE GREEN INK, RIGHT?
USE THIS!
THANKS, HIT.
SPLATT
TATA TATA
LET'S GO!!
SPLISH
WAAAAH!
WHY ARE YOU CRYING?
ZZZZT
THIS ISN'T INK!!
WASABI
URK

EXTRA INK

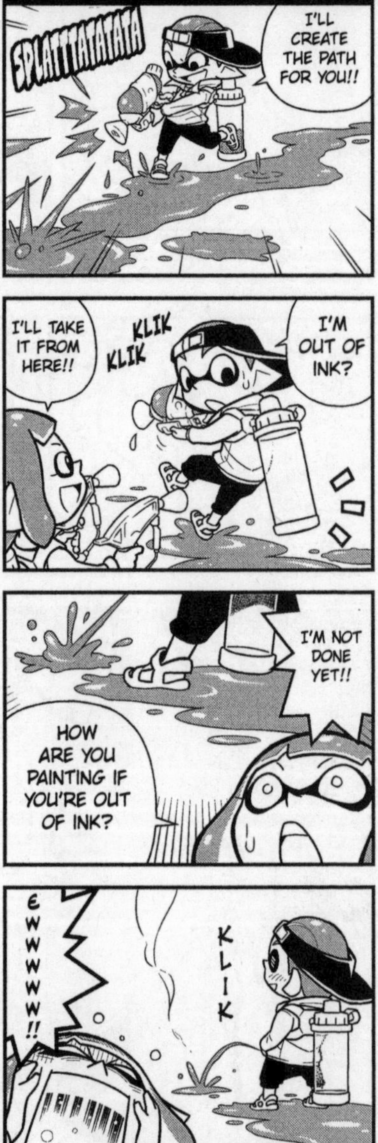
I'LL CREATE THE PATH FOR YOU!!
SPLATTTATATATA
I'M OUT OF INK?
KLIK KLIK
I'LL TAKE IT FROM HERE!!
I'M NOT DONE YET!!
HOW ARE YOU PAINTING IF YOU'RE OUT OF INK?
KLIK
EWWWWWW!!

IN THE INK

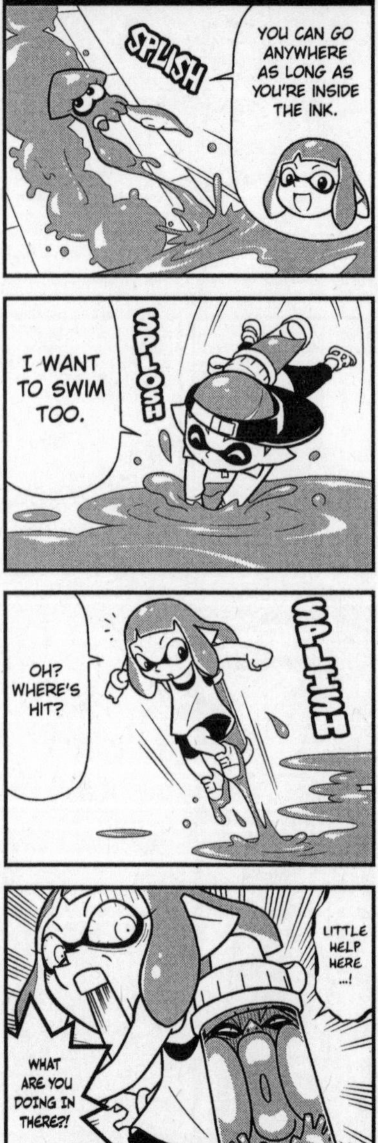
YOU CAN GO ANYWHERE AS LONG AS YOU'RE INSIDE THE INK.
SPLISH
SPLOSH
I WANT TO SWIM TOO.
SPLISH
OH? WHERE'S HIT?
LITTLE HELP HERE ...!
WHAT ARE YOU DOING IN THERE?!

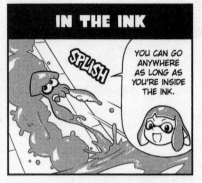

PORTRAIT

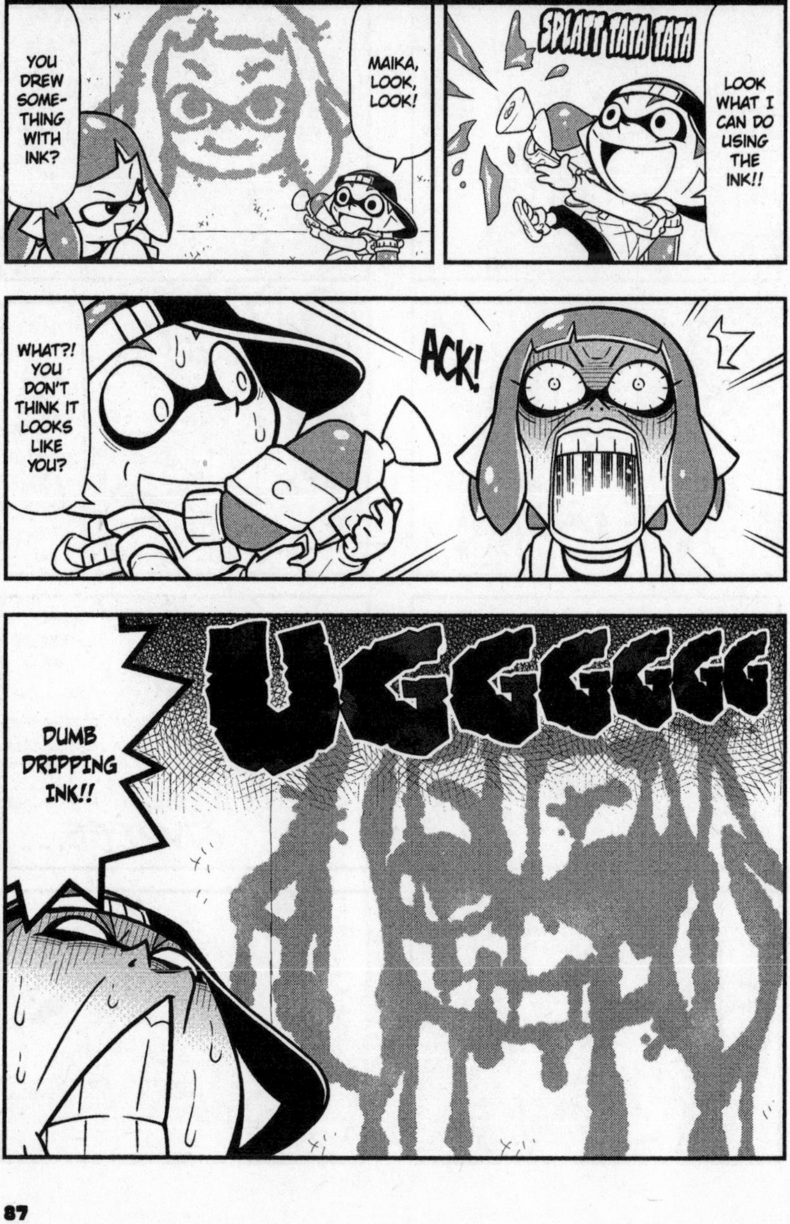
SPLATT TATA TATA
LOOK WHAT I CAN DO USING THE INK!!
MAIKA, LOOK, LOOK!
YOU DREW SOME-THING WITH INK?
ACK!
WHAT?! YOU DON'T THINK IT LOOKS LIKE YOU?
UGGGGGG
DUMB DRIPPING INK!!

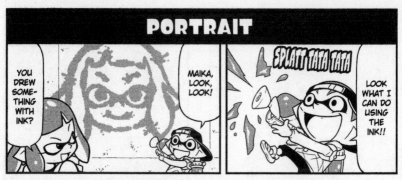

CURLING BOMB

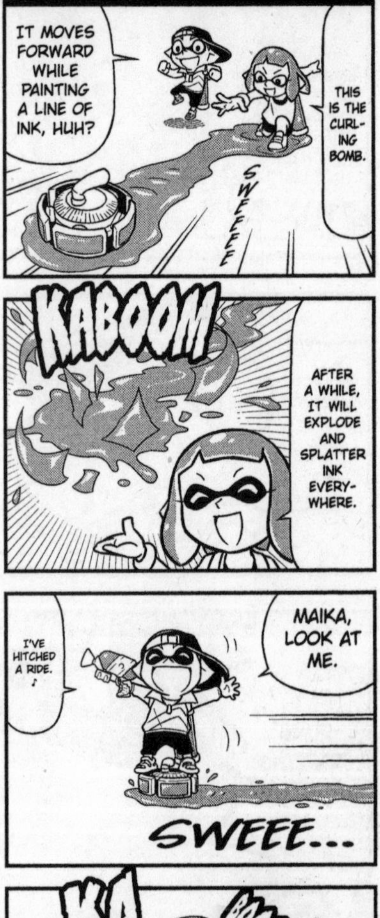
THIS IS THE CURLING BOMB.
SWEEEEE
IT MOVES FORWARD WHILE PAINTING A LINE OF INK, HUH?
KABOOM
AFTER A WHILE, IT WILL EXPLODE AND SPLATTER INK EVERYWHERE.
MAIKA, LOOK AT ME.
I'VE HITCHED A RIDE. ♪
SWEEE...
KA
BOOM

POWER ARMOR

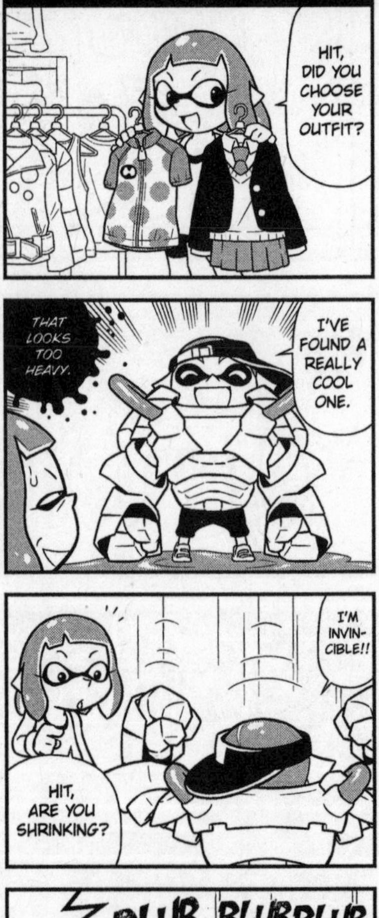
HIT, DID YOU CHOOSE YOUR OUTFIT?
I'VE FOUND A REALLY COOL ONE.
THAT LOOKS TOO HEAVY.
I'M INVINCIBLE!!
HIT, ARE YOU SHRINKING?
BLUB BLUB BLUB
NOT SHRINKING, SINKING!!

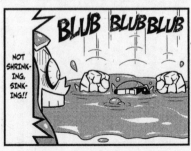

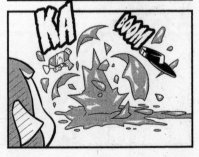

INKJET

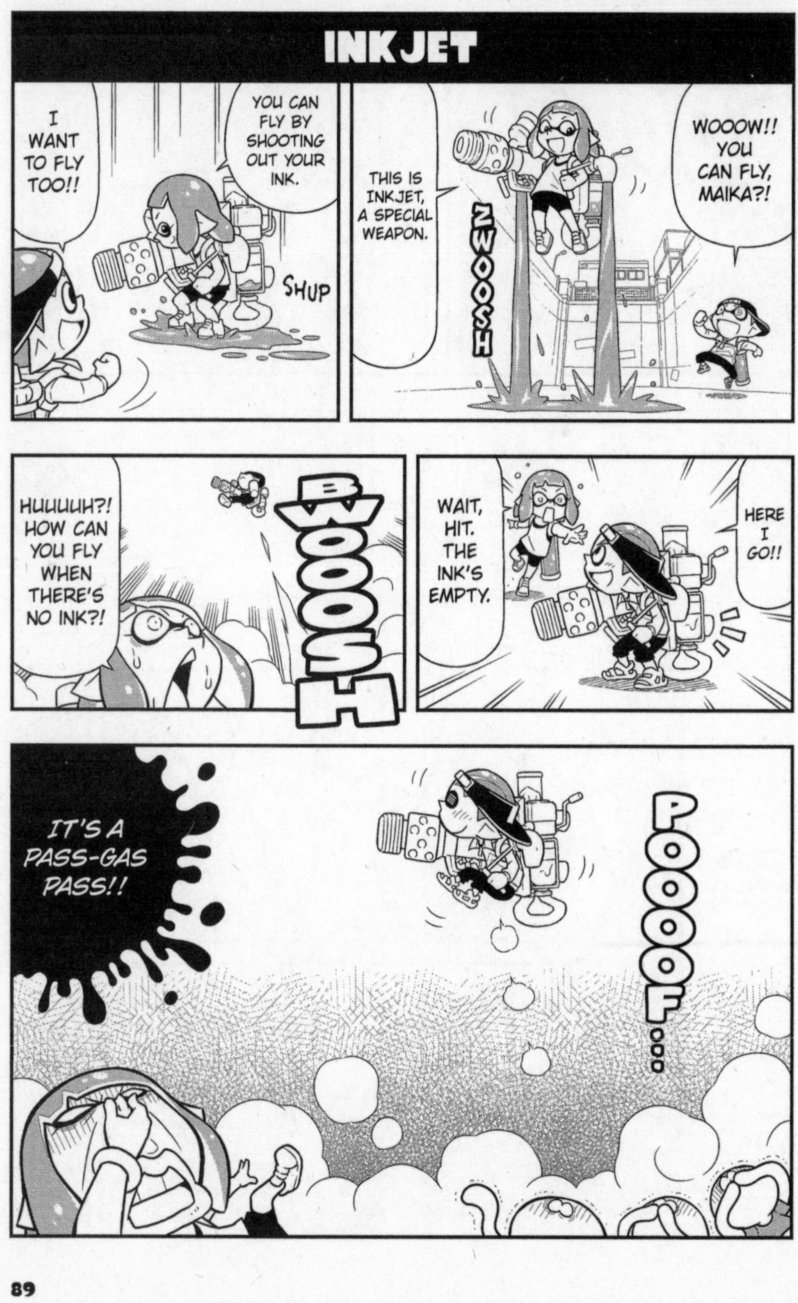
WOOOW!! YOU CAN FLY, MAIKA?!
ZWOOSH
THIS IS INKJET, A SPECIAL WEAPON.
YOU CAN FLY BY SHOOTING OUT YOUR INK.
SHUP
I WANT TO FLY TOO!!
HERE I GO!!
WAIT, HIT. THE INK'S EMPTY.
BWOOOOSH
HUUUUH?! HOW CAN YOU FLY WHEN THERE'S NO INK?!
POOOOF...
IT'S A PASS-GAS PASS!!

FIRING TENTA MISSILES

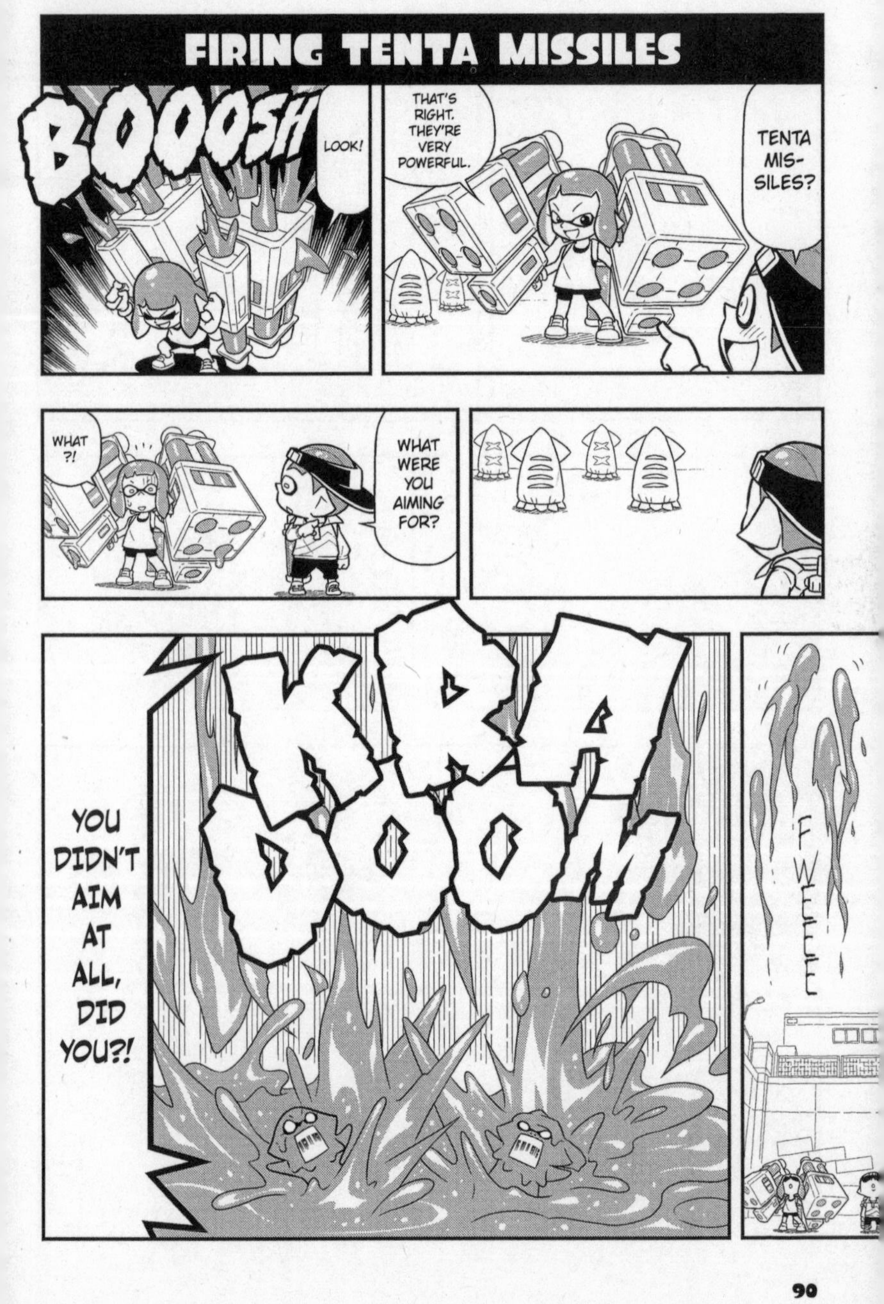
TENTA MIS-SILES?
THAT'S RIGHT. THEY'RE VERY POWERFUL.
BOOOSH
LOOK!
WHAT WERE YOU AIMING FOR?
WHAT ?!
FWEEE
KRA DOOM
YOU DIDN'T AIM AT ALL, DID YOU?!

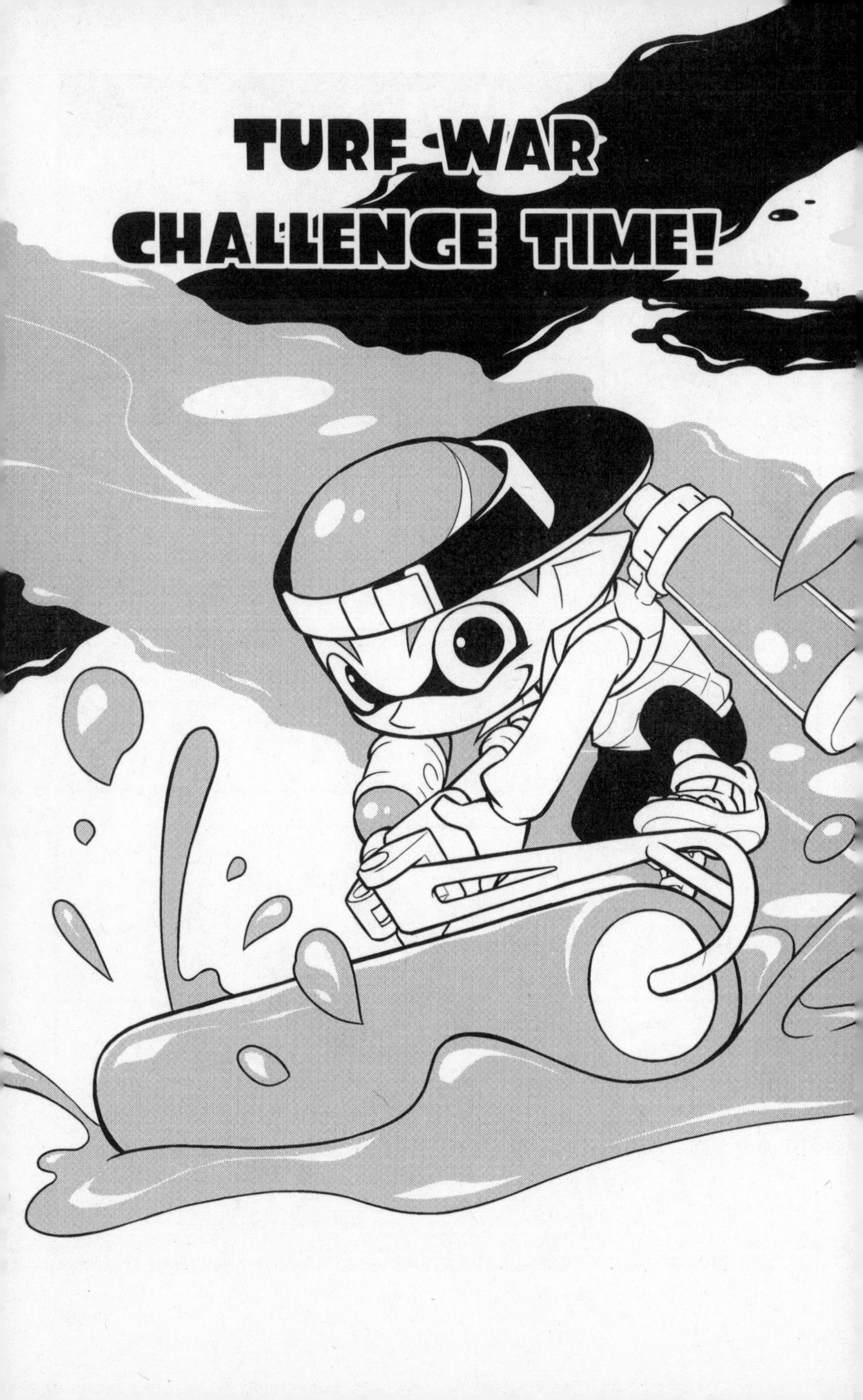
TURF WAR
CHALLENGE TIME!

MY TURF

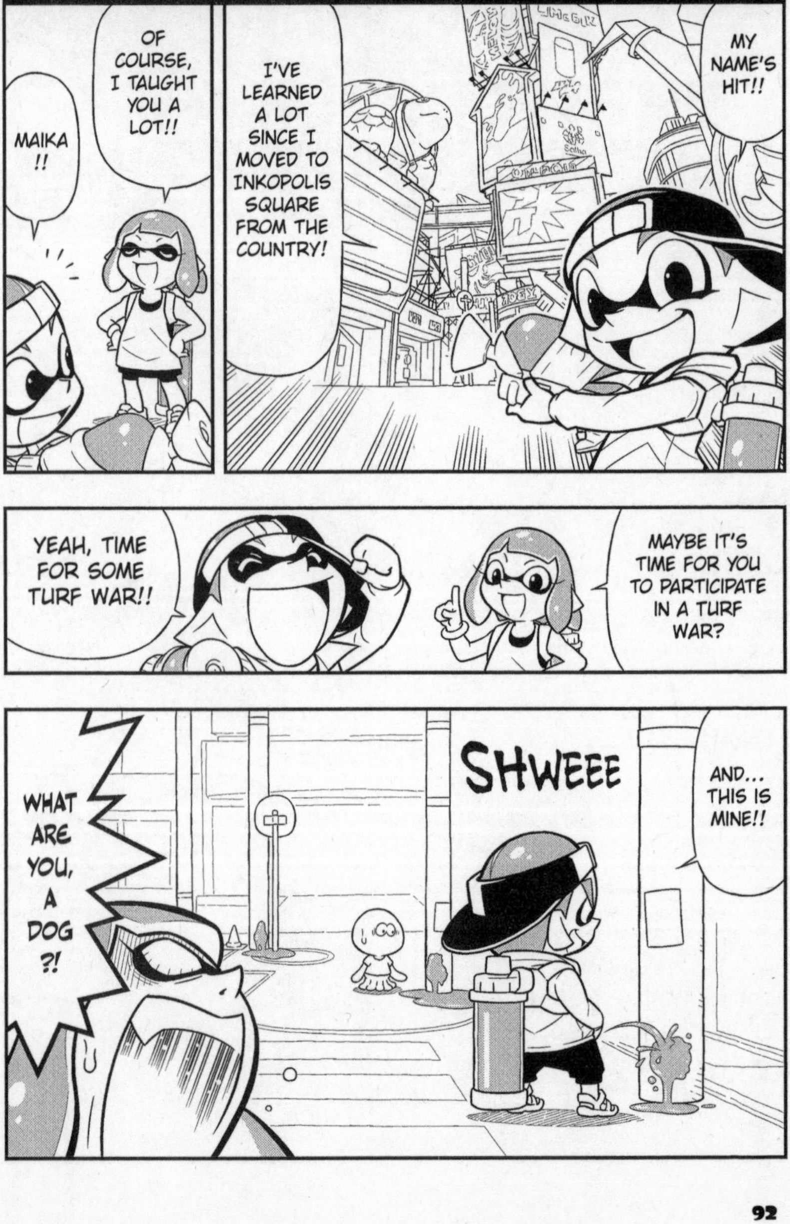
MY NAME'S HIT!!
I'VE LEARNED A LOT SINCE I MOVED TO INKOPOLIS SQUARE FROM THE COUNTRY!
OF COURSE, I TAUGHT YOU A LOT!!
MAIKA!!
MAYBE IT'S TIME FOR YOU TO PARTICIPATE IN A TURF WAR?
YEAH, TIME FOR SOME TURF WAR!!
AND... THIS IS MINE!!
SHWEEE
WHAT ARE YOU, A DOG?!

TEAM MEMBER

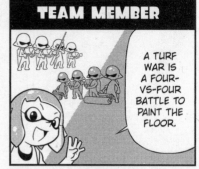

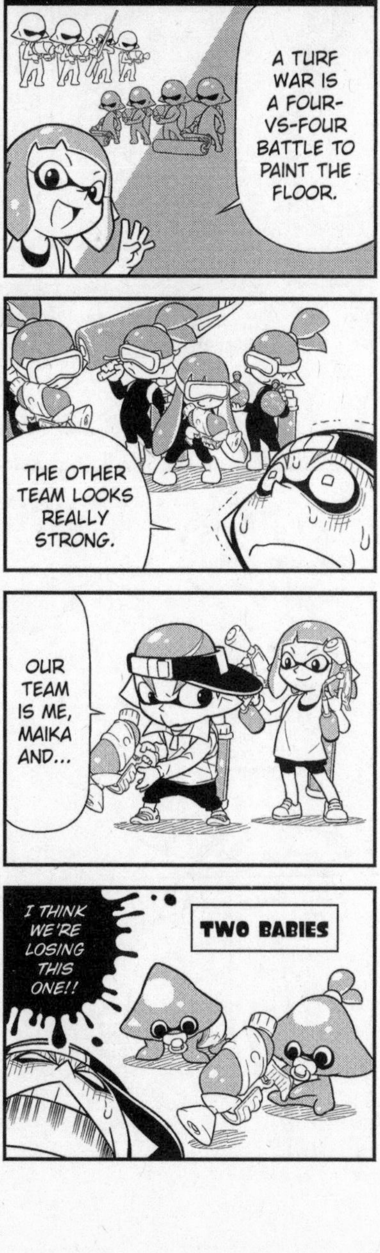
A TURF WAR IS A FOUR-VS-FOUR BATTLE TO PAINT THE FLOOR.
THE OTHER TEAM LOOKS REALLY STRONG.
OUR TEAM IS ME, MAIKA AND...
TWO BABIES
I THINK WE'RE LOSING THIS ONE!!

PAINT THE FLOOR

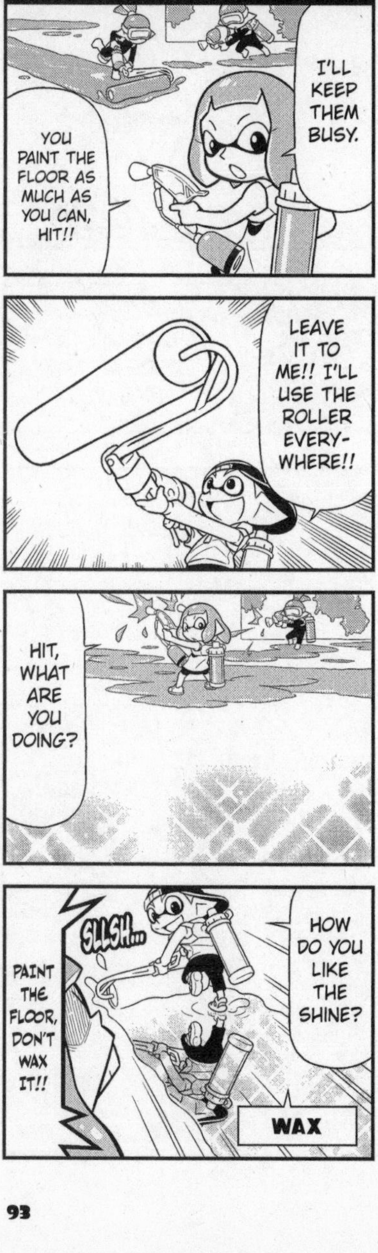
I'LL KEEP THEM BUSY.
YOU PAINT THE FLOOR AS MUCH AS YOU CAN, HIT!!
LEAVE IT TO ME!! I'LL USE THE ROLLER EVERY-WHERE!!
HIT, WHAT ARE YOU DOING?
HOW DO YOU LIKE THE SHINE?
SLLSH...
PAINT THE FLOOR, DON'T WAX IT!!
WAX

TEAMMATE POTENTIAL

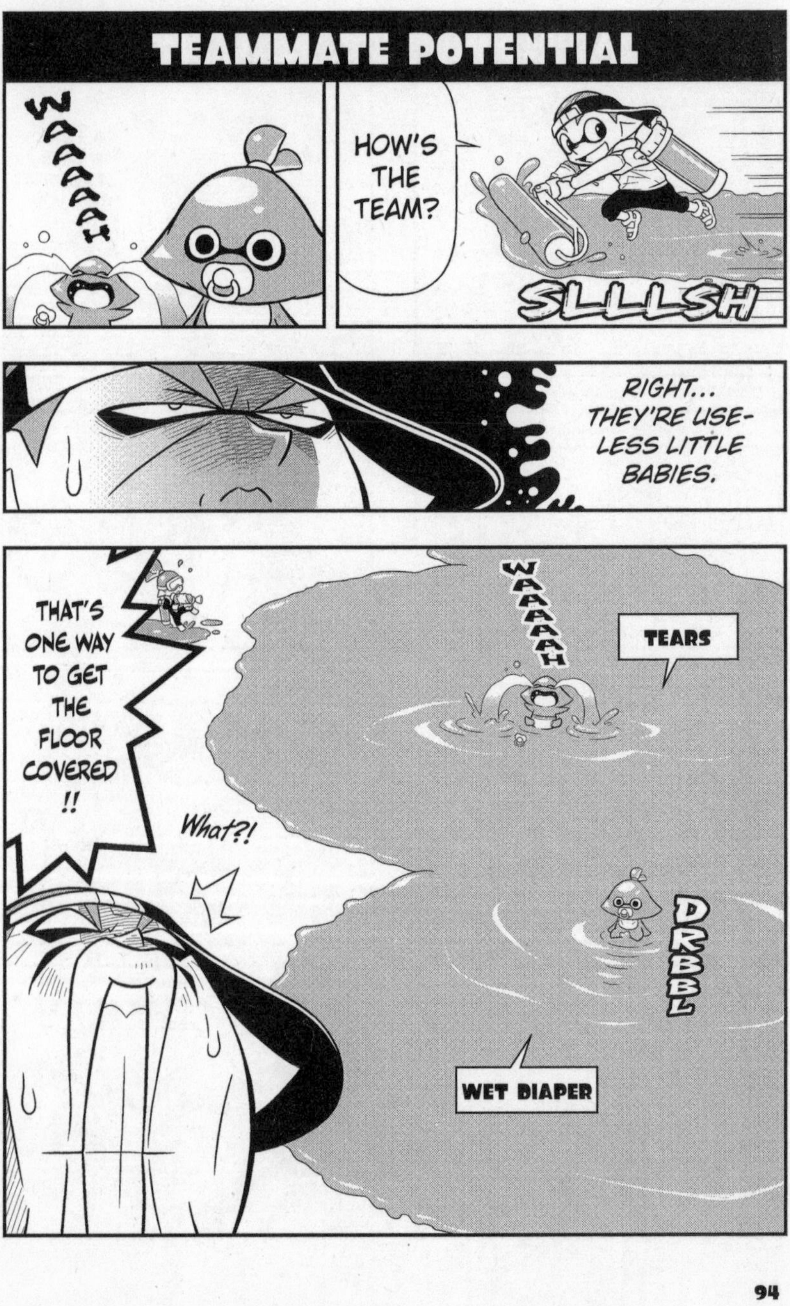
HOW'S THE TEAM?
SLLLSH
WAAAAAAH
RIGHT... THEY'RE USE-LESS LITTLE BABIES.
WAAAAAAH
TEARS
DRBBL
WET DIAPER
THAT'S ONE WAY TO GET THE FLOOR COVERED !!
What?!

DODGE ROLL

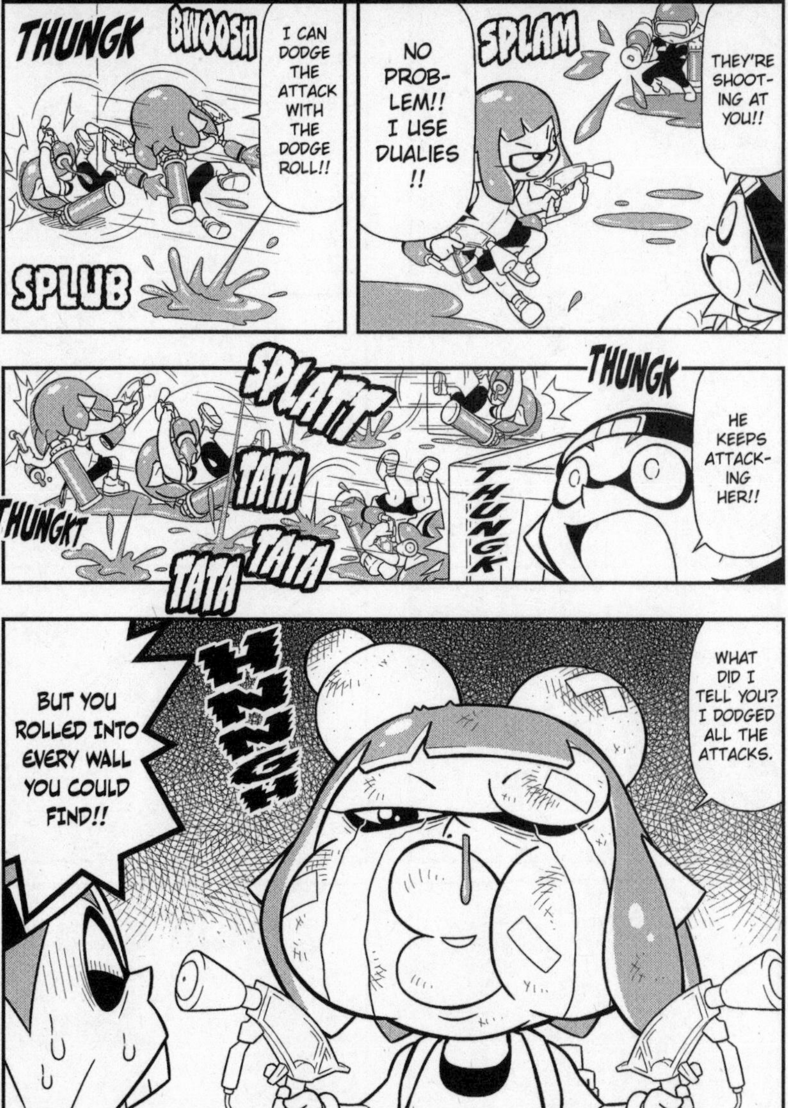
THEY'RE SHOOTING AT YOU!!
SPLAM
NO PROBLEM!! I USE DUALIES!!
I CAN DODGE THE ATTACK WITH THE DODGE ROLL!!
BWOOSH
THUNGK
SPLUB
HE KEEPS ATTACKING HER!!
THUNGK
THUNGK
SPLATT
TATA
TATA
TATA
THUNGKT
WHAT DID I TELL YOU? I DODGED ALL THE ATTACKS.
BUT YOU ROLLED INTO EVERY WALL YOU COULD FIND!!

DIVE

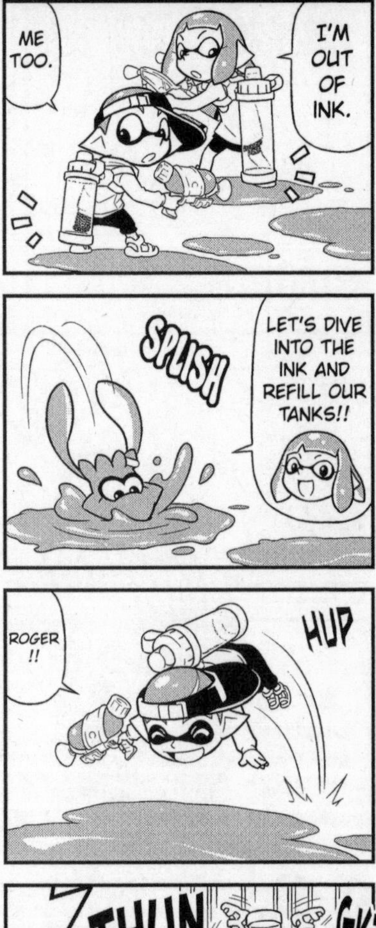
I'M OUT OF INK.
ME TOO.
LET'S DIVE INTO THE INK AND REFILL OUR TANKS!!
SPLISH
HUP
ROGER!!
GKT
THUN
YOU HAVE TO TURN INTO A SQUID FIRST!!

AMBUSH

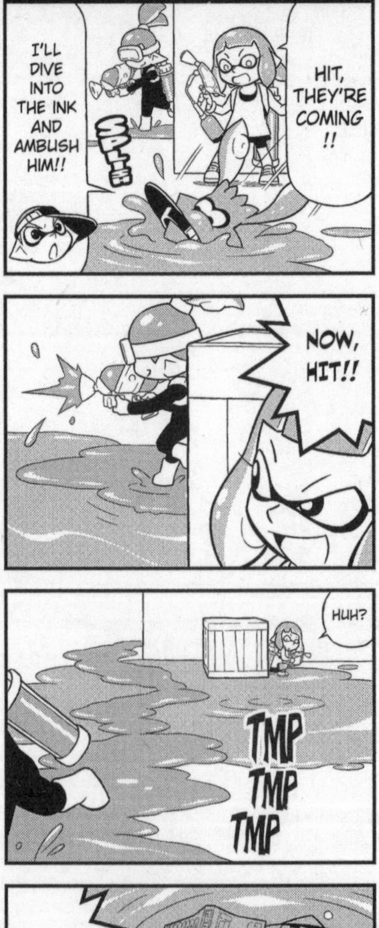
HIT, THEY'RE COMING!!
I'LL DIVE INTO THE INK AND AMBUSH HIM!!
SPLISH
NOW, HIT!!
HUH?
TMP
TMP
TMP
DON'T REST WHILE AMBUSH-ING!!

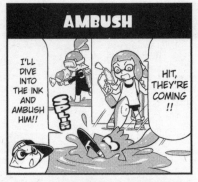

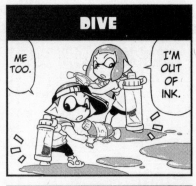

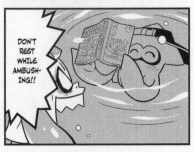

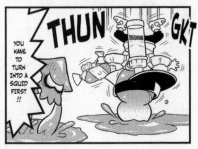

SLOSHER

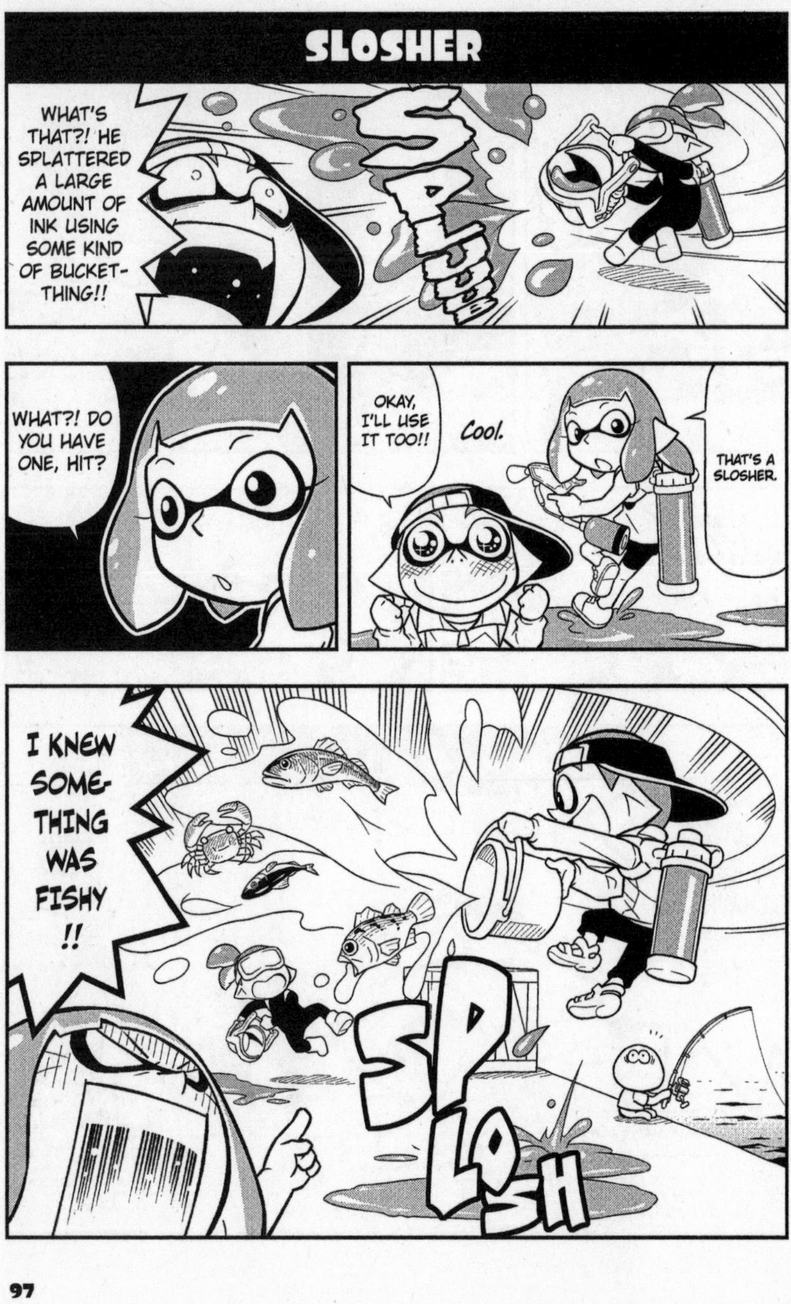
WHAT'S THAT?! HE SPLATTERED A LARGE AMOUNT OF INK USING SOME KIND OF BUCKET-THING!!
THAT'S A SLOSHER.
Cool.
OKAY, I'LL USE IT TOO!!
WHAT?! DO YOU HAVE ONE, HIT?
I KNEW SOME-THING WAS FISHY!!
SPLOSH

PINK

JUDD WILL DECIDE WHICH TEAM WON.
Who won?
MEOW!
WIN!
TEAM PINK
HOORAY!!
WHAT ?!
WHY ARE THEY CHEERING ?!
TEAM REALLY LIGHT RED
28.6%
TEAM PINK
47.2%
I DON'T THINK WE WERE TEAM PINK...
REALLY LIGHT RED?! THAT'S SO CONFUS-ING!!
REALLY LIGHT RED

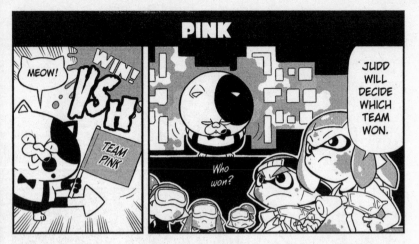

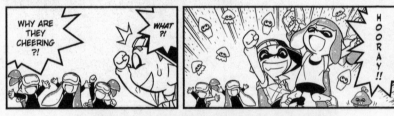

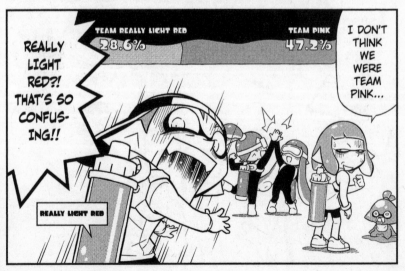

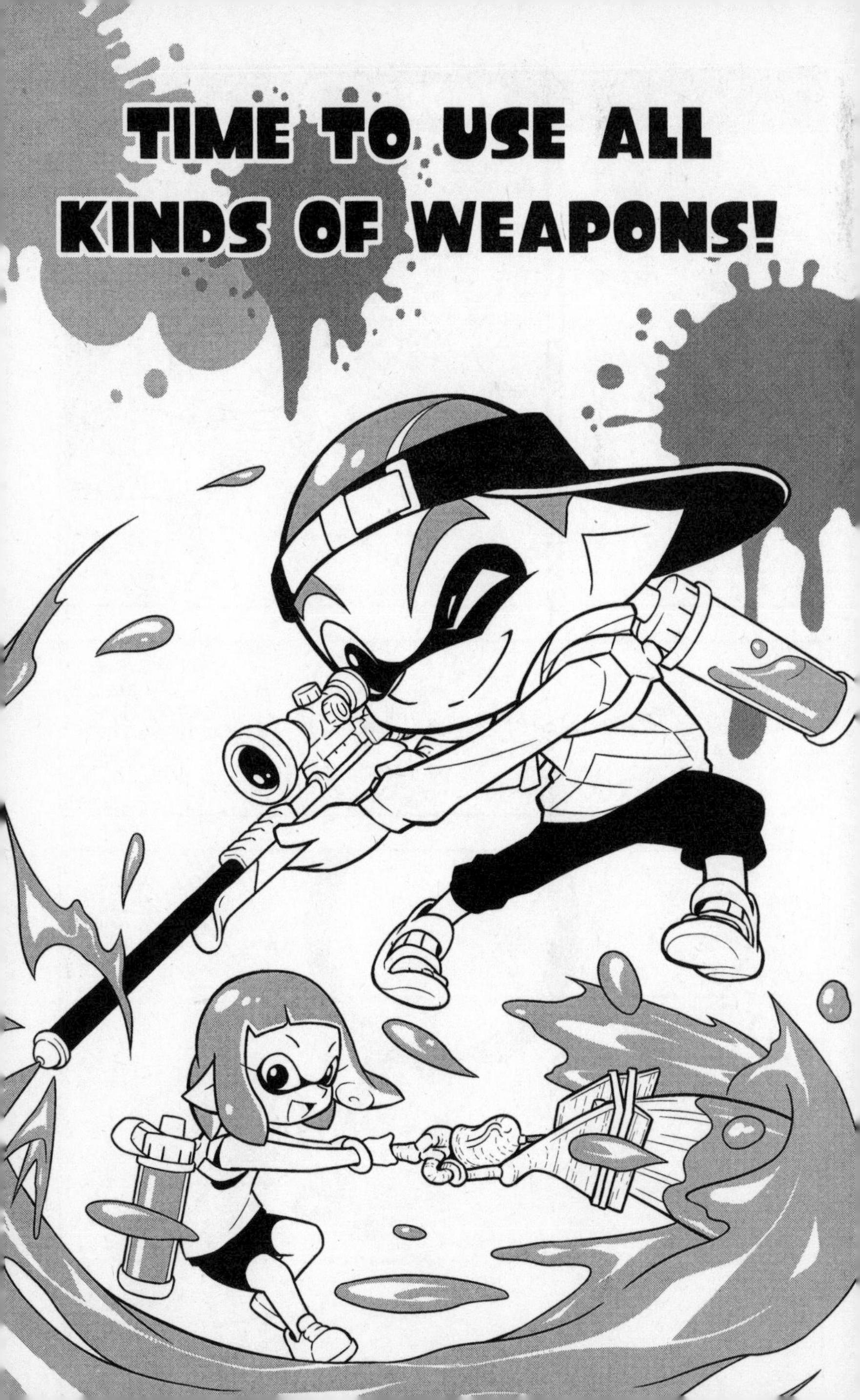
TIME TO USE ALL KINDS OF WEAPONS!

SCOPE

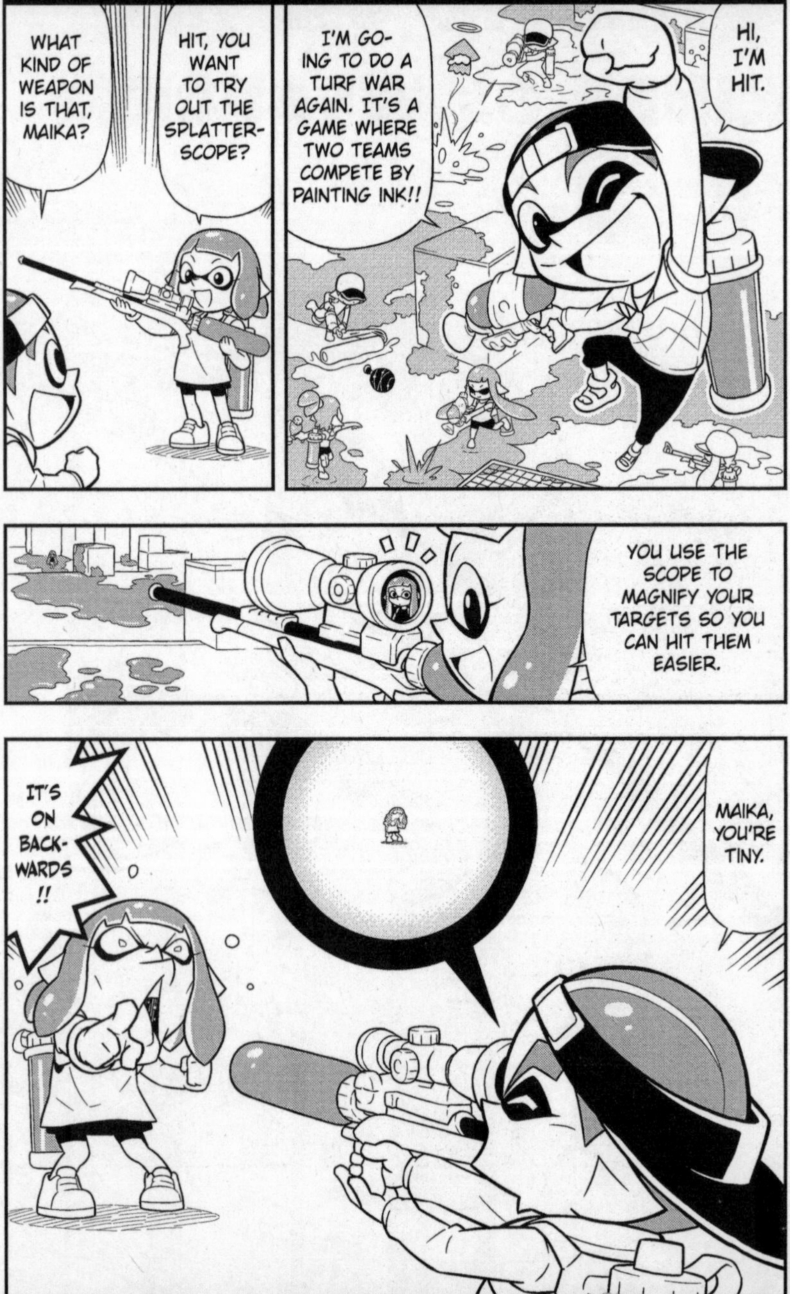
HI, I'M HIT.
I'M GOING TO DO A TURF WAR AGAIN. IT'S A GAME WHERE TWO TEAMS COMPETE BY PAINTING INK!!
HIT, YOU WANT TO TRY OUT THE SPLATTERSCOPE?
WHAT KIND OF WEAPON IS THAT, MAIKA?
YOU USE THE SCOPE TO MAGNIFY YOUR TARGETS SO YOU CAN HIT THEM EASIER.
MAIKA, YOU'RE TINY.
IT'S ON BACKWARDS!!

PAINT AWAY!!

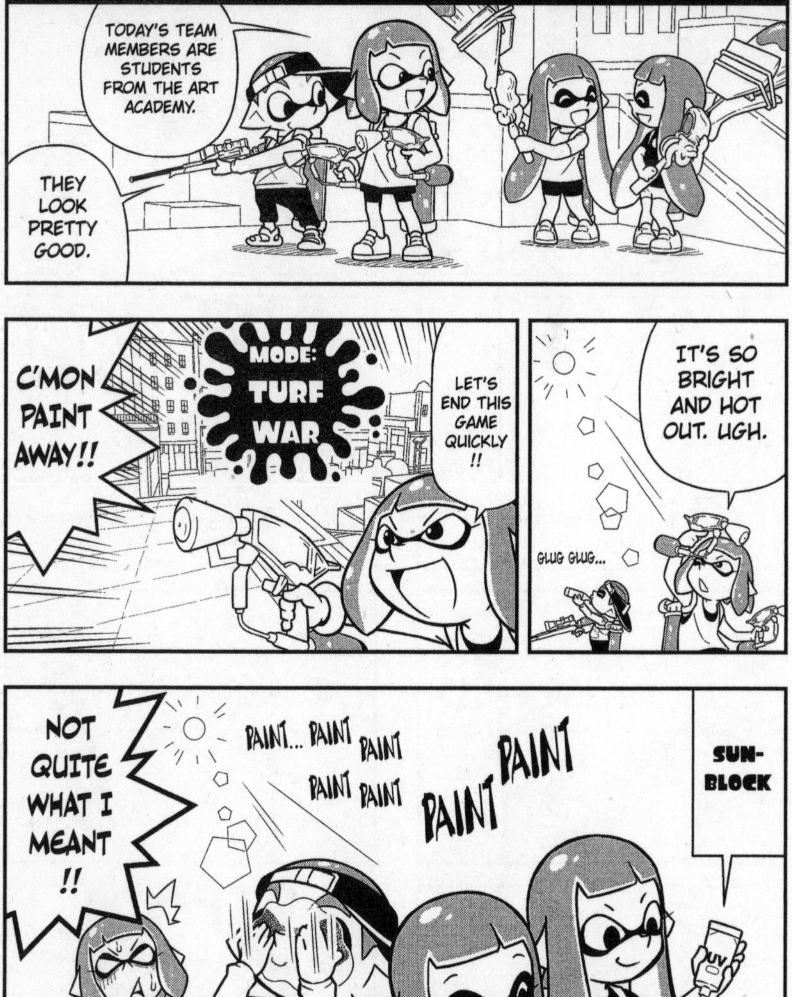
TODAY'S TEAM MEMBERS ARE STUDENTS FROM THE ART ACADEMY.
THEY LOOK PRETTY GOOD.
IT'S SO BRIGHT AND HOT OUT. UGH.
GLUG GLUG...
LET'S END THIS GAME QUICKLY !!
MODE: TURF WAR
C'MON PAINT AWAY!!
SUN-BLOCK
UV
PAINT PAINT
PAINT... PAINT PAINT
PAINT PAINT
NOT QUITE WHAT I MEANT !!

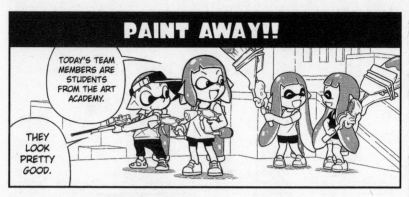

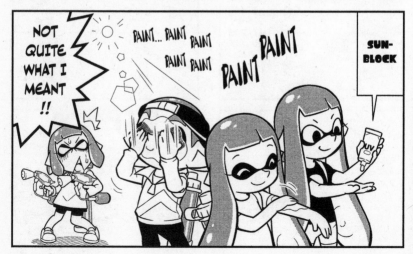

I'LL FIND HIM

Whoa.
WHO SHOT THAT?!
SPLUB
SPLAM
LEAVE IT TO ME!! I CAN SEE THROUGH MY SPLATTER-SCOPE !!
SPLUB
BULL'S EYE!!
LIGHT SWITCH
P
PA
CAN YOU GET HIM?!
There he is!

AUTOBOMB

MAIKA, LOOKY HERE!!
THAT'S THE NEW SUB WEAPON, THE AUTO-BOMB.
ONCE IT DETECTS ITS TARGET, IT WILL FOLLOW THEM AND EXPLODE.
TMP TMP TMP
THE OPPO-NENT'S HERE!! HURRY, HIT. TIME TO USE THE AUTO-BOMB.
HOLD ON.
KRRCH
KRRCH
A WINDUP AUTO-BOMB ?!
You're losing him!!

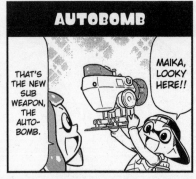

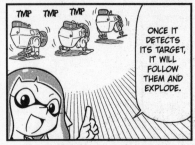

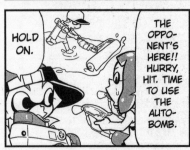

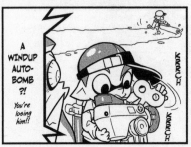

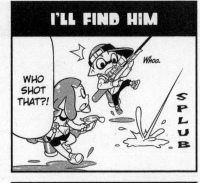

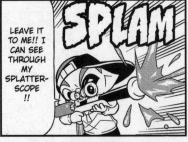

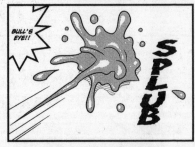

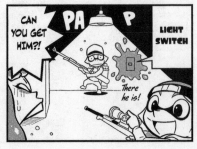

BACK SPLASHING

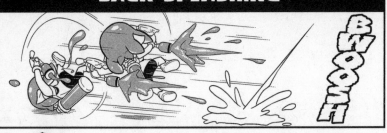

BWOOSH
YOU CAN MOVE QUICKLY BECAUSE INK SPURTS OUT FROM THE BACK OF THE DUALIES.
It's the dodge roll.
COOL, ISN'T IT?
SPLAM
THEY'RE SHOOTING AT YOU AGAIN!!
BWOOSH
SPLUB
HIT, WERE YOU SHOT?!
JUST BY YOU, MAIKA...

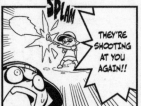

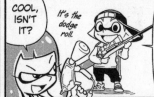

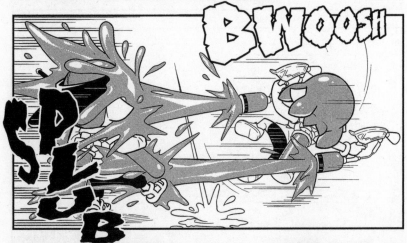

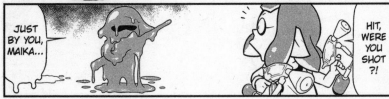

ART ACADEMY SKILLS

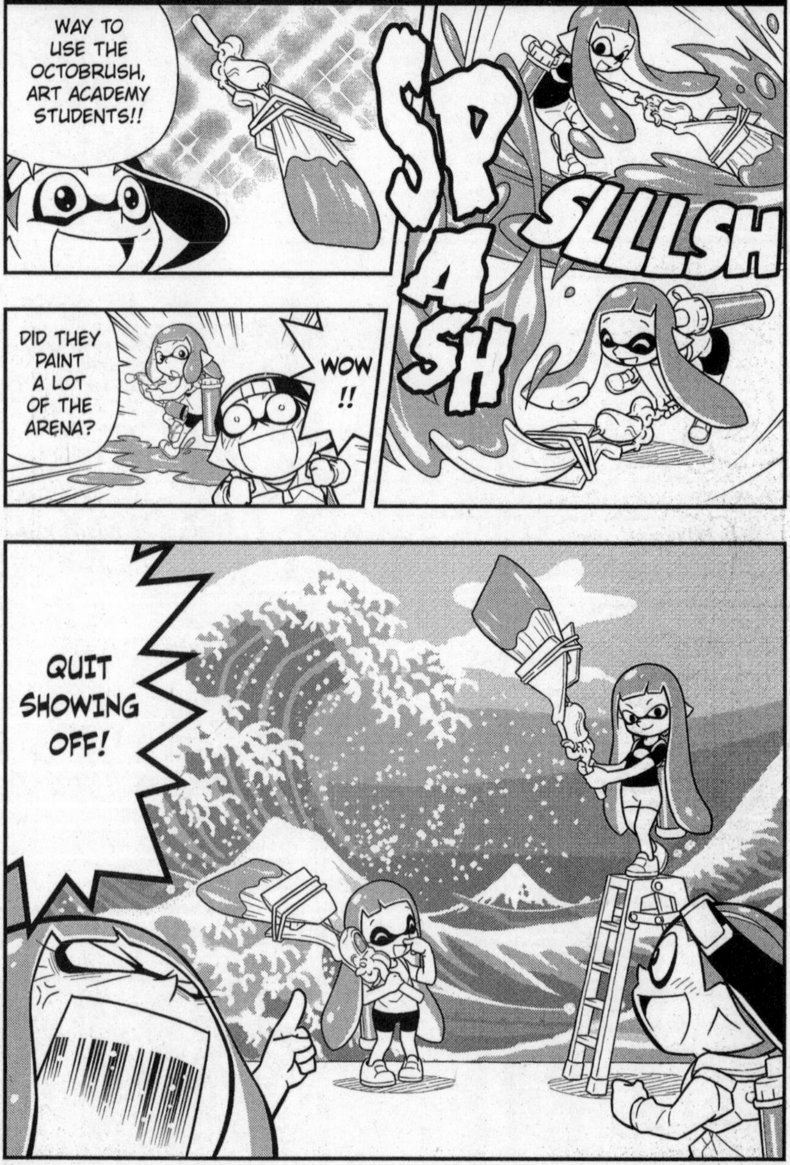
SPLASH
SLLLSH
WAY TO USE THE OCTOBRUSH, ART ACADEMY STUDENTS!!
DID THEY PAINT A LOT OF THE ARENA?
WOW!!
QUIT SHOWING OFF!

BRUSH ATTACK

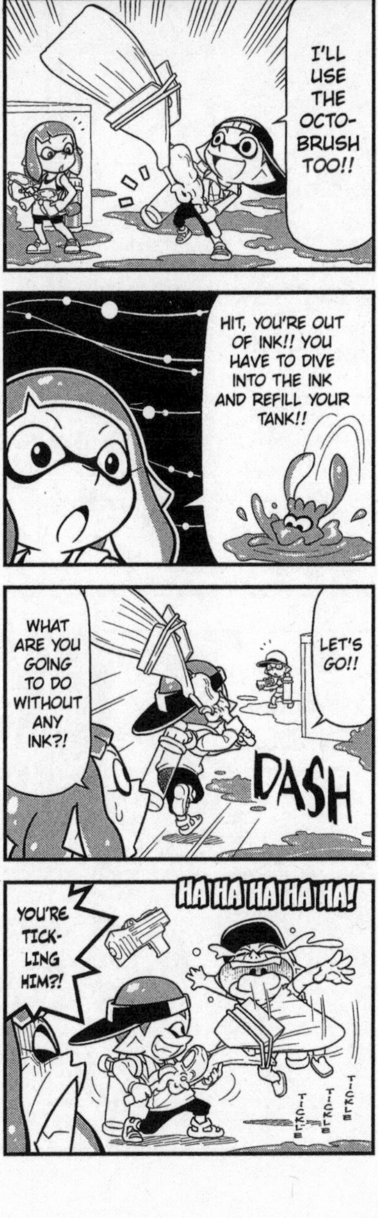
I'LL USE THE OCTO-BRUSH TOO!!
HIT, YOU'RE OUT OF INK!! YOU HAVE TO DIVE INTO THE INK AND REFILL YOUR TANK!!
LET'S GO!!
DASH
WHAT ARE YOU GOING TO DO WITHOUT ANY INK?!
HA HA HA HA HA!
TICKLE
TICKLE
TICKLE
YOU'RE TICK-LING HIM?!

PAINT TOGETHER

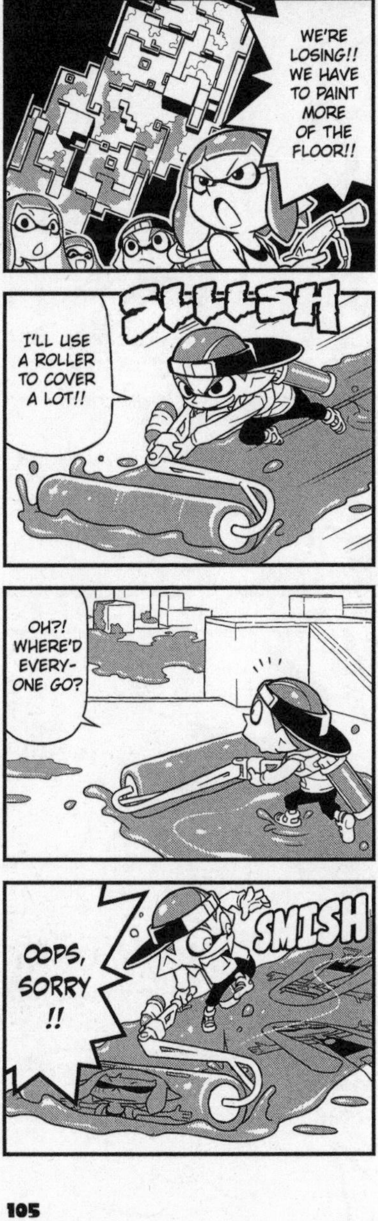
WE'RE LOSING!! WE HAVE TO PAINT MORE OF THE FLOOR!!
SLLLSH
I'LL USE A ROLLER TO COVER A LOT!!
OH?! WHERE'D EVERY-ONE GO?
SMISH
OOPS, SORRY!!

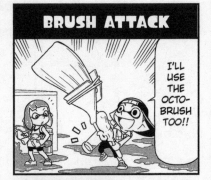

GOT THEM ALL

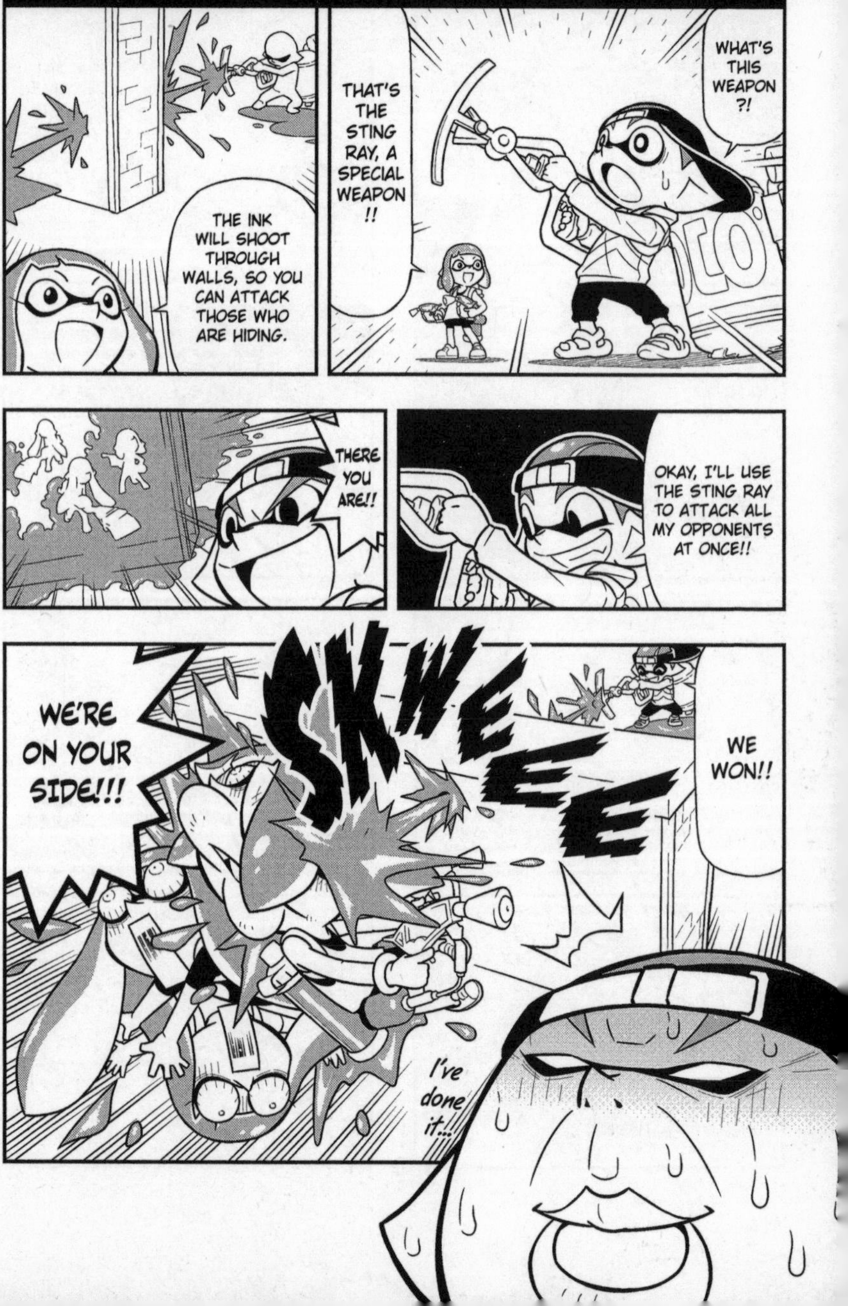
WHAT'S THIS WEAPON ?!
THAT'S THE STING RAY, A SPECIAL WEAPON !!
THE INK WILL SHOOT THROUGH WALLS, SO YOU CAN ATTACK THOSE WHO ARE HIDING.
OKAY, I'LL USE THE STING RAY TO ATTACK ALL MY OPPONENTS AT ONCE!!
THERE YOU ARE!!
WE WON!!
SKWEEEE
WE'RE ON YOUR SIDE!!!
I've done it...

TIME TO AIM FOR VICTORY WITH THE SPECIAL WEAPON!

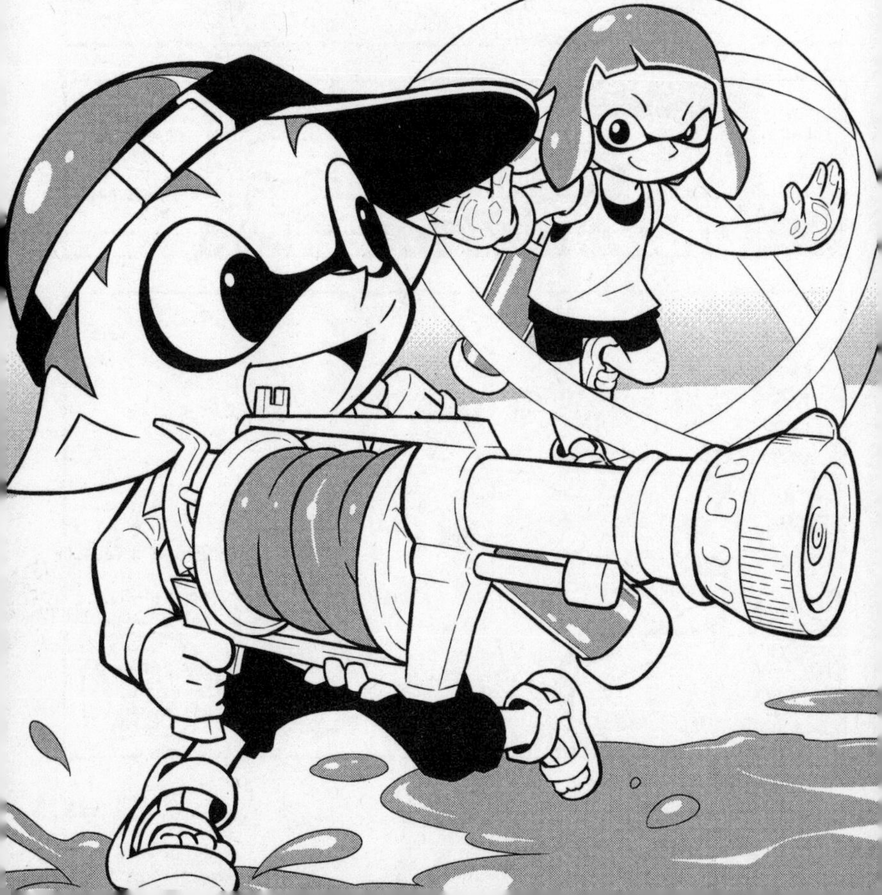

A NEW WEAPON

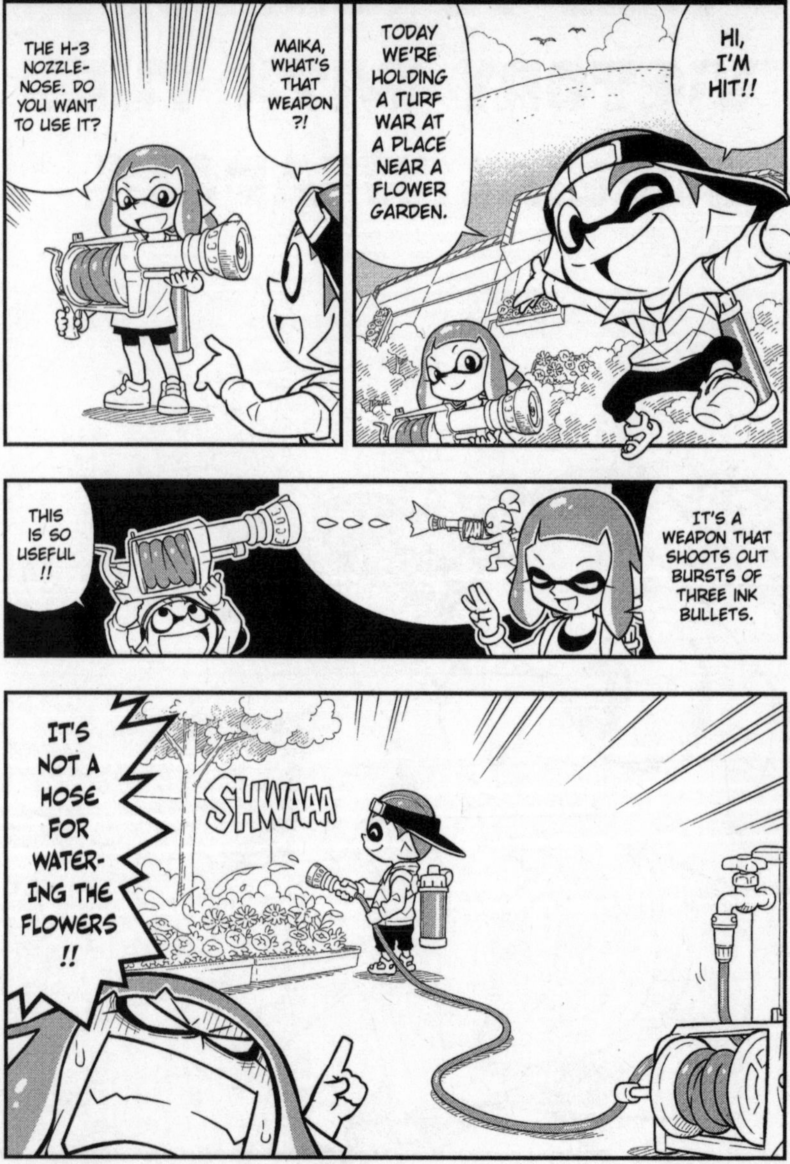
HI, I'M HIT!!
TODAY WE'RE HOLDING A TURF WAR AT A PLACE NEAR A FLOWER GARDEN.
MAIKA, WHAT'S THAT WEAPON?!
THE H-3 NOZZLE-NOSE. DO YOU WANT TO USE IT?
IT'S A WEAPON THAT SHOOTS OUT BURSTS OF THREE INK BULLETS.
THIS IS SO USEFUL!!
SHWAAA
IT'S NOT A HOSE FOR WATERING THE FLOWERS!!

GETTING READY

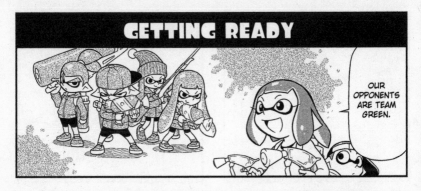

OUR OPPONENTS ARE TEAM GREEN.
I'LL STAND IN FRONT.
SUP-PORT ME FROM THE BACK, HIT!!
WAIT, MAIKA!!
I'M STILL GET-TING MY WEAPON READY.
BUT THERE AREN'T ANY WEAPONS THAT TAKE TIME TO PREPARE.
I WAS JUST FINISHING WATERING THE FLOWERS.
SHFF
SHFF
SHFF
IT'S A WEAPON, NOT A HOSE!!
H-3 NOZZLENOSE

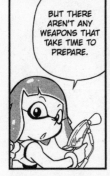

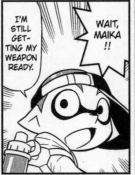

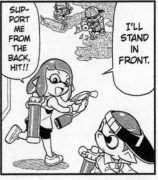

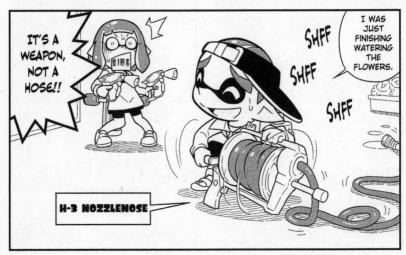

SPRINKLER

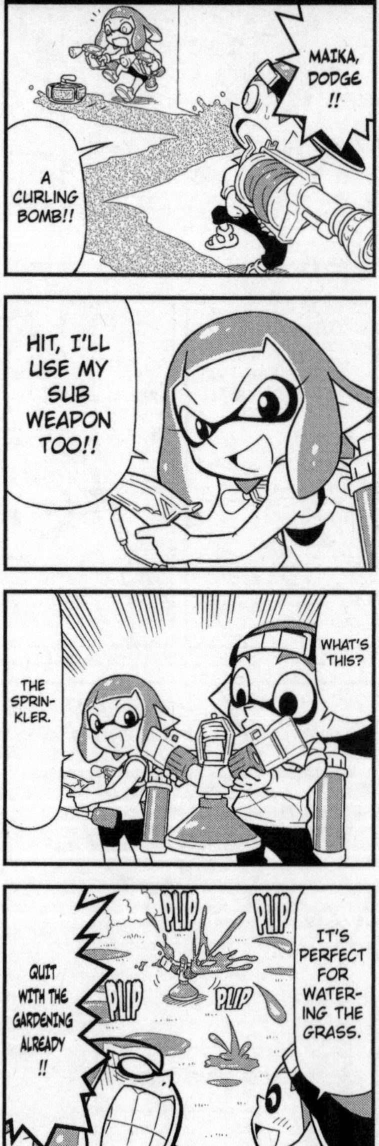
MAIKA, DODGE!!
A CURLING BOMB!!
HIT, I'LL USE MY SUB WEAPON TOO!!
WHAT'S THIS?
THE SPRIN-KLER.
PLIP
PLIP
PLIP
PLIP
IT'S PERFECT FOR WATER-ING THE GRASS.
QUIT WITH THE GARDENING ALREADY!!

FLOWER PATTERN

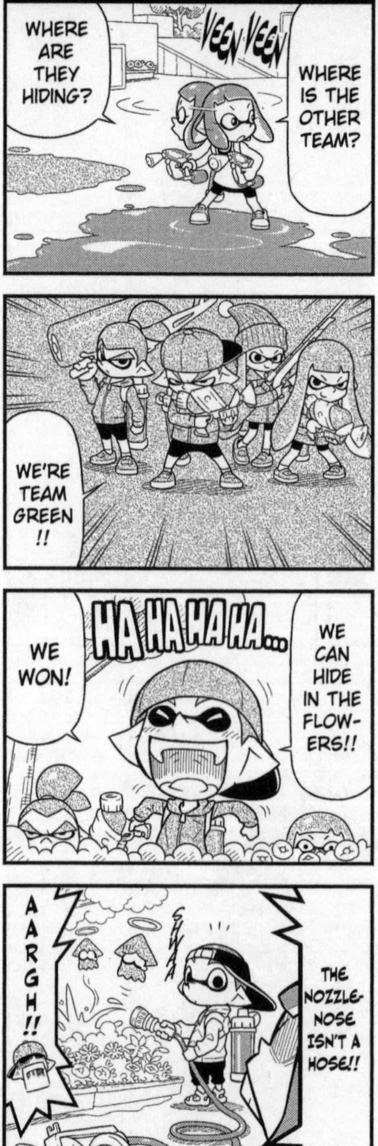
WHERE IS THE OTHER TEAM?
VEEN VEEN
WHERE ARE THEY HIDING?
WE'RE TEAM GREEN!!
WE CAN HIDE IN THE FLOW-ERS!!
HA HA HA HA...
WE WON!
THE NOZZLE-NOSE ISN'T A HOSE!!
AARGH!!

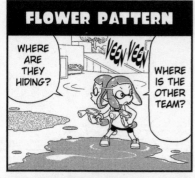

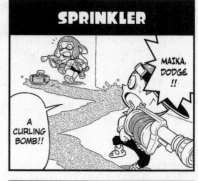

TOXIC MIST

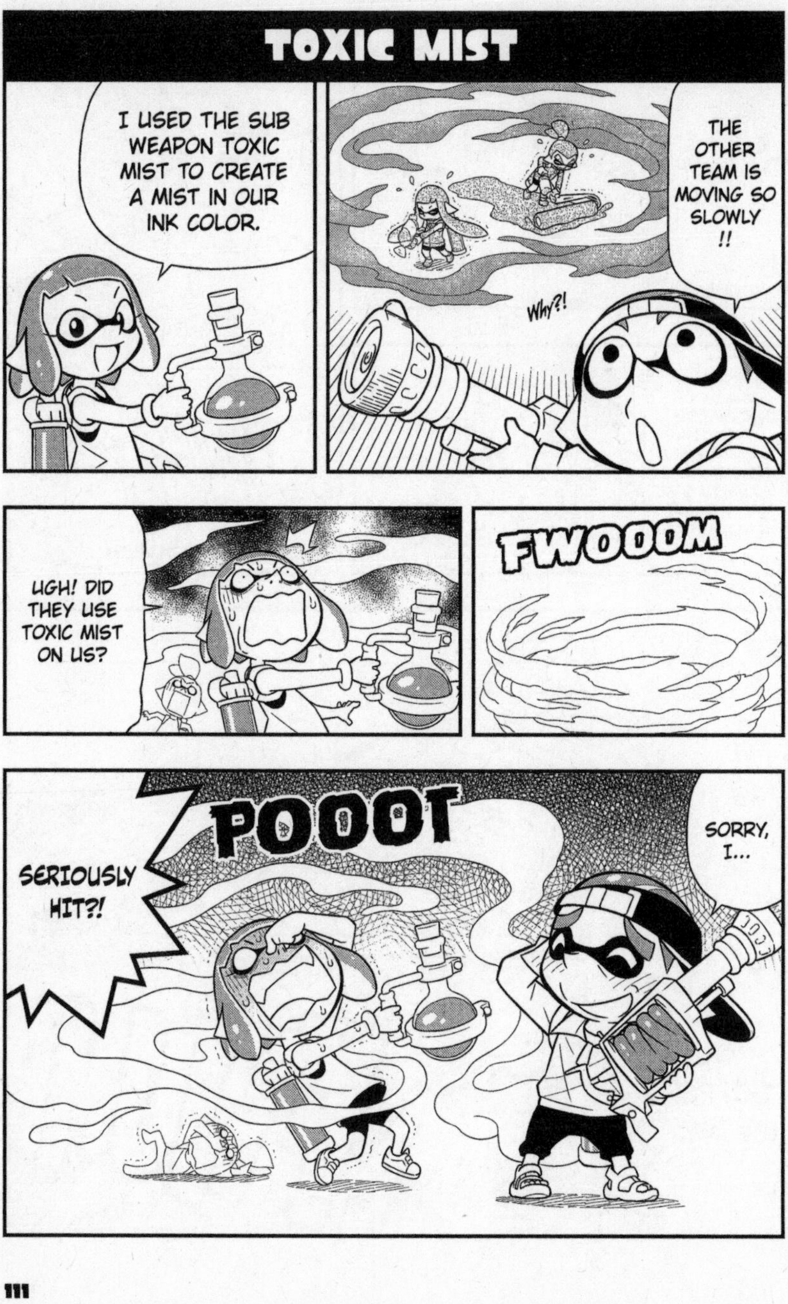
THE OTHER TEAM IS MOVING SO SLOWLY !!
Why?!
I USED THE SUB WEAPON TOXIC MIST TO CREATE A MIST IN OUR INK COLOR.
FWOOOM
UGH! DID THEY USE TOXIC MIST ON US?
SORRY, I...
POOOT
SERIOUSLY HIT?!

GOTCHA

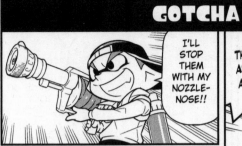

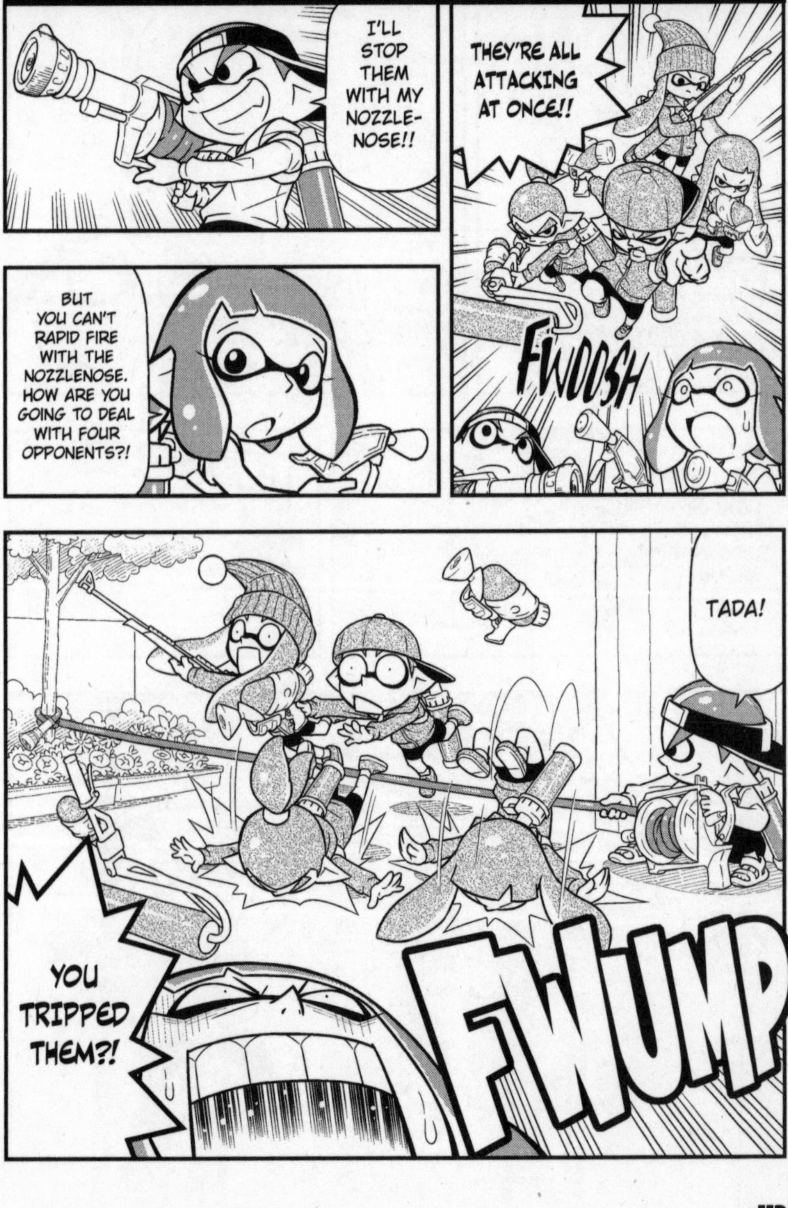
THEY'RE ALL ATTACKING AT ONCE!!
FWOOSH
I'LL STOP THEM WITH MY NOZZLE-NOSE!!
BUT YOU CAN'T RAPID FIRE WITH THE NOZZLENOSE. HOW ARE YOU GOING TO DEAL WITH FOUR OPPONENTS?!
TADA!
FWUMP
YOU TRIPPED THEM?!

TAKE THAT!

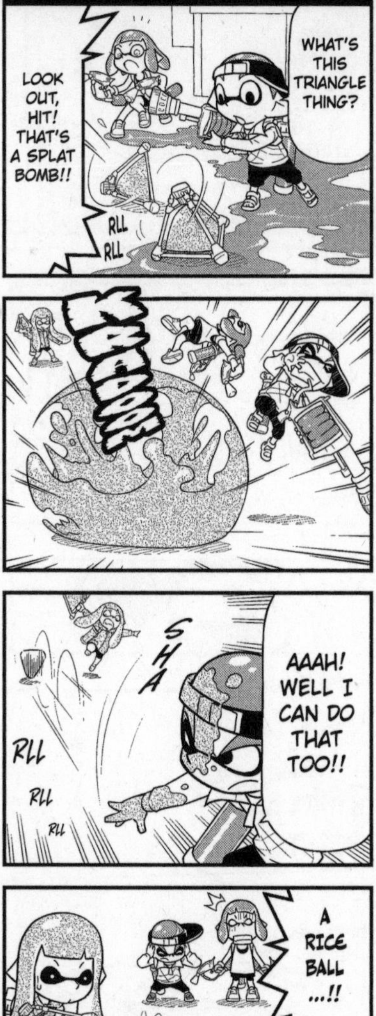
WHAT'S THIS TRIANGLE THING?
LOOK OUT, HIT! THAT'S A SPLAT BOMB!!
RLL RLL
AAAH! WELL I CAN DO THAT TOO!!
SHA
RLL
RLL
RLL
A RICE BALL ...!!
RLL
RLL

BALLER

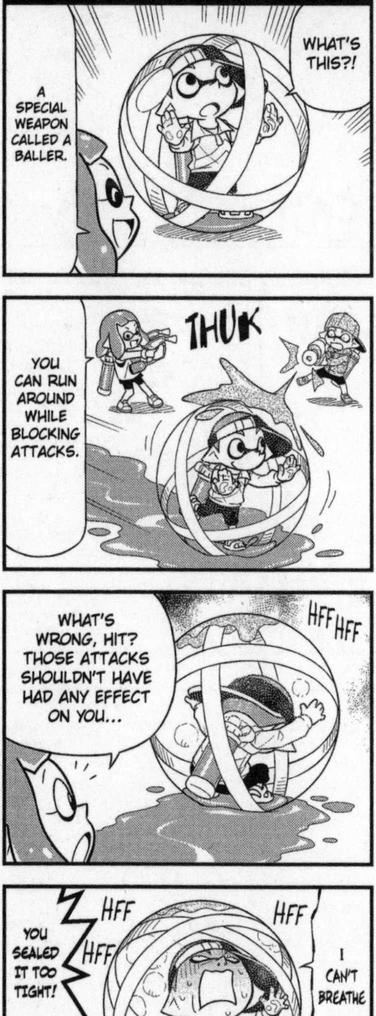
WHAT'S THIS?!
A SPECIAL WEAPON CALLED A BALLER.
THUK
YOU CAN RUN AROUND WHILE BLOCKING ATTACKS.
HFF HFF
WHAT'S WRONG, HIT? THOSE ATTACKS SHOULDN'T HAVE HAD ANY EFFECT ON YOU...
I CAN'T BREATHE ...
HFF
HFF
HFF
YOU SEALED IT TOO TIGHT!

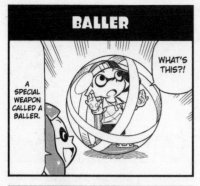

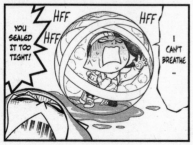

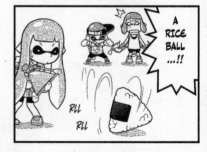

SAFE ON WATER

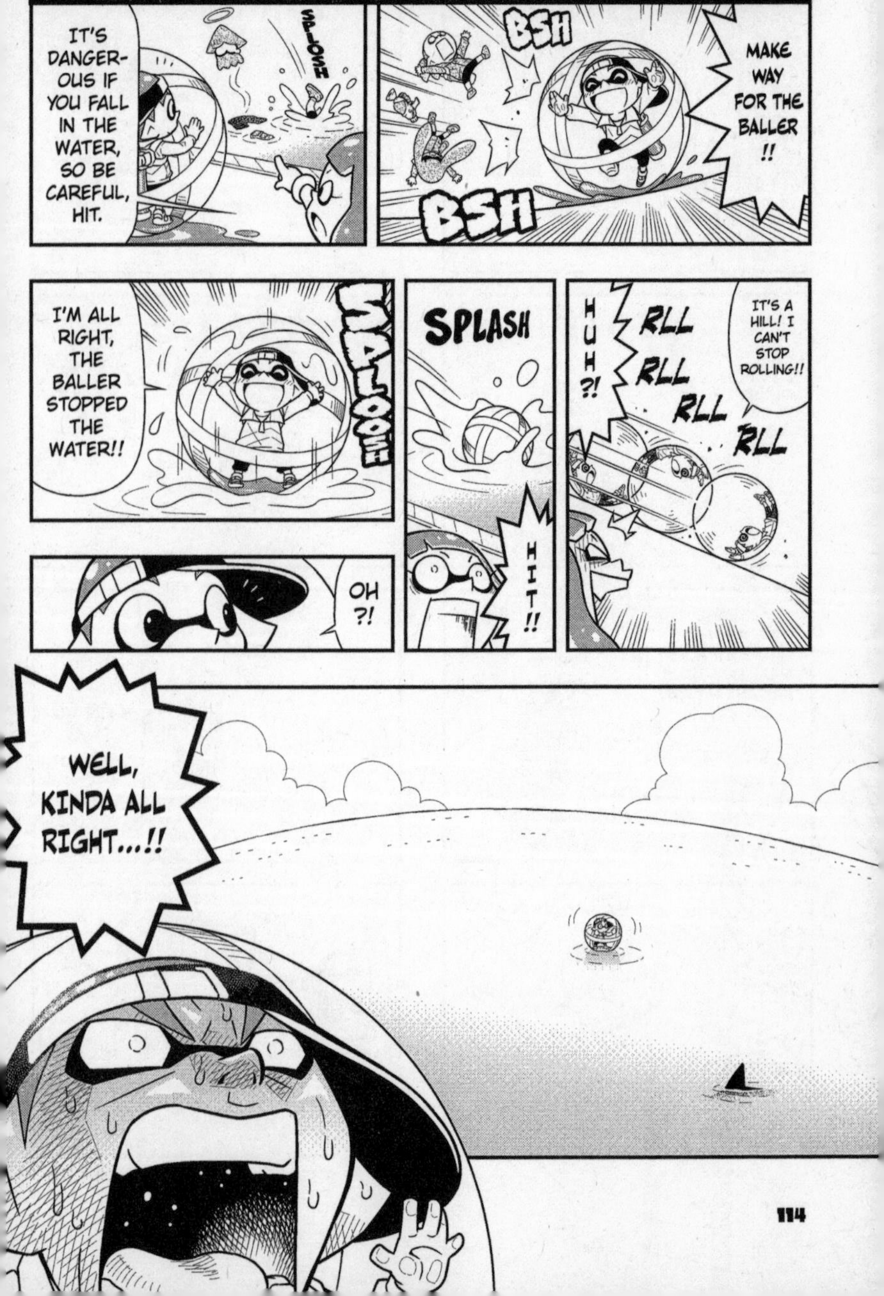

BSH
MAKE WAY FOR THE BALLER!!
BSH
SPLOSH
IT'S DANGEROUS IF YOU FALL IN THE WATER, SO BE CAREFUL, HIT.
IT'S A HILL! I CAN'T STOP ROLLING!!
RLL RLL RLL RLL
HUH?!
SPLASH
HIT!!
SPLOOSH
I'M ALL RIGHT, THE BALLER STOPPED THE WATER!!
OH?!
WELL, KINDA ALL RIGHT...!!

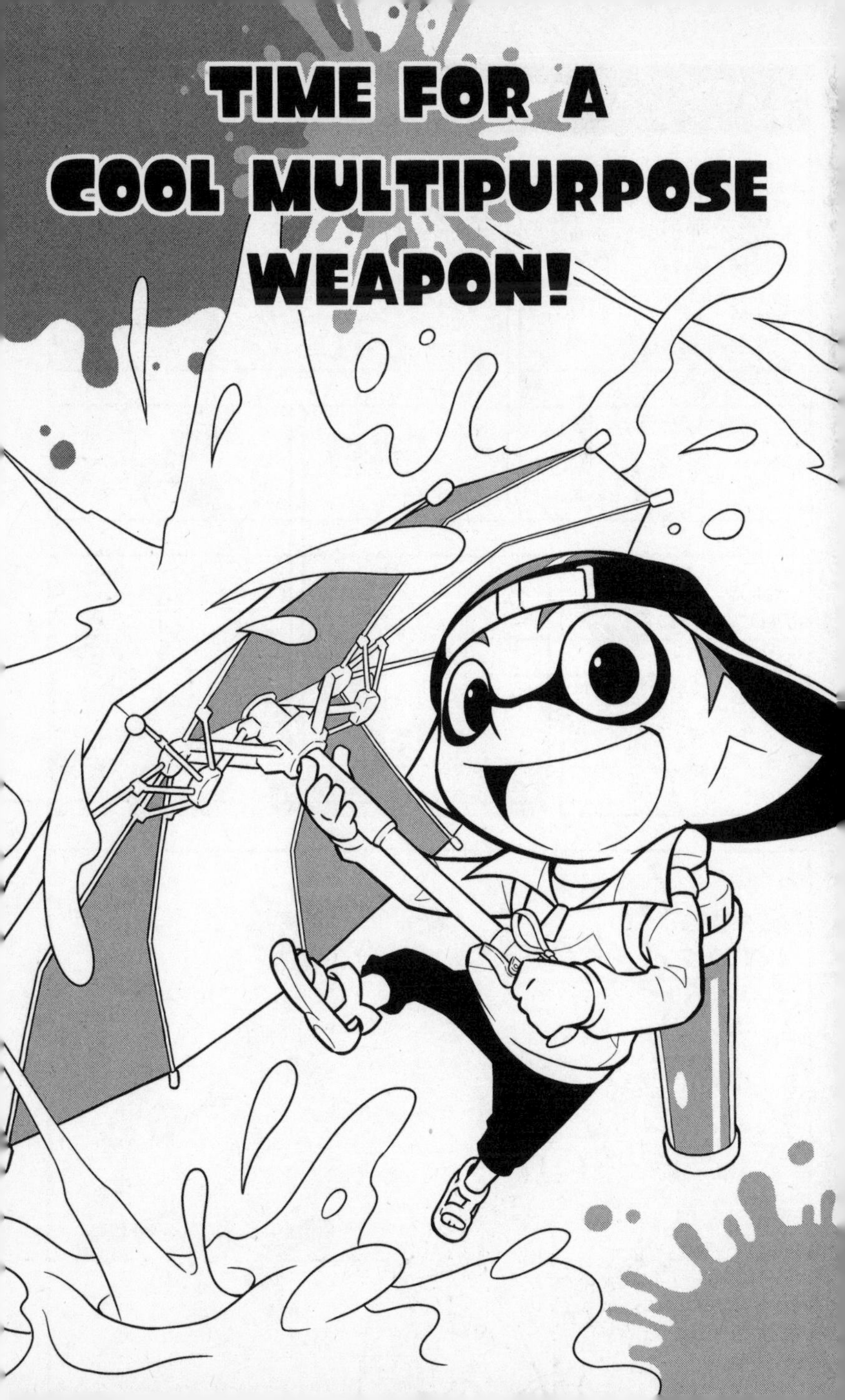
TIME FOR A
COOL MULTIPURPOSE
WEAPON!

SPLAT BRELLA

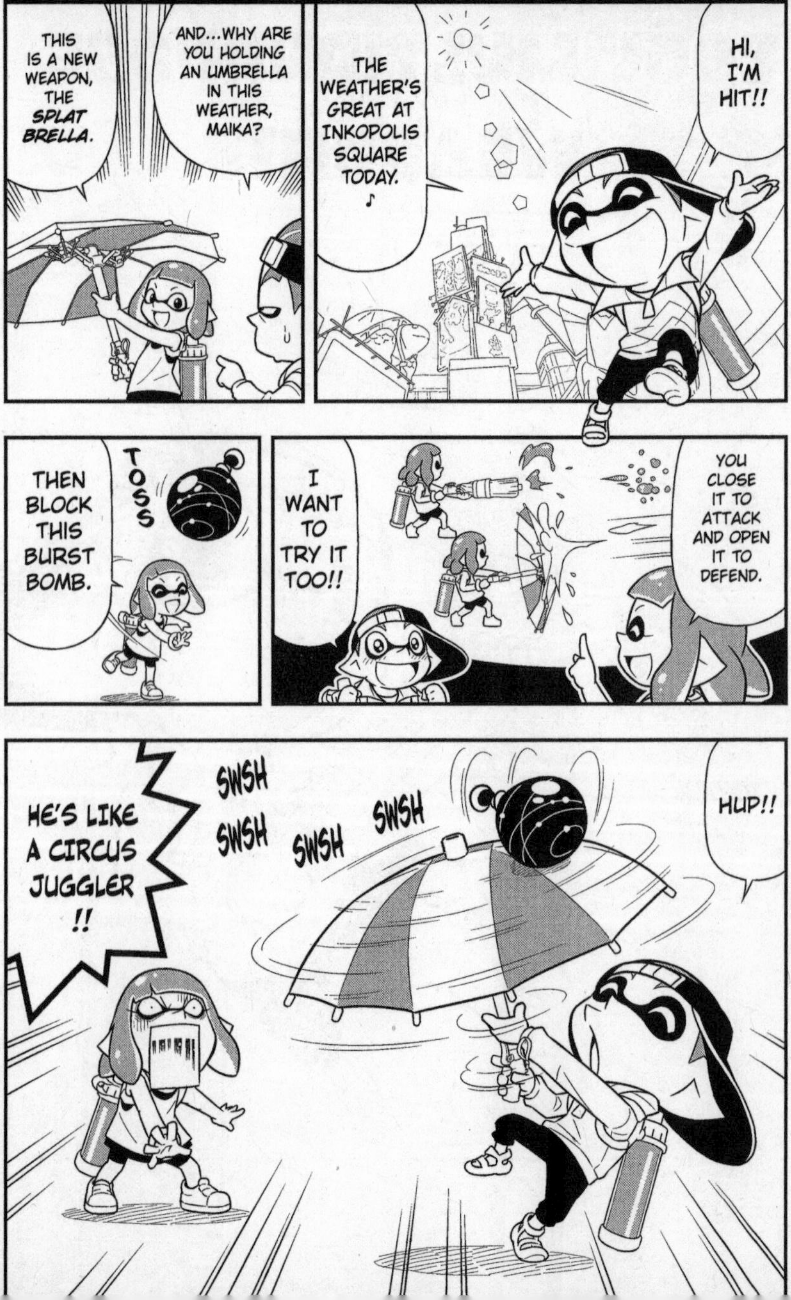
HI, I'M HIT!!
THE WEATHER'S GREAT AT INKOPOLIS SQUARE TODAY. ♪
AND...WHY ARE YOU HOLDING AN UMBRELLA IN THIS WEATHER, MAIKA?
THIS IS A NEW WEAPON, THE *SPLAT BRELLA*.
YOU CLOSE IT TO ATTACK AND OPEN IT TO DEFEND.
I WANT TO TRY IT TOO!!
TOSS
THEN BLOCK THIS BURST BOMB.
HUP!!
SWSH
SWSH
SWSH
SWSH
HE'S LIKE A CIRCUS JUGGLER!!

LAUNCH

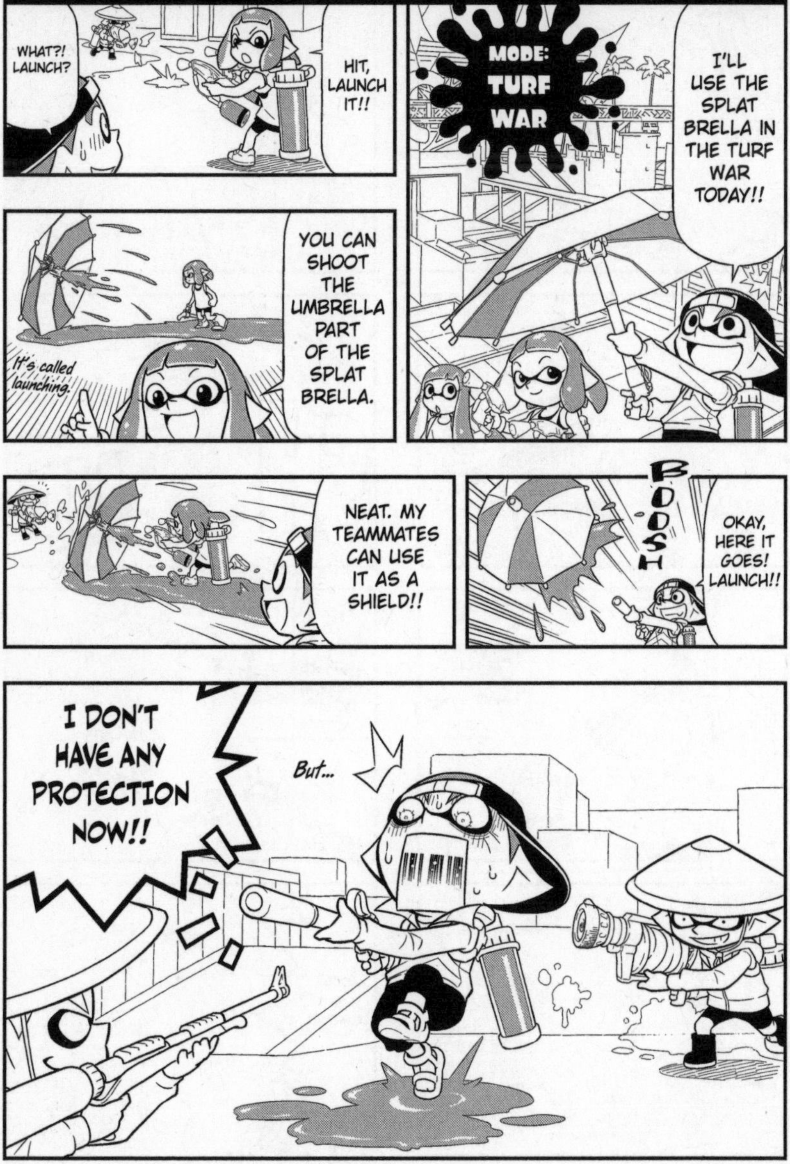
MODE: TURF WAR
I'LL USE THE SPLAT BRELLA IN THE TURF WAR TODAY!!
HIT, LAUNCH IT!!
WHAT?! LAUNCH?
YOU CAN SHOOT THE UMBRELLA PART OF THE SPLAT BRELLA.
It's called launching.
OKAY, HERE IT GOES! LAUNCH!!
BOOSH
NEAT. MY TEAMMATES CAN USE IT AS A SHIELD!!
But...
I DON'T HAVE ANY PROTECTION NOW!!

PARACHUTE

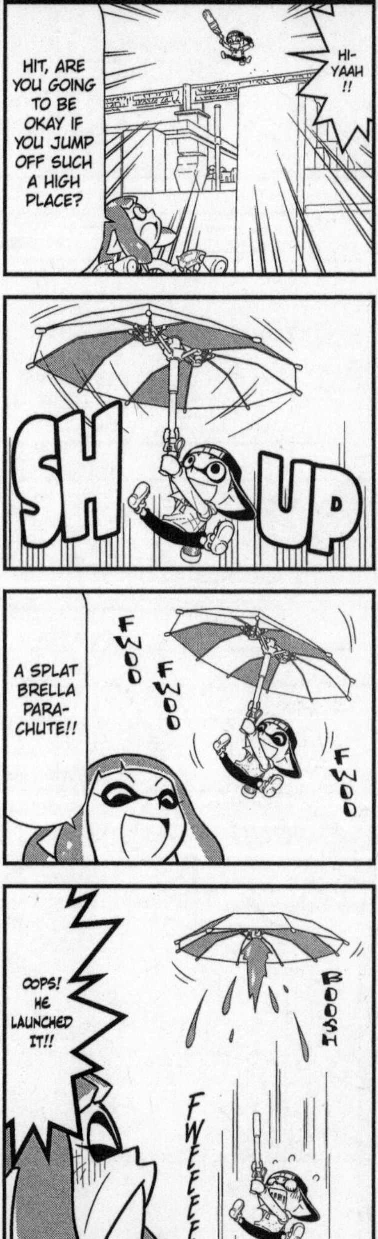
HI-YAAH!!
HIT, ARE YOU GOING TO BE OKAY IF YOU JUMP OFF SUCH A HIGH PLACE?
SH
UP
FWOO
FWOO
A SPLAT BRELLA PARA-CHUTE!!
FWOO
BOOSH
OOPS! HE LAUNCHED IT!!
FWEEEE

RAPID FIRE

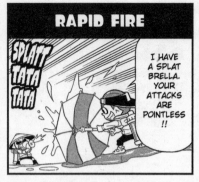

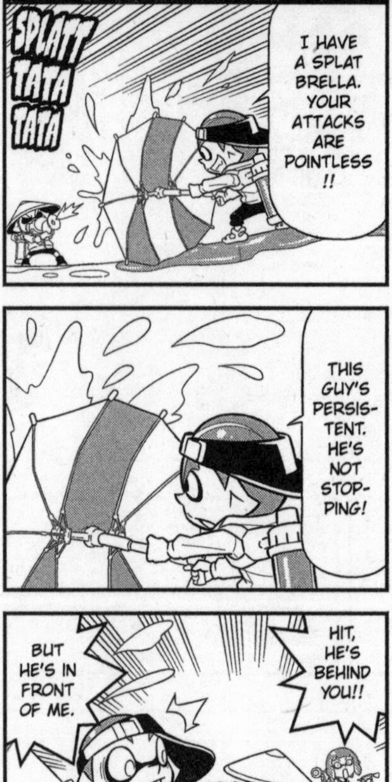
I HAVE A SPLAT BRELLA. YOUR ATTACKS ARE POINTLESS!!
SPLATT TATA TATA
THIS GUY'S PERSIS-TENT. HE'S NOT STOP-PING!
HIT, HE'S BEHIND YOU!!
BUT HE'S IN FRONT OF ME.
PLIP PLIP
PLIP PLIP
HE STUCK A SPRINKLER ON MY SPLAT BRELLA!!

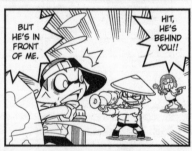

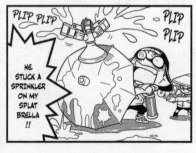

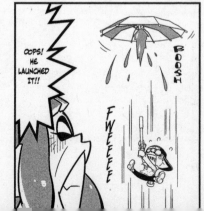

UNOPENABLE SPLAT BRELLA

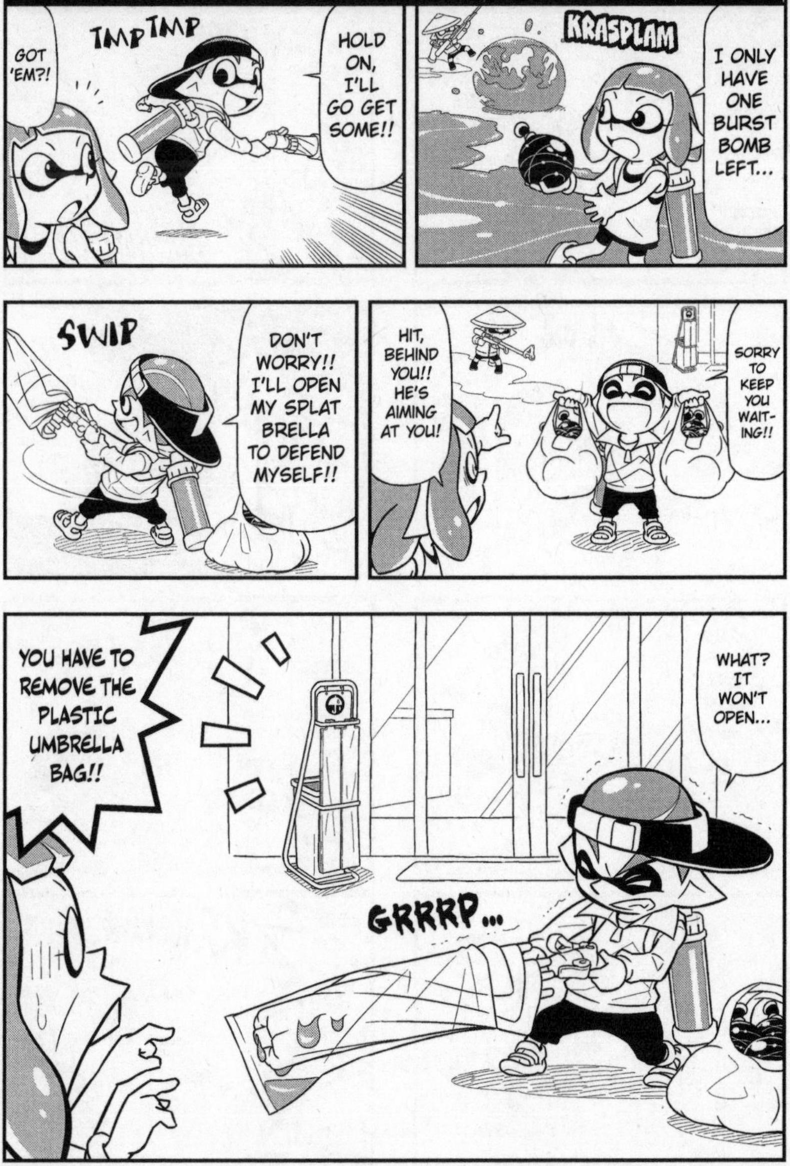
I ONLY HAVE ONE BURST BOMB LEFT...
KRASPLAM
GOT 'EM?!
TMP TMP
HOLD ON, I'LL GO GET SOME!!
SORRY TO KEEP YOU WAIT-ING!!
HIT, BEHIND YOU!! HE'S AIMING AT YOU!
DON'T WORRY!! I'LL OPEN MY SPLAT BRELLA TO DEFEND MYSELF!!
SWIP
WHAT? IT WON'T OPEN...
YOU HAVE TO REMOVE THE PLASTIC UMBRELLA BAG!!
GRRRP...

WINDSHIELD

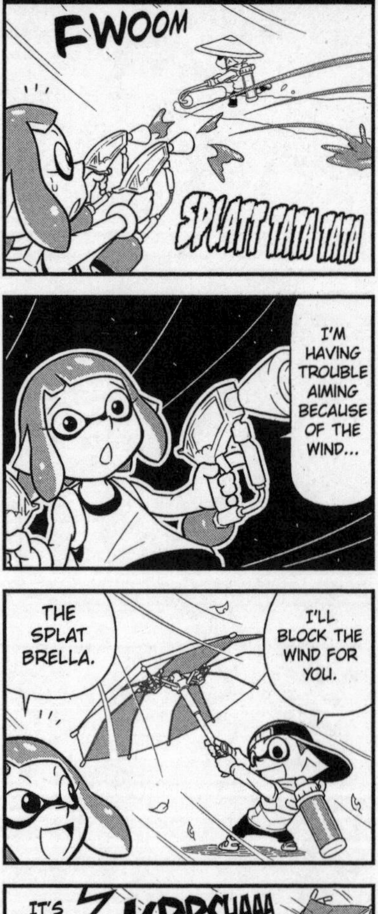
FWOOM
SPLATT TATA TATA
I'M HAVING TROUBLE AIMING BECAUSE OF THE WIND...
I'LL BLOCK THE WIND FOR YOU.
THE SPLAT BRELLA.
KRRSHAAA
IT'S NOT HELPING!!
BWOOOOM

SPLAT BOAT

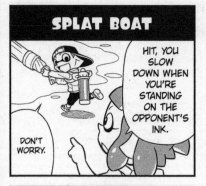

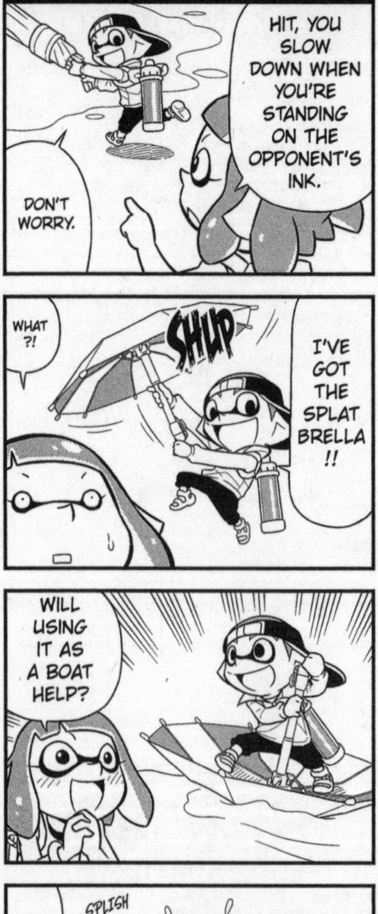
HIT, YOU SLOW DOWN WHEN YOU'RE STANDING ON THE OPPONENT'S INK.
DON'T WORRY.
I'VE GOT THE SPLAT BRELLA!!
SHUP
WHAT?!
WILL USING IT AS A BOAT HELP?
Humph! Humph!
SPLISH SPLISH
NOPE.

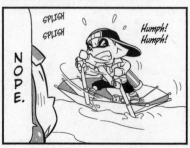

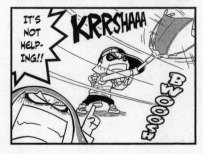

SPLAT BRELLA ATTACK

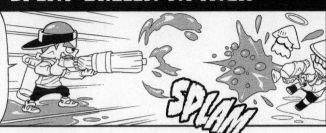

YOU DIDN'T SEE THIS COMING, DID YOU?! THE SPLAT BRELLA CAN EVEN ATTACK!!
SPLAM
KLIK
HIT, TURN INTO A SQUID AND DIVE INTO THE INK!!
KLIK...
YOU'RE OUT OF INK!!
I CAN STILL ATTACK!!
SHUP
NOT WITH AN OPEN UMBRELLA!!
SWIP SWIP SWIP
I WAS WRONG!!

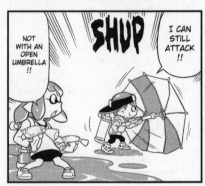

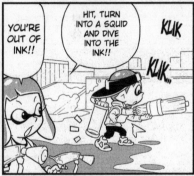

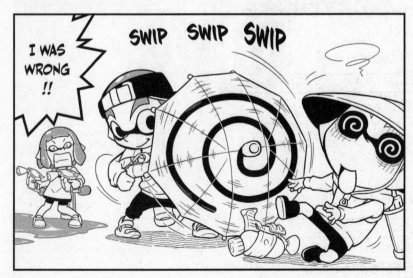

UMBRELLA SHARING

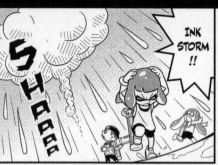

SHOOM
HE'S USING A SPECIAL WEAPON!!
INK STORM !!
SHAAAA
IT WON'T WORK ON ME!!
OPEN, SPLAT BRELLA !!
SHUP
LET ME IN TOO!!
BUMP
HEY ...!!

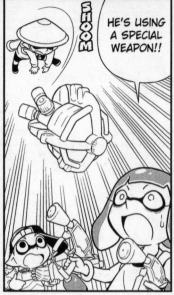

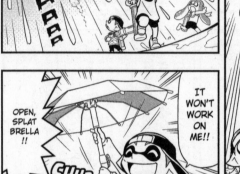

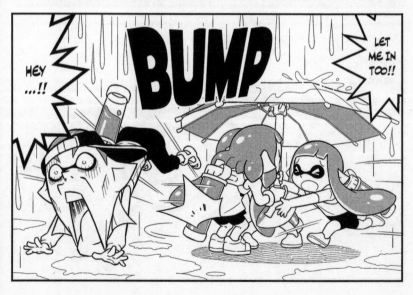

EXTRA MANGA: JELLYFIIIISH

CLOTHES

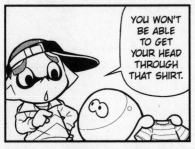

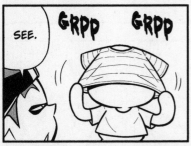

YOU WON'T BE ABLE TO GET YOUR HEAD THROUGH THAT SHIRT.
GRPP GRPP
SEE.
SQUEEPP

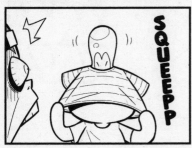

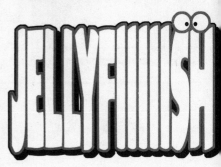

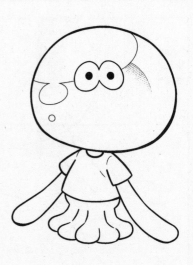

SHOES

SUPER-POPULAR SHOES
NOW IN STOCK
RRRMMBBLL
ONE SET LEFT
I MANAGED TO BUY IT. ♡
AWWW
TOO MANY FEET

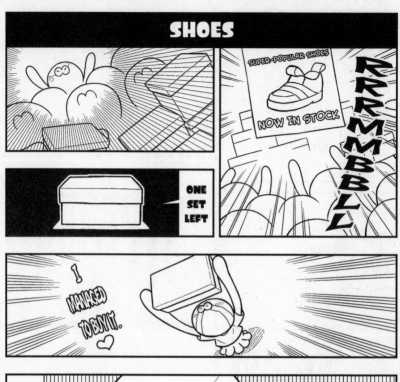

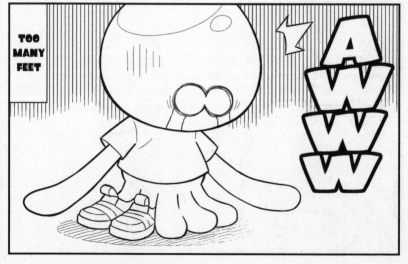

THE HEAD

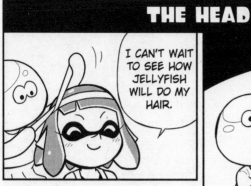

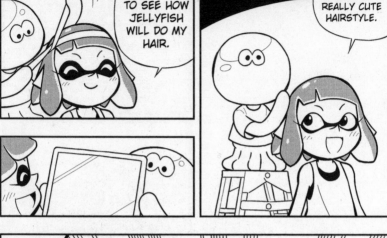

I WANT YOU TO GIVE ME A REALLY CUTE HAIRSTYLE.
I CAN'T WAIT TO SEE HOW JELLYFISH WILL DO MY HAIR.
UGH, I SHOULD HAVE KNOWN !!

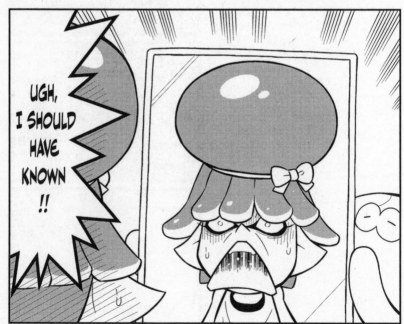

COVER COLOR CONFUSION
THANKS FOR READING THE PINK VOLUME, SPLATOON: SQUID KIDS COMEDY SHOW, VOLUME 1!
WE'LL SEE YOU AGAIN IN THE GREEN-COLORED VOLUME 2, AND THE ORANGE-COLORED VOLUME 3!
YEAH, LET'S SUPER JUMP TO THE NEXT VOLUME!!
BWOOOSH
The green one right?
WAIT, THOSE ARE ACTUAL ORANGES. YOU DON'T LISTEN! ALSO... THE NEXT VOLUME IS GREEN, NOT ORANGE!
SPLUUUB
SALE
MANDARIN ORANGE
50 CENTS EACH

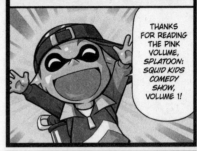

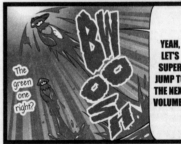

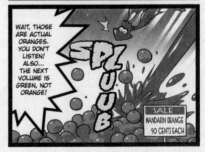

HIDEKI GOTO

I get scolded for spilling
paint and ink. But I'm
splattering as much ink as
I can inside the manga. ♪

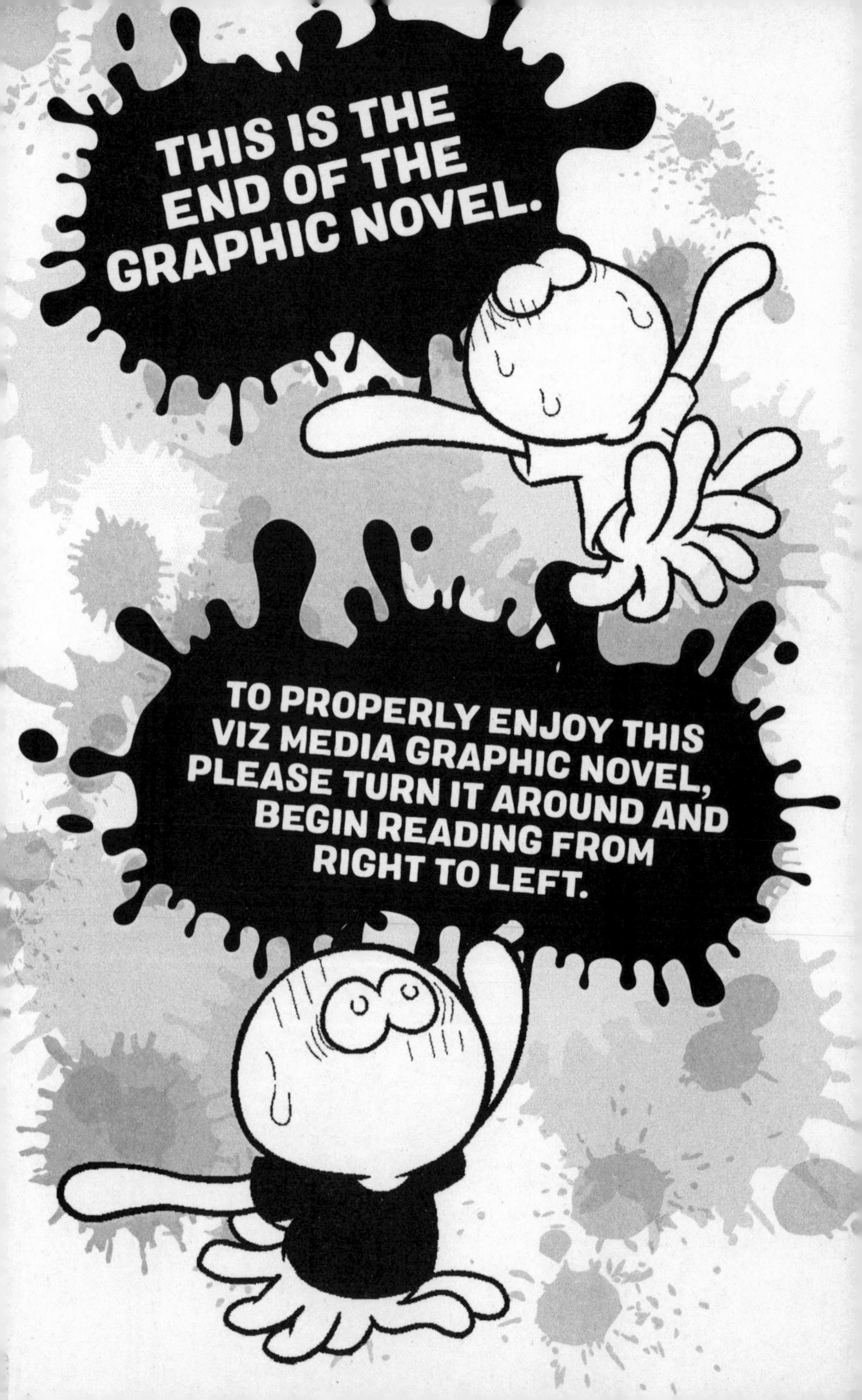
THIS IS THE END OF THE GRAPHIC NOVEL.
TO PROPERLY ENJOY THIS VIZ MEDIA GRAPHIC NOVEL, PLEASE TURN IT AROUND AND BEGIN READING FROM RIGHT TO LEFT.